TO CURSE A KNIGHT

ALL THE QUEEN'S MEN, BOOK 2

BY CORA FLYNN

Edits: LZ Edits

Cover Design: Artscandare Book Cover Design

Paperback ISBN: 978-1-0689780-1-2

E-book ISBN: 978-1-0689780-4-3

CONTENT NOTICE

This book is intended for mature audiences, recommended for readers 18+ years only as it contains profanities, sexual innuendo, and detailed sexual scenes.

This book is my darkest yet. Hillary's story begins to unravel, and with it comes a lot of deeply violent baggage. With that in mind, this book includes:

Skin flaying, torture, gruesome death, drugging, genital mutilation, sexual abuse, graphic rape (not main characters), witnessing murder, captivity, guns, child soldiers, murder, removal of body parts (head), anxiety, insomnia, discussions of depression, emotional manipulation, mentions of dead parents, deterioration of a parent/child relationship, grooming, child grooming, humiliation. Sexual scenes include anal sex, double vaginal penetration, snowballing, and unprotected sexual activity (all consensual).

For a full list of content notices, please check my website: www.coraflynnauthor.com.

This is a Why Choose/Reverse Harem romance novel, meaning the FMC will end up with more than one love interest and will not have to choose between them to find her HEA. The characters are bisexual and eventually enter an ethical poly relationship.

This novel is written in American English by a Canadian author, and the spelling, terminology, and grammar have been edited accordingly.

This book has been edited multiple times by multiple people, both personally and professionally, but the imperfection of human beings is a beautiful and inevitable thing. If you notice a typo, please choose to contact me at coraflynnauthor@gmail.com with the subject "Typo Found" so I may fix it.

Thank you!

xo
Cora Flynn

ACKNOWLEDGEMENTS

This series has been one wild ride. What you're about to read is what I believe to be my best book, both in storytelling, character development, structurally – all the author things – and that is because I have an entire team of incredible people supporting me.

Megan and Jennifer – you two joined me on this author journey and are now my best friends in this entire world. Megan, you are the world's greatest Alpha reader/ PA/ graphic designer/ sounding board/ human extraordinaire and I'd be lost without your morning texts and calendar reminders. Jennifer Larkin, you are, hands down, the world's best book coach. Your feedback has made this my greatest work of art. I can't wait to see where your career takes you (and please remember me when you're famous)! Thank you from the bottom of my heart.

Brandi and Paula – you are the best Alpha team! Your reader feedback and enthusiasm and helpful suggestions helped make this book the best it could be. Thank you!

Vanessa, Becky, Marina, Kristie, and Emmi—your thoughtful beta feedback and hilarious comments (and voice messages) brought me so much joy, especially your thoughts on that cliffhanger (cue evil laughter). I love working with you.

My friends, family, and coworkers—half of which do not understand Why Choose and are not allowed to read this book series, yet still choose to support me and celebrate my wins.

My husband, who made writing this book on an insanely tight deadline possible by being Super Dad and Super Partner. Thank you for supporting this dream through your words *and* your actions.

Lara, my editor—you are so valued and appreciated. Thank you for making my words better.

Maria of Artscandare—your cover design is stunning, as always.

And of course, you—my readers. Thank you for choosing this book from the mountain of your TBR and diving into the made-up worlds of my head. You've made this small-town Canadian's dreams come true.

XO,

Cora

For every woman whose rage could castrate
A man with a single glare ...

I hope it happens one day.

...

CHAPTER 1

Kellan

What in the ever-loving *fuck* was going on with my night right now?

What was supposed to have been an honorable fight to the death—by all accounts, Rodriguez's death—on the wrong side of town, had become a brutal battle between me and the insufferable woman who couldn't help inserting herself into every facet of my business.

Instead, the blood spatter of three different signatures painted a gruesome picture across the brilliant blue tarp on Rodriguez's floor, and the living portrait of us wasn't much better.

Aaron looked half-dead—without Hillary's cock-sure intervention, he would have been. His aristocratic face had smeared layers of dried blood and fresh cuts, his eyes so swollen I barely saw the dark irises beneath.

Hillary's eyebrow had split open when she was just a microsecond too slow to block my punch. The pouty lips I loved to bite were sliced and puffy, and her arms were littered with welts that would become dark bruises by the morning.

The rising ache in my joints and oozing fluid on my face and knuckles told me I hadn't fared much better. I was still standing, and so were the two people beside me. Admittedly, the fact we were all still alive was the highlight of this shit show of an evening.

My Killer had no idea when to quit; protecting her from her enemies in the shadows alone was a full-time job—but protecting her from herself would be the fucking death of me.

Rodriguez and I flanked her sides when she cocked the little pistol I'd gifted her and held it to the annoying Irishman's sweaty head. In the many years of fucking her or fighting her—sometimes both at the same time—I had never seen such an unfiltered view of her power.

It was infuriatingly intoxicating.

"You shouldn't have followed me, Lucky." Fiery blue eyes burned a hole through his thick skull as she held the gun tight in her fist at close range. A tingle of pride crept up the back of my spine, but I swiftly tamped it down.

Not the time, not the place.

"Yeah, gatherin' that," the incessant pain-in-the-ass shot back, though his normally confident retort was considerably toned down. His gaze flicked between the three killers towering over him. "All hopes of an orgy party are out of the window, then?"

My left eye twitched in a barely stifled eye roll. The bastard really didn't know when to shut up. I'd stared down death hundreds, if not thousands, of times in my almost forty years, and even I wouldn't have the balls to joke while my little Killer held a gun to my head.

I'd made the mistake of ignoring this man, even though now, in hindsight, he was a glaring red flag.

I was slipping, and that needed to change now. If I hadn't been so tied up with Antonio's vendetta or trying to cover Hillary's ass, I would have paid more attention to Lauchlan's convenient appearances at my gym haunt and seen through his invitation to Jediah's sham of a party.

That run-in had been enough to surprise me, but apparently, I was off my game enough I hadn't put two and two together. The little fucker was up to something, had some powerful people in his pocket, and by the fury embedded in Hillary's face, he was playing her, playing me, or both.

The abrupt click of the safety releasing finally caused a flicker of fear to flit through our hostage's pretty eyes.

Good.

I tucked my gun back into its holster. Hillary could take the lead on this one.

Shifting my weight onto my heels, I added an inch to my height and folded my arms across my chest. The power stance had made bigger men than Lauchlan piss their pants in fear, but he barely spared me a glance, his gaze trained on the whites of my Killer's eyes.

"So, who am I fighting to prove my worth as a man?" A bratty smirk played across his lips; I wanted to spank him until it fell right off of his face. Abruptly, his expression turned into a neutral stare. "What's it going to take for me to walk away from this, love?"

The man's voice didn't waver—his tone even and cool. Someone practiced in hostage negotiation, or at least someone who had deescalation training. I watched him fold in on himself but maintain his composure, subtly assuming a submissive pose without moving a solid muscle.

Who the fuck is this guy?

Aaron shifted beside me, and I almost startled; I'd almost forgotten he was there.

Almost. I'd underestimated his strength and sheer determination, and he'd impressed me with his fortitude. Antonio would be on the warpath if I allowed him to leave here alive tonight, but we'd have to figure it out. With Hillary's determination to step into the ring and Lauchlan's interruption, I wasn't in the mood to carry out my father's wishes, no matter the cost to my own life.

Antonio needed me, so I wouldn't die at his hand. I wasn't able to make the same promise to anyone else.

Hillary's body coiled like a snake around the handle of the small gun, but I knew she'd keep her wits about her. For all her faults, she was calculating, not impulsive, but I wouldn't bet a nickel on what was about to come out of her mouth. I didn't have a fucking clue.

"Sweet Lauchlan," she cooed. Her saccharine tone tasted disgusting on even my tongue. "Explain to me"—she paused just long enough to nod her head side to side—"to us," she amended, "what you want with Alvarez? Your answer literally decides where you end up tonight."

She rolled her neck and shrugged her shoulders as if she was stretching after a workout, but her grip didn't relax for a nano-second.

That's my girl.

"He took something from me." Lauchlan's response was direct and assured, with enough of a bite I believed him. "Something priceless, and I'm plotting payback."

They stared at each other for a long minute. Aaron and I stood silent like the trained bodyguards we were, knowing this was Hillary's mercy or punishment to deliver.

"Who'd he take from you?" She delivered the question knowingly—my Killer saw through the mask and into the pain of his statement. She would have made an effective

FBI agent—even though she'd never follow orders and her attitude was shit.

"Someone important." The haunted shadows of tormented men filled the Irishman's gaze. He stared through the other side into Hillary's fierce expression, but didn't say another word.

"Is that why you followed me here tonight?" She lowered the gun only slightly, but relaxed her posture. I'd seen Hillary shoot at a range firsthand—she'd get off a kill shot within a second if she changed her mind—but I doubted Lauchlan knew that.

His own posture loosened, and the cocky gleam reentered his stare; a soft smirk spread across his features.

Insufferable.

"Nah, love. I followed yeh 'cause I was bored and hoping for a lay. Never imagined I'd run into two lays at once. Happy coincidence." He dipped his head toward me—I could have strangled him with my bare hands—but he didn't elaborate.

He gestured to the gun still held tight in her right hand, though now dangling by her side.

"Are yeh gonna kill me, Blondie?" He winced and made slow movements to push himself off the ground, never breaking eye contact. "If you're reconsidering, can I stand for a minute?"

Her blue eyes darkened to raging seas. "Try anything and you'll lose a kneecap."

"Wouldn't dream of it, love."

He rose to his full height—taller than Hillary, shorter than Aaron and I—and rolled his shoulders, as if we were equals in this conversation.

"I dunno what kinda shyte I stumbled in on, but if you're taking Alvarez out, I want a seat at the table."

Aaron snorted in disbelief, his sneer cracking the layers of blood on his cheeks into flaking paint chips. "You have nothing to offer, *Rojo*. We have bigger problems to contend with." His swollen gaze met my own, the commanding presence of a leader still bleeding through. "I have an incinerator nearby. That will do, no?"

"Ay, rather than be barbecued," the Irishman interrupted, "I have something to offer, and I doubt you lot can match it."

Soft green eyes flitted between the three of us, calculating and determined. "I'm an inside man, with access to his networks. It's only a matter of time before I break the firewall. I've a plan to expose every sordid, shady, fuckin' detail that family has ever done. You want an inside man? *I'm* that man."

Hillary's shoulder brushed mine as she shifted her weight and cocked her head in consideration. The murderous look slowly leached from her eyes. "You work in tech…"

"Yes, Blondie. Tech."

A silent conversation passed between them, intense stares of hopeful consideration and hesitant mistrust expanding into the room.

Finally, Hillary broke the deafening tension.

"I don't trust you whatsoever, Lucky. But I believe you could be our inside man."

She turned her attention back to Aaron and me. "He was having dinner with Gertie Baker, Marco's executive assistant, a few weeks ago. She told me they both work for him. It supports this half-cocked theory, anyway."

I had no idea who Gertie was, but I trusted Hillary's assessment. My life was complicated enough—I hated killing men who didn't deserve to be killed, but I was on board with Aaron's cremation idea. Adding the irritating Irishman to our mix was going to cause a whole other host of problems I didn't have time to deal with.

Especially now we'd have to hide Rodriguez from my father, and risk the brutal torture that came along with that decision.

Aaron and I shared a dark look—the glare seeping through the slits of his eyes would have made lesser men tremble. Whatever was coming, we weren't going to like it.

Once this was settled, we'd talk about the inevitable price on Rodriguez's head. We'd have a day—two max, to come up with a plan, or Antonio would make sure someone else finished the job I'd come here to do.

And I'd enjoy a pleasantly delivered torture session for my insolence. Another branding to remind me of my duty.

"You're still living with your mother?"

Hill's question caught me off guard, snapping my attention back to the two of them. Lauchlan's brows crinkled in confusion, but he nodded.

"Not anymore. You're moving into my condo tonight. Kellan's going to outfit you with a tracker, and you're going to tell us everything you have planned. No surprises. No bullshit."

I whipped my head around. No. He was not living in her space. Fuck that.

"We're going to kill him," I growled. "I'm not letting him live with—"

"You're not letting me do anything," my little Killer shot back, her blue eyes flashing with dangerous defiance. "This is the plan, Kellan."

Brat.

I blew out an angry breath of frustration, but knew I was stuck. Aside from killing him, I couldn't think of a solution that covered our bases more than this one. For now.

I was now responsible for two men I really want nothing to do with. Fantastic.

She sauntered over to her surprised captive, her lithe body gracefully moving between three of us helpless to escape her orbit. A wicked glint lit her eyes.

"Looks like you're ours now, little Lucky."

Cora Flynn

CHAPTER 2

Hillary

"I don't like this plan at all, Killer."

Kellan's glower was as familiar to me as my own reflection in a mirror. A foreboding presence, he stood in the doorway of Aaron's warehouse. We'd just collected our weapons, returning indoors to formulate some semblance of a plan before we stepped back outside and left this terrible memory of an evening behind.

"Big surprise, Viking." I rolled my eyes at his overbearing, broodish facade. "But I'm not killing him tonight, and you two are in enough trouble."

Raising an eyebrow, I pointedly looked down my nose at the two men in front of me. Lauchlan currently stood outside, handcuffed to Kellan's passenger seat, despite my explicit instructions he was to come home with me. I'd agreed to one night of interrogation, but Kellan was to bring him back to me in the morning—preferably in one piece.

I didn't have high hopes. The cartel King made a show of smashing Lucky's head against the door frame as he shoved him into the vehicle like he was a wanted felon.

The truth, really.

Lucky's admission had come as a surprise, but in a way, also completely expected. Lauchlan had already proven himself to be a cunning opponent, and learning I wasn't the sole focus of his attention validated my previous thoughts. He was smarter than he let on, leading a shell game with the practiced slight of hand of a talented magician.

Now, though, I had far larger concerns than an intriguing game of cat-and-mouse with a sexy con man. That he'd tracked and followed me here might have been another element of our veiled competition, but he'd chosen the wrong night to up the ante.

So now, he'd be under lock and key with... me. I wasn't looking forward to having another person in my space, but that would be a future-Hillary problem. It hadn't slipped my attention there'd been no mention of his alleged profession—he was still keeping his identity a secret. I was curious if a little one-on-one 'attention' could make him crack. I looked forward to finding out.

First, we had to deal with Aaron.

I shifted my ire to the badly beaten man in front of me. Even covered in blood and bruises, he radiated the calm poise of a self-assured man. He stood tall and proud, arms wrapped around his chest in disapproval, but after he had first voiced his suggestion of burning Lauchlan alive, he'd remained quiet. Observant. Waiting.

"Your suicidal tendencies aside"—I glared poison-dipped daggers at my frustrating Dark Knight, but he didn't give me so much as a twitch in return—"we're going to have to get you somewhere safe. And my condo is now taken." I dipped my head toward the door to emphasize the point.

"I will not need to retreat yet." He casually wiped the stream of blood from a reopened cut on his lip into the sleeve of his destroyed white dress shirt. "I have a few days, yes?"

"Barely," Kellan responded, the exasperation in his tone barely overshadowing his concern. "Antonio didn't give me a timeline, but he is not a patient man. He'll expect this to be done this week."

"Okay." I nodded my head. "A few days is good. You're going to need a lot of makeup, but a public appearance over the next day or two would be a good thing. It will make your retreat from public life a little more believable."

Aaron cocked his head and a subtle grimace of pain flitted across his features. "How do you propose, *Mi Reina*?"

"I have a safe house about an hour out of town." My gaze landed on the Viking's icy stare. "Kellan—do you have connections we can use? With your—other—organization?"

I hesitantly searched his eyes, not about to give up his most guarded secret, but hoping it would have some use against Antonio's vendetta against the Rodriguez family. If he wanted to massacre Aaron's parents and extended family, I'd stand back and let natural selection have its vengeance, but I wouldn't let a single hair on Aaron's head be touched going forward.

Aaron didn't know about Kellan's FBI employment; I was sure of it. The only reason I knew was I'd been involved in Winter's family drama years ago. At every party or social interaction, like Jediah's, Kellan represented the Carlos Cartel and the Carlos Cartel only.

The blond God shook his head, clumped strands of bloodied dreads swaying around his face.

"I'm about to have a turf war on my hands. If I bring him into a safe house, I can't guarantee that they won't try to use him as a pawn to bring in his parents. Antonio's still off the table—barely—but Veronica and Vicente would be a huge win for them."

Aaron's brow furrowed in confusion, but he waited, expectantly.

My business partner was always the most patient man in a boardroom, waiting for others to confess their sins while he silently stared into their souls. Watching him apply this tactic to Kellan would have been amusing in different circumstances.

Instead, I stood between them with knots in my stomach, wordlessly counting the number of secrets I was going to have to manage between the three men.

Kellan sighed and the noisy burst of air forced his cracked lips apart. He scrubbed his large palms over his dirty face.

"Fuck it," he murmured as his gaze dipped to the rough floorboard beneath our feet. He lifted his eyes, steely resolve darkening the rich blue to navy, as he stared directly into Aaron's caramel brown slits.

"I'm a double agent with the FBI. It's a long story, one we will likely never get into, but now that I'm fucking responsible for your life, too"—he threw an unnecessary glower my way—"you should know what you are getting into. I'll do my best to protect you, but I can't guarantee it. I can't guarantee my own life with Alvarez and Antonio about to go head to head."

To his credit, Aaron's face remained an unreadable mask, save for a micro-crinkle of his left eyebrow I had learned was his tell. His emotionless stare drifted to mine for a brief moment, then resolution entered his own gaze.

Steel entered his spine, and he rose to his full height, now within an inch of Kellan. He stuck out his palm in an extended handshake, the image of a formidable businessman ready to enter a company shakedown. "Nice to finally meet you, *hermano*. Let us take down the devils that sired us together. Keep me hidden, and I'll use my networks to avenge us both."

Kellan's poker face all but evaporated. His eyebrows shot up in surprise, eyeing the offered hand with incredulity. Aaron didn't concede, leaving it awkwardly hanging in the air between them.

"You're a relentless fucker, I'll give you that." His lips twitched in the faintest ghost of a smile, then he clasped Aaron's hand within his own rough palm. "It's a battle ahead, brother. Death is a more peaceful alternative."

"One I will face once my parents have filled their own coffins."

Raw power emanated from within Aaron's bronzed skin, encasing the three of us in a cloud of bitter determination. He and Kellan exuded the earned confidence of men who had built a legacy of destruction and sin.

I stepped back, needing distance from the overpowering layers of emotion.

"As much as I'm thrilled to see you two getting along"—I grabbed my sweater from the floor, feeling the sharp sting of chilled air now that the adrenaline had worked its way out of my system—"we need an actual plan for the week. Aaron—two days maximum, okay? Office and home, no deviations. I don't trust Antonio not to have a contingency plan."

Kellan grimaced in agreement.

"Get your affairs in order, move what you can over to my office and pack a bag. Tell no one—not even Jacques— where you are going. I'll have Joey deliver you to my safe house, and we will work out the details this weekend, okay?"

This really was a terrible plan. My safe house apartment was in the basement of my private, heavily secured warehouse. Aaron wasn't privy to my after-hours activities, and Alec's cell on the upper level would have to remain a secret—for how much longer, I didn't know, but I wasn't willing to reveal everything tonight—no matter how much I cared about him.

Still, I wouldn't be able to secure another piece of real estate close by in just two days, even with all my connections. It was probably safer, but I selfishly didn't want Aaron leaving the state, if it meant I couldn't keep an eye on him. This seemed the best option in a sea of really shitty ones.

Aaron reached for me, and with a light tug on my wrist, drew me into his arms. He stank of iron and salt, but the underlying scent of his familiar body wash—sandalwood and vanilla—still clung to his skin like a comforting blanket. I sank into his embrace. The recent memories of being held in the quiet of his office brought me a rare sense of peace. I closed my eyes for a brief second, listening to the muted thump of his heartbeat against my cheek.

He gently kissed the top of my head, then nuzzled me backward to stand next to Kellan once again.

"And text me when you get home. Both of you. Please," I tacked on, no longer in the mood to issue orders that affected yet another man's fate. I was desperate to get to my condo, have a shower, and crawl into bed.

My already waning mood turned sour when I realized I would have a house guest for the foreseeable future.

"You can deliver Lucky to my guest suite tomorrow evening, Viking. I'll deal with him then."

Not waiting for his response, I pulled open the dented metal door that had just changed the trajectory of my entire life and stepped out into the damp night air.

I hoped Sammy found me a new playmate this week. It was time to let off some much-needed stress.

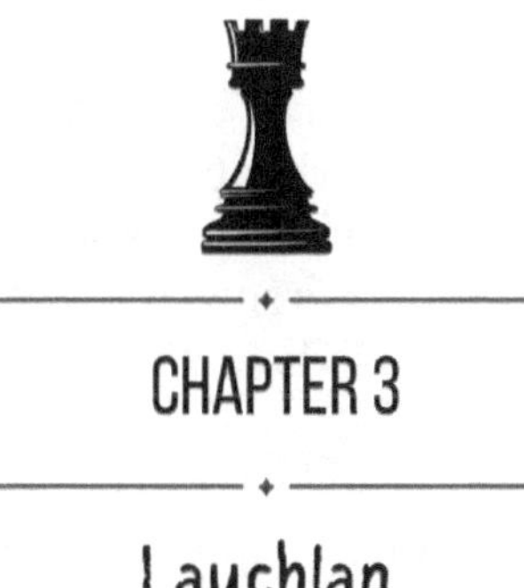

CHAPTER 3

Lauchlan

Fuck.

My body felt like I'd gotten railed by a steel rod up my arse through to my skull. Ol' Conan musta had fun with me after he'd shoved a tranq in my arm.

Last thing I remembered, I was handcuffed to Kellan's seat and then—a vicious slash of a sexy-as-fuck Viking mouth before I was injected with a tasty little cocktail.

Kinky fucker.

Even kinkier—my eyes were covered by a hard leather blindfold, and by the feel of things, it was attached to a harness strapped around my head. Not my first rodeo with

BDSM toys, not by a long shot, but not quite what I was expecting from the brute.

I knew I wasn't in for a good night's sleep when Blondie let him take me to his cozy little cartel den, but even in my dirtiest dreams, I never pictured being tied up by the big guy.

This was what soaking wet dreams were made of.

Had one of these just 'lying around' here, did ya ol' Kell Bell?

My cock aside, I needed to find a way out of this situation. At least loosen the handcuffs. I didn't want to escape from my Barbarian, but I wasn't willingly playing the role of sitting duck. I knew a trick, but Kellan must have known it, too, because he'd placed a metal rod through the center of the chain.

Smart fucker.

Fighting the dizzy fuzz bouncing around in my brain, I reach out to my trusty five senses to make sense of my situation.

Small metal chair—check.

Arms bound behind me with the cuffs. Check.

The air was freezing, but it would have been warmer if he'd kept my clothes on. I'd been stripped in my unconscious state and wore nothing but my favorite red silk boxers and a pair of dress socks.

Not a foot fetish guy, then. Noted.

I was in a basement, judging by the damp smell of concrete and mold, but it might have been a basement in Timbuktu for all I knew.

How long ago did you put me out, Conan?

Stilling my body and slowing my breathing, I listened hard to my surroundings. Con men—good con men, at least —trained themselves to be observant through all the senses. It had saved my life on more than one occasion.

We were patient creatures—willing to put in the time for the payoff. I blocked out my own breaths and shivers in the barbarian's basement to really hear the surrounding room.

Ahhh. There it was.

The faint, almost inaudible sound of another body breathing offered the slightest echo against the concrete near my head.

"You like watching another man cuffed in his drawers, do ya?"

My voice drawled sluggishly—I still had a good bit of drugs in my system—but no amount of drugs could mask my Irish sense of humor.

No response. But I'd have bet my left testicle he was in the room with me. Somewhere to my... right.

"What'd you dope me up with, Kell Bell? I'm having déjà vu of my college days."

Better—less slow-motion action sequence and more coherent. I swore I heard a light snort, but still no confirmation came.

My theory Kellan couldn't resist a good brat was about to be tested, and I was a snuffling little piglet on a platter.

"Not my first torture session, Conan," I mused while wiggling some feeling back into my fingers. "Gonna have to try harder next time—got some nipple clamps back there?"

A wicked grin crossed my lips when a satisfying shuffle of feet came closer. Hints of lemony citrus and warm amber wafted toward me before I was hit with a whole wall of Kellan's man-scent.

Intoxicating, really. Wish we weren't in a real torture scenario, or this whole thing would have knocked a tasty little fantasy off the old bucket list.

The warmth of his body radiated against the freezing flesh of my own. He was hovering close. I licked my lips in anticipation.

Hard clips latched onto my tiny pink pearls and I squealed like the little metaphorical piglet I was. The familiar voice of buttered gravel growled above the shell of my ear.

"Your wish is my command, *Caperucita Roja.*"

Little Red Riding Hood. Cute. And I thought this grumbly bear wouldn't know a joke if it kicked him in the teeth.

"Now," he continued, heated form directly in front of me. "We're going to play a little game. I'm going to ask questions, and you're going to give me answers. *Capisce?*"

Not bloody likely.

I chose peace instead of violence.

"Sure, big guy. Ask away. I'm an open book. Practically the Bible, really, with all the—"

A large hand gripped my bare thigh, the rough calluses catching on the soft layer of hair there. The squeeze was firm but gentle—a warning.

"Why did you follow Hillary tonight?"

"No secrets—already told you that one. Had a taste of her already, and now I'm taken with the woman. Was hoping for another taste. You wouldn't know anything about that, would ya?"

A blind man could have seen how the mafia man looked at my Blondie. Broody and protective, his attention never straying from her for longer than a few seconds. A man in love, or at least a man as obsessed as me.

"Don't talk about her that way," he spat. Bingo—man in love, no question.

"Talk about her like what? Like she didn't give me the best fuck of my life? Sorry, Conan, our '7 Seconds in Heaven' shower fuck was good, but I'm gonna need a whole lot more than that, if you want to measure up to Blondie."

The grip on my skin tightened, the heat of his palm branding my frozen skin. That was the extent of it, though – I was impressed with his control. It would be even more satisfying to make him lose it.

"Why are you here?"

"In a feckin' basement?" I feigned confusion. "Some pervert drugged me and brought me here."

The blunt nails of his hand might have punctured my skin with the vise-like hold, but I was on a roll. Kellan's weakness was the need to tame an insolent brat—and here I was, at his disposal.

"Why. Are. You. Here?"

"Stop asking questions you know the answers to." I shot back, goading him. "Work in tech, remember? Infiltrating Alvarez's tech company. Gonna bring the baddies down. Weren't you in the room when we had this conversation? Wait—what's your IQ?—not related, just curious."

To my disappointment, he removed his hand, and I heard the shuffle of his feet against the pavement floor moving away. A jolt of electricity shot into both of my nipples. My back arched off the chair and I howled. The handcuffs pulled painfully at my wrists from the spasm.

Jesus, fuck, that hurt. But my dick disagreed, because my shorts were fully tented, dick loud and proud, ready for more.

Fucking masochist, my dick.

A dark chuckle reverberated off the walls and deft hands unlatched the leather eye covering from the harness.

Blinking rapidly, my eyes adjusted to my dim surroundings. We were in what looked like a workshop; a collection of saws, hammers, and screwdrivers on a pin board in front of me. Unease settled into the pit of my stomach.

Did Kellan make children's toys, or were those meant for torture? Definitely the latter. I just hoped he wouldn't touch my face. I really liked my face.

Rough pads of his hands landed on my shoulders from behind, sliding down the front of my chest to tweak the nipple clamps. My body twitched again from the sensation, but my dick practically leaped out of my boxers.

Traitor.

"You've got a tracker under there." Kellan casually slapped the fleshy part of my shoulder from behind, a dull ache settling deep into the muscle tissue. "Ankle monitors can be too easy to manipulate. I made sure that one was deep, so you won't be able to tamper with it. Since you work in 'tech'."

Didn't need to see him to catch the air quotes on that one. But fuck, internal hardware had not been part of the plan.

"You're not just a cocky little shit," he mused, his hands moving from my arm to slide excruciatingly slowly over the planes of my chest. "You're trained for interrogation."

Coarse hair tickled my cheek when he lowered his mouth to my ear. Warm, soft lips gently traced the shell before a hot tongue laved down to the lobe and he sucked it gently between his teeth.

I squirmed in the hard seat. With nowhere to go, if this was how Kellan wanted to test me into spilling my secrets, I'd at least spill my load in the process.

Bristles of his beard brushed against my neck as his mouth moved southward, pressing bruising kisses along the taut muscle.

Fuck it. I melted into the seat, rolling my head to the side to give him better access. I could be a pliant subbie with the right motivation.

"Why are you here?"

The words weren't a demand anymore; they were coaxing, commanding. Like a sexy siren call—if the siren was a buff gladiator.

Closing my eyes, I caught another strong whiff of his scent before whispering back the words he wanted so badly to hear.

"Tech. Revenge. Another ass-fucking by a billionaire."

I practically leaped off the chair, chains and all, when he took a raging bite out of my shoulder.

"The fuck, Kell!" I shouted in alarm; positive I was bloody bleeding all over the nipple clamps.

The sexy oaf finally moved around to the front of me and I got a good look at him.

Yeah, he fucking broke skin, all right. Blood coated his lips, the red tint staining the hair around his mouth. But the wolfish, satisfied smirk stopped me from unleashing a torrent comprised of every curse word I had ever learned.

Kellan, Viking God of all that was holy, was dressed in nothing but a pair of red and black plaid flannel pajama pants; every muscle, tattoo, and faint curl of blond body hair on display.

Sure, I'd already seen it before. I got a nice little eyeful when we were crammed up in the gym shower. But there was something about a man, shirtless and dressed in nothing but cotton pants, that just did something for me. Bubble butt outlined; sack perfectly molded as an imprint within the fabric...

I'd fucked a lot of men in my day—sexy men, ugly men, that Russian mark one time—but Kellan's body might be the prettiest.

Even with my blood coating his tongue. Okay, *especially* with my blood coating his tongue. My cock was so solid it was going to force its way through my shorts at any moment. A small wet patch sat on top; what I wouldn't do to have his mouth on me ...

He spun around to the bench behind him and grabbed something plastic from the tabletop. I craned my throbbing neck to see.

Two sets of zipties. What the—

My questions were answers when he lowered himself to my feet and secured each ankle to the leg of the chair. His kneeling made him eye-level to my dick; He openly stared at the patch of pre-cum, his eyes now a dangerously dark blue.

Without warning, he buried his face in my crotch, sucking at my throbbing shaft through the silky fabric. My legs tensed, thighs bucking up in a sorry attempt to ride his face. My muscles cramped hard against my new restraints. His hands held my thighs down as he buried his face deeper against me. His pillowy lips mouthed the underside of my cock before his teeth nibbled a path up to my trapped head. His mouth closed over the wet patch, his tongue pulling up on my sensitive head over and over until my spine erupted with tingles and—

Just as abruptly, he stopped and pulled away from me. Fierce determination filled his stormy eyes. He didn't stand, though, his hulking body still kneeling at my feet in the sexiest form of dominance possible.

"Why are you here?" he repeated, a new dangerous edge in his tone.

I can't say I'd ever trained to withstand edging torture, but I was into it—so into it. I'd add this to my training roster once this was all over and he handed me back to Hillary in pieces.

Blowing out a breath of desperate lust, I levelly met his gaze.

"I was hoping to get a chance to ass-fuck you. That still on the table, Kell Bell?"

The Viking God snorted, his eyes flashing with a combination of lust and irritation. "I don't bottom."

"Yeah, yeah." I taunted. "You don't do a lot of things. Doesn't explain that chub you've got going on for me, does it?"

I couldn't see it, but I knew it was there. Men like Kellan Carlos didn't bury their face into some guy's dick and not get a hard-on. I'd bet good money this man was a pleasure Dom, when he wasn't all torturey and stuff.

Heat blazed through his eyes before a mask came down so hard I couldn't read him anymore. Now *that* was a skill he'd be able to use as a con artist.

In one quick movement, he yanked my boxers over my ass down to my knees and unwrapped my very ready package for him. My cock sprang free, jutting into the air like a sword ready for battle.

Before I had blinked, my dick was in his mouth with no barriers between us. The smooth, silky wetness wrapped tightly around me like a pure pocket of Heaven.

He shoved his tongue into my slit and I saw stars—galaxies, even—his mouth expertly hitting every nerve in my cockhead and I couldn't move, couldn't breathe, until I was going to come down his throat.

But he didn't give me the chance. The moment I was about to blow, he'd pull back, my squirming, sweaty body needy as fuck and begging for his mouth again.

"Why are you here?"

Softer voice this time. Coaxing again. Tender.

"Needed a face to fuck." I grunted, bucking upwards into freezing airspace instead of his orgasmic mouth hole.

A burning pain met my answer as the Neanderthal bit a chunk out of the inside of my thigh. I gaped at the bloody ring of teeth marks two inches from my taint and glared daggers into his eyes.

That fucker was going to scar.

"Fucking hell, Conan!" I shouted as my quad cramped hard from the pain. I was definitely reconsidering my pleasure Dom assessment. "Seriously?"

"I can break every finger and toe in your body." His face was now a completely neutral mask, like a trained serial killer. "Be grateful."

Aye, when he put it that way—

"I already told you why I was here, you caveman," I spat. I was desperate for a release, but his pit bull style—if not a little unorthodox—questioning was exhausting. He wasn't going to get the answers he wanted. I wasn't a small-time mamby-pamby pussy—I was a professional. Hardening my stare, I stuck out my chin in defiance.

A moment of silence passed between us—the sorry stubborn sap in the vintage chair and the lumberjack torturer with a blood fetish—we faced off like dueling partners of a bad porn script.

He unclipped the nipple clamps and threw them to the floor. He lifted the chair, then carried me toward the room's rear wooden stairs.

Well, this was a new one.

My head smashed against the low beam up the stairwell, but I stifled my cry of pain. I was way too curious to see where I'd end up. That, and I knew I'd end up leaving here alive, if Kellan wanted to leave here alive, too. I didn't mind being under Blondie's protection.

He carried me face-forward down a dark, carpeted hallway, then deposited me in a simple white bedroom with a king bed, nightstand, and dresser.

Wordlessly, he uncuffed my legs from the chair, then lifted me effortlessly onto the bed, spread me out and attached my bound hands to a metal ring on the headboard.

Kinky, kinky, kinky.

My head was pounding from the solid whack to the beam, but my heart pounded even harder. Was he going to break my fingers now? My dick?

Kellan stepped back from the bed and assessed his handiwork, his cock swollen underneath those sexy PJs. Slowly, he shucked them down his legs and the massive length of him sprang free, like an adult Jack-in-the-box.

Holy shyte. Is this—am I—what?

He pulled my legs to the end of the bed. My arms strained against the cuffs as he lifted my upper body into the air. Spreading my legs wide, he brought his dick to my ass, and rubbed the head all over the sensitive ring of muscles. The wetness of his pre-cum slid over me.

Reaching into his pocket, he pulled out a shiny blue foil packet of lube. It wasn't going to be enough.

Ripping the packet open with his teeth, he slowly spread the lube over the crown of his head and down the length of his shaft. My dick twitched in response, in a fucking tailspin over this sudden turn of events.

Torture by fucking. Other than some disturbing porn I'd watched as a teen, this was definitely a new one for the books.

My Viking Dom released his hold on his coated cock and reached for me. Gripping my thighs so tight I'd have thumb prints all over them in the morning, he forced his head into my tight hole. Painfully stretched, I saw stars behind my eyelids. He looked down at the space where our bodies met and aimed a huge gob of spit onto his dick.

He thrust into me, hard. I cried out, in pain, in pleasure, in fucking delicious lust. He withdrew and thrust back into me again, holding me completely fucking hostage by my hands and thighs and dick.

I took it. Welcomed his dick inside me and squeezed him as fucking tight as I could. I opened my body to take more of him as he loomed over me, sweat matting the long hair against his brow.

His face betrayed nothing, but those sexy stormy eyes said everything. How much he wanted me, how much he hated me, how much he needed to fucking rail me into these sheets to punish me.

I bucked against him, my dick ready to explode all over his stomach. My back arched painfully upward...

Edging fucker.

He pulled out and flipped me over on my stomach; the handcuffs chafed hard into my skin. He clenched my hips and notched himself into my hole again, but he didn't move anymore, despite me pressing my ass into him, begging for more.

"Why are you here?"

Sweat beaded my brow, my whole body on fire.

"For this, you cunt. I'm twenty moves ahead of yeh, and knew you couldn't resist a—a"

I jolted forward as his cock threatened to break me in half, his rutting so frenzied, I was afraid for the sanctity of my asshole for anyone else. I'd gloat about the ability to unravel this man later. For now, I needed to just. Fucking. Come.

His hand reached around and stroked my cock in time with his thrusts, and fuck me, I was going to come—finally come—I—"FUCK!" I cried out when he pulled away again in the nick of fucking time. "Just FUCK ME, you wanker!"

He resumed his thrusting, harder and faster, rubbing my cock, massaging my balls, bringing me right to the edge again, and pulling away, over and over, until I had almost come 47 times.

I whimpered and writhed, now completely at his mercy. Fuck, I needed to come. I needed to come, I needed to—

"Why are you here?"

His thrusts were slow, torturous, and easy now. His hands stroked down my back in a sensual massage as he soothed my aching form. He had to need to come by now, too. What was bloody wrong with him?

I wasn't in my right mind anymore, every brain cell glazed with drugging desire and the raging need to feel his cum flood my asshole. Every cell in my body was completely on fire.

Fuck me. Just fuck me, dammit.

His pace increased by a thousand. I couldn't handle another edging—another disappointment. If he didn't let me explode right now, I was going to dive into a pit of absolute madness.

I was there—right there—my balls drawing upward and my spine tingling with electricity. Tears sat at the edge of my eyelids as I inwardly begged for my redemption.

Swallowing hard, I gave him a tidbit—something I hadn't planned on giving up, but I needed to get my happy ending, or I would die on this bed from sexual dissatisfaction.

I was already caught in their snare, anyway. One piece of information wouldn't destroy everything I was working towards.

Please, let me come.

"He killed my sister."

Kellan made no acknowledgment of the admission. Instead, his thrusting became that of a man possessed, driving me into the bed with such force I knew I wouldn't be able to sit down in the morning. Or ever.

Worth it.

I gave a deep-throated cry, the sticky jets of my cum shot all over my stomach and the comforter as he let out a bear-like growl from deep in his chest.

I collapsed into the sheets, shoulders on fire from the handcuffs, and buried my face into a puddle of my own tears. The euphoria of my release turned my whole body into a shaking, spasming mess.

He'd won this round—I had never planned to give him a damned thing. But I'd won, too—there's no way Kellan-the-controlled-Cartel-king had planned on losing his mind with me tonight.

So now I knew for sure; the man had a weakness for cocky Irishmen. And you'd bet I was bloody going to use that power to my advantage.

Tomorrow.

The last thing I remembered was a warm cloth over my backside and a blanket pulled over my lifeless form before I fell into a blissfully dreamless sleep.

Touché, Conan. Touché.

Cora Flynn

CHAPTER 4

Aaron

If you cheat, may you cheat death.

The proverb danced around in my mind as I entered the red double doors to Club 7.

The long hallways of dark velvet and dim lighting no longer offered me the warm, familiar comfort I had felt since I was sixteen. Club 7 had once been my haven; the palace in which I held court.

Walking through it now, it felt more like a dungeon of my demise; the thick carpeting and soothing music suffocating reminders of the empire I would soon lay to ruin.

Cora Flynn

In my thirty-five years, I had become many shades of gray to rule this world as if I owned its bounty. Profiting off humanity's most basic desires was an easy leash to hold; a simple product to sell.

Knowing my hedonistic castle was to be transformed into a den of sexual slavery turned the acid in my stomach to lava, but I would have to endure this place one more day.

One more day before...

For the first time, I didn't have the answer to where my next day would take me. I had to trust in *Mi Reina* and the man who should be my greatest enemy. Here I stood, putting full faith in two people who would have handsomely profited if they'd buried me in a shallow grave outside the city.

Instead, Kellan had offered me a dignified end, and she—she fought for my honor when I had nothing left to give. They were now the only allies I had in this world, unaffected by the poisonous taint of my parents' touch.

Kellan had entrusted me with his greatest secret; I would carry it to my grave. I could only ask for the gift of time to avenge his enemies before I rested there.

If either of you dies, Kellan, I might as well be dead, too.

The words were recorded in my mind and imprinted on my soul. Wherever fate led me, my path was destined to be intertwined with hers, and through that admission—his.

I was not a hopeful man, nor a trusting one. Resignation was not pushing me forward. Faith in her—and him, by proxy, would lead me through this next phase of uncertainty. I would hide in the shadows while they played their pieces on the board. Then I would bury my parents in the coffins I'd promised them.

The Irishman, however—that man would not live under my watch. *Mi Reina* believed he could be manipulated to be useful—I would not hesitate to slit his throat if he proved otherwise.

"Mr. Rodriguez?"

The short blonde woman—Rosa—who ran the front end of Club 7, interrupted my thoughts, her squeaky voice at odds with her sultry exterior.

Her eyes darted nervously across my battered face; the cuts and bruises were healing and covered with a high-quality foundation, but still visible. Fear crossed her features, confusing me. I was not a man to admire, but I'd garnered respect from my employees, if nothing else. Never fear.

"I'm sorry, sir, we weren't—ah—expecting you this evening. She is not ready for you."

My attendee—the woman whose name I still did not know—whom I hadn't seen since the ribbon cutting, when she'd mysteriously appeared in the crowd.

I'd remained committed to *Mi Reina*. I had not touched the woman since I'd failed to get my cock up in her presence the last time. I was resigned to my future with a woman who wanted me, but wouldn't commit to me, and found myself uninterested in the cunt of another.

In my current circumstances, I would likely only receive gratification from the touch of my own hand and the vivid memories of her riding me into the carpet of my office.

"I am not here for pleasure." I brusquely moved past Rosa into the stairwell behind her that led to my office on the floor above. "I will only be here for an hour to review some paperwork. Please do not disturb me."

Her nod was hesitant, but she said nothing else, so I left her to play host to our guests. Wednesdays were quiet, but she'd be busy enough with the regular clientele to ensure I wasn't interrupted.

The office was a glorified closet; the tight space offered a desk, a chair, and a few cabinets behind a locked door. My father and I were the only two people with access.

Surprise filled me as I unlocked the door and found I was not alone.

A male figure sat at the end of the desk, his trousers down around his ankles; a dark head of black hair bobbed between his legs.

The woman obviously worked here, dressed in the Club 7 uniform—a micro-pleated black skirt and black sequined bustier, with red sequined 4-inch stilettos tied around her feet. Employees could only service clientele in the provided rooms downstairs, as a protective measure. Whatever this was, it was not a client call.

My father's taunting grin, a grin too close to my own when I bothered to smile, stared back at me. It molded into a vicious sneer, reinforcing my thirst for blood and revenge.

I said nothing as the woman completed her task. Vicente's eyes finally left mine and rolled upward as he forced his putrid cum down her waiting throat.

"*Tonto*," he purred, as he gripped the woman's jaw in a tight hand and pulled her to her feet, cutting off her air supply as he did so. Her body jerked forward, the lack of oxygen causing her limbs to spasm in my father's hold.

Within seconds, I was upon them. I ripped her from his grasp and shoved her behind me. One look at her face told me she was my regular attendee.

Aside from the rage I felt at her mishandling, our contract stated clearly that she was mine and mine only. She was not to be touched; whether or not I was fucking her, she was paid handsomely, and the agreement was still in place.

Her selection today had been intentional.

A furious growl escaped my lips and I scowled at the half-naked man smirking back at me. Vicente's figurative balls were far larger than his physical set, the shriveled sacs hanging from the desk like the pathetic disappointments they were.

"She is not to be touched, *Veijo*." I stepped into his space and loomed over his body as he made no attempt to pull his pants back up. "Cover yourself and leave. I am still building your coffin."

His eyes darkened at the challenge. He stood tall and assured, his height within millimeters of my own, as though attempting to force me into submission.

I hadn't bowed to this man in years. Today would be no different.

"She will pull them up for me," he commanded, eyes full of malicious intent as he dipped his head toward the woman behind me.

"She will not," I spat. Losing my patience, I yanked them up for him, keeping my face as far away from his sack as possible. I shoved the unbuttoned folds of fabric into his own hands.

"Leave, or I will hand the keys of this entire network to Lane Enterprises, and she can do what she will."

It was the most dangerous threat I could manage. This man cared not about money or weapons or morals. He had mastered manipulation and would carefully disseminate many rumors to ensure my downfall. But to endanger his business by handing it to an American woman, one with more wealth and power than him?

It was the most revolting premise to his kind of man.

The wrathful hate in his gaze reinforced what I knew in my heart to be true. I was nothing but a sacrificial lamb. His critical mistake was to mislabel me as such—I was the dark wolf in sheep's clothing, waiting patiently for the kill of a lifetime.

"You are a castrated man, *mi hijo. Los débiles.* You are no son of mine."

"As you are no *padre.*" I hardened my stare and grabbed his bicep tightly. "Leave, now."

I shoved him past his captive, who'd remained where she was, despite the door still wide open to the hall.

He hovered in the doorway, disheveled and glowering.

"I am unafraid of making a scene, father." I levelly met his glare with a calm, patronizing stare. "Leave."

With a final fierce scowl of loathing, he brushed himself off, then proceeded down the stairs.

Resolution filled me; I had planned on today being my last day on the premises, but I had a responsibility to protect the people under my care. Even if it was to be a temporary measure.

My attention landed on one such person. She'd averted her gaze to the floor, her head bowed in submission.

"Are you alright?"

It was not my nature to care for anyone's needs but my queen, though I was compelled to ask the question. The woman's gaze rose to meet mine for a moment before falling back down to the ground.

"Yes."

Her gesture was compliant, but the assurance was spit out in bitter anger between gritted teeth.

I ignored it. I could not soothe the sting of my father's venomous bite. But I could grant her leave to escape this place before my parents inevitably turned the safe space into a predator playground.

"I can dismiss you today, with pay. You will not need to see him again."

Moving around the desk, I grabbed a pen and notepad from the drawer to proceed with just that.

"No." Her head snapped up, her eyes flashing in a fierce defiance I knew very well. "He doesn't get that kind of power. I choose to stay."

I took her in, truly looking at her for the first time in weeks. She was quite striking even in the dim confines of the office. Dark features, thick lustrous hair, broad hips and a lithe, muscular body—still feminine enough to be considered pretty, but with enough of a flair to stand out in a sea of beautiful escorts. She'd come highly recommended from an associate, and my people hired her on the spot.

"Very well." I dropped the pen onto the desktop. "But I must inform you, I will no longer be needing your services. If you are to stay, you must take a new assignment. I'll be upping security measures, and I expect you to report if you've been treated poorly."

Long brown lashes blinked rapidly, but her face remained impassive and unreadable. "Yes, sir."

I gestured to the hallway, dismissing her. "I'll speak to Rosa today. Please speak of this to no one."

I ushered her through the doorway and closed it shut, locking it before I sat down behind the desk.

Closing my eyes, I took a moment to center myself and bury the rage simmering below the surface of my skin. There was no time to be angry; I had to remove a few key files and abandon this place with a handful of directives to my top staff. Primarily to enforce the rules, and keep employees safe until my parents rendered them useless.

Then I would change the locks on the office and the facility. It was the petulant gesture of a spoiled child, but it would impede my father inflicting damage, even for a day.

The other brothels under our ownership would have to fend for themselves. The hourglass of my day was running out of sand—I couldn't waste another moment.

I cleared out the desk, sent off a few messages, and quietly locked the door behind me, taking the discreet entrance into the back stairwell to avoid another run-in with Rosa with a stack of files in my arms.

Gabriella awaited me at the company office—the company office that would be entirely under Hillary's control as of tomorrow.

Despite my accomplishments being swept off to others, all I felt was relief.

Kellan's mercy and Hillary's interference had gifted me a new opportunity—one I would not squander. Legacies were built and rebuilt.

Cora Flynn

I would mortar each brick of my next legacy with the blood of my enemies. Beginning with Marco Alvarez and ending with Vicente Rodriguez.

"You good?"

Kellan's gruff tone interrupted my thoughts as I gazed onto the landscape of a bustling city below my office window, the people scurrying along sidewalks like ants in the freshly fallen snow.

Perhaps this would be the final time I looked out on this view. Would I return from the dead one day to retake my castle and my rightful place as leader of this company? Would I even desire such a thing after a true taste of freedom?

I didn't know the answers. A familiar numbness had spread through my limbs and into the fabric of my heart, keeping my emotions at bay. A protective shield I was well used to wearing.

Kellan and I had strategized my death through the cloak of private telephone calls and text messages—never in person for risk of being seen.

My executioner could not fraternize with his victim without a mark placed on his own head.

I'd gotten to know the man in this brief window of time, in far greater capacity than any of Jediah's showy parties. He was very calculating, a strategist—and his ideas were well deliberated.

For years, I had considered him the masculine oaf to scratch Hillary's itches, and I was pleased to learn my judgment had been misplaced. His fierce loyalty to her and the vicious hatred he held for his family ties mirrored my own—I felt bonded to this man who had once been a stranger.

"I am good, *companero*." I nodded though he did not see it. "I am ready to shed this skin and leave it to rot."

Hillary's Viking partner chuckled low through my headset, and the sound brought a smile to my own lips.

"Good." He responded succinctly, in the way I was learning Kellan did. The man spoke only when he had something valuable to say, in order to command attention when he did.

I liked that about him.

"He's already at the restaurant," Kellan continued in my ear. "You'll want to leave in the next five."

"It is done," I assured him and turned on the spot to pull my coat from its rack and the small messenger bag with my things. "Jacques will take me now."

"Remember," he reminded me, "no threats on your end, but make sure he gives you something we can use—goad him until you do."

"It is done," I repeated, exiting through the entrance doors of my empire without a backward glance. "I will call shortly."

We hung up as Jacques rounded the corner of the parking area, having been waiting for me. I directed him to the restaurant of the evening and he drove us there with impeccable timing, as always. Of all my staff, I would especially miss this man.

Exiting the vehicle with instructions for him to wait for me, I straightened my tie and walked through the barrel door alcove, waving the hostess off as I searched for my prey.

I stalked to him, pores already clogging from his greasy aura; the coating of malicious intent slicked my skin with a noxious film.

"You are a challenging man to track down, *Culicagado*."

I spat the Colombian insult as I stared down at the white-collar businessman, seated alone at his usual table in Les Augustin. A hearty spread of filet mignon and lobster filled the plates on the table, an exorbitant amount of food for one.

Marco Alvarez grinned up at me, his arrogant shark-tooth smile alight with undisguised delight and his shiny teeth glowing in the dim light of the café.

"Aaron Rodriguez," he boomed, dipping his fingers in the lemon water cleanse in front of him and wiping them between crisp linen napkins. "I'm surprised to see you here. Didn't your parents kick you to the curb?"

His words were dipped in acid, intending to burn; this man did not know I was already marked for death—the words of little men were of no consequence.

Scoffing brusquely, I took the seat in front of me, directly across from him, ignoring his useless taunt. Being rid of my parents would be the most positive outcome of my disappearance. Soon, I would make their riddance a permanent state of being.

"My parents will plead temporary insanity one day soon."

I reached for the basket of bread rolls in the center of the table and cracked one open with my hands. I began buttering it from the whipped pat beside it. "You are misguided if you believe I am nothing without them. Hillary and I have more than enough prospects to rival your newest arrangement."

I shrugged and leaned back in my chair, as if I were unaffected by his moves on the board. "I have no need for false promises for more money and power. Veronica and Vicente would whore themselves out for an additional ounce of either."

I bit into the bread roll, tasting nothing as I chewed and swallowed the crusty dough as Marco Alvarez chuckled heartily.

"Your parents were easily swayed," he said, agreeably, slicing into his rare steak and taking a bite. "You and

Hillary may be harder to break, but I assure you, you will break."

The amusement in his eyes morphed into the steely determination of a jungle cat hunting an elephant—the look of a man whose hubris far outweighed any source of sense. He was cunning and ruthless, certainly—only such people would dare get into bed with my parents, let alone vie for their attention.

His threat was confident, his intentions clear. It was not enough he was challenging Antonio and pulling down the sheets for the bed he'd made with Veronica and Vicente—he was determined to remove Hillary and I from the board as well.

A false prophet was dangerous when he believed in his own rhetoric.

"We are not breakable," I mused, pouring myself a glass of red wine from the table, raising the glass to him in a toast. "But if you choose to invest resources to discover this for yourself, you'll invest poorly. Be my guest."

I drew a sip of the rich, earthy wine and mulled it with my tongue, enjoying its delicate sweetness and sharp finish as my opponent watched me with hawkish eyes across the table.

His medium build had rounded over the years; his body no longer held the threatening aura of a hardened criminal. He drew fear from his eyes, able to shift from content family man to cold-hearted murderer with a single blink; a psychopathic light switch.

I held no fear of the pathetic visage of a man in front of me. He was another stooge in a sea of small men, determined to rise on the backs of others by breaking spines and snapping necks.

True power came from resilience and resolve; a cause worth fighting for. I had been an aimless man before now, handcuffed to my wealth and tethered to the expectations of others. I would now bask in my freedom from a gilded cage, though far freer than I'd ever been in this lifetime, under the protection of a woman who cared for me.

Hillary was now my purpose. Trusting her and keeping her safe by temporarily removing myself from the equation. Trusting in Kellan to protect us both while we knocked more pawns off the board.

Weak men rush into battle without swords and shields, proving their stupidity, not their bravery. Patience is a virtue, and I had it in spades. I would bide my time until I inserted the knife into Alvarez's heart myself.

"I am here as a warning." I fingered the stem of the wineglass and eyed the tawdry man over its rim. "Your entire operation will be exposed within days if you come after Lane Enterprises, or any of our outstanding contracts. I am still aligned with our previous friends, and they will not take kindly to your interference."

An outright lie—Antonio expected me dead and buried any day now, but Kellan had assured me the hit on my life was a private request. None of what I said mattered, regardless. Today wasn't about taunting Alvarez into useless confessions. It was about being seen, and hopefully, heard.

Alvarez chewed, looking thoughtful as his gaze never left my face, scrutinizing my intentions.

"You're bluffing, Rodriguez. Run home and hide before I come to get you. You're next."

There it was; the thin wisps of a threat, but there it was.

Satisfied, I rose from my seat and stared down at the man who would be tortured by my hands soon enough.

"Even great men bow to the sun," I quoted one of my favorite poets as my bulk loomed over his thin form. I smiled. "Consider me the star in your night sky."

Walking down the restaurant aisle, I dialed a number and hovered in the entryway near the hostess desk, where a petite Latina woman was sanitizing menus.

"If anything happens to me, it'll be Marco Alvarez's doing." I growled into the phone within earshot. "He just threatened me."

"Good," came Kellan's reply. The masculine roughness of his voice slightly filtered through the phone line. "And you got the recording?"

"Yes," I said succinctly, eyeing the woman who was poorly eavesdropping, as I'd hoped.

"Good work." Kellan's praise slid over me like a warm blanket; I was surprised by how much I enjoyed its comfort. "That'll be all we'll need when the time comes."

I hung up without another word, bracing for my incoming life of solitude and seclusion, a temporary reprieve while we made our next move.

Revenge was a dish best served cold. Alvarez would soon be knee-deep in gazpacho, his blood the broth, his bones the bread.

A feast fit for a king.

Cora Flynn

CHAPTER 5

Hillary

I awoke with a massive headache, the shrill screech of my alarm pulling me out of another terrifying nightmare.

They were getting worse; each evening brought far more hellish landscapes along with it, despite the emphatic promise from my doctor my brain would not be capable of dreaming under the effects of a newly prescribed sedative.

I didn't have time to be tired. As usual, my day was packed with meetings, with one particular presentation I wouldn't be missing, migraine be damned.

Pulling off my puffy pink eye mask and noise canceling earphones, I filled my lungs with three head-clearing breaths to calm my nervous system.

Cora Flynn

No amount of breaths in the world was going to bring me peace today. I needed to hit something.

Padding to my ensuite, I took my time getting ready, letting the steam from my shower seep into my pores and cleanse me from the inside out. I carefully tended to the cuts and bruises all over my body. Thankfully, my face hadn't taken the hardest hits; expensive makeup, dark lipstick and strategic hairstyling would cover the majority of it.

I finally stepped out of my soapy cocoon, applied my makeup and dried and curled my hair into loose waves. I rarely curled my hair—it took too much time, and I had too many more important things to do—but I couldn't force myself to rush out into the real world today.

The shattered shards of the last seventy-two hours had finally embedded themselves into my skin, and the pain of almost losing Aaron, the necessity of standing up to Kellan, and now having to keep Aaron safe from Mafia hit men, and keep Lucky under lock and key had shifted the trajectory of the next several weeks. I couldn't afford the detour.

I couldn't keep Alec in an offsite facility forever. No amount of picking off individual predators would ever bring my Cariña back. One judge or one family having their daughter returned to them wouldn't avenge Isabella.

I'd been searching for a way to honor her life for years; to avenge the gruesome way it had been stolen. The nightmares were wedging their way into my daily consciousness, as if her ghost was haunting me for failing her. For not loving her enough to see the grooming signs.

I hadn't been strong enough to save her.

My vendetta was for her; to avenge her death by removing all predators from our state. The only way to do that was to take out the head of the organizations providing them with fodder in the first place. Managing these additional complexities would take energy and time—time I didn't have.

When I finally made it out into the kitchen to make my morning cappuccino, the freshly prepared mug sitting on the countertop surprised me, complete with heart-shaped white foam nestled on top.

Right. My house guest.

The muscular form of a man in a navy suit lounged on my white chaise lounge in my periphery. I turned to Lauchlan O'Donnell laying on the settee with his arms behind his head, eyes closed to the ceiling.

So much for handcuffing him to my bedpost, Kellan.

"Was wondering when you'd join me." His Irish brogue broke through my usual morning quiet, but those sparkling, sea-glass eyes remained closed. "Heard your shower running and almost stepped in to join yeh."

He'd arrived late into the evening last night, after Kellan had installed the tracking chip under his skin as promised. All he'd brought with him was a travel case and a suit bag—and a bag of snacks because *'I know you're not gonna have anything good to eat here.'*

Ignoring the mug left for me on the counter, I made my way to the espresso machine that took up most of my counter space, and removed my favorite hand-potted mug from the hook on the wall. I turned the machine on to warm it back up—he'd had the courtesy to shut it off when he was done with it, at least—and turned my attention back to my wayward ward.

"Good thing for you, you didn't. I know how to castrate a man."

His eyes snapped open, but a playful grin danced across his tempting full lips. His gaze landed on mine, showing no sign of fear or hesitancy, just intrigue.

Apparently, very little made this man shake in his boots. I looked forward to testing that bravado soon.

"I'll bet you do, Blondie. Do yeh bathe in the man's tears afterwards? Or just collect them for your potions?"

A snort escaped me despite myself. Lucky O'Donnell was a brat.

And a con man—that little piece of information was still hanging between us. As far as I knew, Lucky didn't know I was privy to his actual day job—regardless of his side gig and crusade against Marco Alvarez. And as far as I knew, Kellan and Aaron weren't aware of it, either.

Lauchlan couldn't possibly know about Kellan's FBI ties; I was surprised Kellan had told Aaron about that part of his life, but it certainly made plotting my next steps with the two men easier. Fighting to the death in a gentlemen's agreement apparently developed an instant bond of sorts, which should prove useful in the days ahead.

Neither Lauchlan nor Aaron had any inkling of my evening activities—although, now I knew Lauchlan tracked my phone, I'd have to walk a much more careful line while delivering justice this week.

What an interesting circle of secrets among the four of us.

And I was the only one who knew them all.

Cocking my head, I assessed Lucky, who still leisurely took up space in my living room. I could call him on his shit right here and now, metaphorically castrate his agenda, and shift the power balance between us—but I didn't know enough yet. Someone had hired him; I needed to know who and what they'd hired him to do.

If he was going to steal something, he might as well get it over with while living in the lion's den—but the simplicity of that plan didn't sit well with me. A thief didn't need to follow me in the middle of the night to keep up the pretense. There had to be more to the story—a lot more—and I was determined to find out.

So, instead of pinning him to the wall with all that I knew, I raked my eyes over the well-honed biceps and thighs trapped in his form-fitting suit, sprawled out in all their glory, and enjoyed the view for a second longer than I should before responding.

"I drink them in my coffee, and it looks like I'm fresh out. I wouldn't test me."

Swinging his legs down to the floor, he settled into a seated position, resting his elbows on his knees, gaze peeking out from beneath long lashes, locked on mine in an intense stare of feral hunger.

"Oh, how I'd *love* to test you, lass."

Warmth spread deep in my belly and directly into my silk panties. His heated suggestion contagious, I tossed ice-chilled water on the fire before it could build further. Lauchlan O'Donnell was a tool to be wielded against the Alvarez empire; nothing more. Sexual attraction and chemistry be damned.

"I'll bet you would." I said, intentionally tossing his words back at him then poured his bribery caffeine down the sink and finished making my cappuccino.

He didn't take the bait, silent gaze on me as I worked; his stare burned a tiny hole through my shoulder blades, like I was an ant beneath his magnifying glass.

Having someone else in my space—especially *him*—was going to take some getting used to. With any luck, we'd be able to find an in to take down Alvarez as quickly as possible. For Aaron's sake, and for mine.

Speaking of—it was time for Lauchlan to earn his keep around here.

"Alright, Lucky," I sat on the sofa across from him, crossed my legs, and stared into the cocky recesses of his soul. I'd have to sip my coffee while conducting this small impromptu business meeting.

"It's time for you to spill. Your sister..." I prompted, eyeing him expectantly.

The playful nature that always danced behind his eyes dissipated instantly, the glow within the sea-glass going eerily blank. Still, his smile remained. He steepled his fingers in his lap and brought them up to rest on his lips.

"Fecking Conan." He shook his head, his smile morphing into a pained grimace. "He had to fuck me to get it out of me, but yeah, my sis."

My perfect brows rose to my hairline as I nearly choked on the drink halfway down my throat. Sputtering, I wiped the dribbles of coffee off my mug. "He failed to mention that part."

"Did he, now?" Lauchlan's eyes lit up again in amusement, the familiar cocky grin taking over his features. "Well, that won't do, will it? No secrets among the musketeers now, aye? Tied me to the bedpost and fucked me till I spilled my secrets and my cum all over his bedsheets. Would have been a great torture porn."

Shifting back into his seat, he eyed me in challenge. He clearly thought he'd shocked me.

As if I hadn't read the sexual tension between them months ago.

"Couldn't have been too great of a fuck if he only got one secret out of you." I raised a brow and took another, more cautious sip of my coffee. "Perhaps a woman's touch was needed."

He relaxed further into the cushion, his brows knitting together into a serious frown.

"I have no more secrets to spill, love."

He was so good at duplicity; it was truly astonishing to watch—not a single standard tell to show he was lying. When all the cards were on the table and I truly had him at my mercy, I would force him to teach me—I could use that level of skill in the boardroom.

"And your sister?" I prompted again, determined to get one story—a real one—out of him.

He tore his gaze from mine and rubbed a hand over his jaw, his calloused palm scraping over the two-day-old stubble atop his cheeks. Taking a page out of Aaron's patience book, I waited, sipping what remained of my coffee as I tried to assess every nuanced shift of muscle in his face.

"Shayna is—was," he corrected on a sigh, his stare downcast into the couch cushion, "my half-sister, but she might as well have been my parasite for how close we were."

"Da had an affair after a family job when I was nine. Ma came to America, and I stayed with him—he didn't marry her, but she had a child out of it, and Shayna became my world. Tiny little thing in need of protectin', so I became her protector."

My stomach twinged, the admission forcing pricks of unease down my spine. I didn't want to see similarities in our situations. Lucky was a chess piece. Anything else would be too... complicated.

"While I was away in college—I have a degree in 'tech', by the way." He smiled ruefully. "Software Engineering. Anyway, she got on with the wrong set of blokes. Groomers. She was fourteen, young and stupid, and they convinced her to do some things on cam. Then they blackmailed her with it to do other... things."

Groomers. That word... That despicable, disgusting word. I froze in my chair, willing the memories to remain under the surface. I was the one interrogating Lucky; I would not fall apart in his presence.

He blew out a harsh breath, shifting in his seat uncomfortably before his gaze finally met mine, his eyes crinkled with sorrowful regret.

Finally, a genuine emotion from his carefully crafted facade; The raw agony in his features took me back—a mirror of my pain.

Still, I stayed silent.

"She ran away at sixteen. Came to America, with two men younger than me who'd sold her on the land of opportunity, when they'd just sold her body to the highest bidder. Alvarez."

A raw timbre shook from his throat on the last word, as if Alvarez had stolen a part of his soul—just as he'd stolen a piece of mine. I tried to swallow the golf ball of emotion firmly embedded into my throat, but the bitter feelings only lodged deeper into my chest.

Mournful green eyes remained fixed on the rug, his hands clenching and unclenching in his lap, as if squeezing out his hidden hurt.

"Took me years to find out—to track down her whereabouts—and she was last seen in Chicago. And then she was a Jane Doe in the morgue. Da used a contact on this side to confirm it—pretty sure the heartbreak killed him."

Glossy eyes rose to meet mine. For a second, we were trapped in time, our tragedies inextricably intertwining our heads and our hearts.

A rosy flush crept up the sides of his neck to the tops of his cheekbones. He shook his head emphatically, as if clearing himself of the haunting memories and the ache that came with them.

I knew that pain. The rawness of it; how it scraped across every part of your insides with violent claws. I buried all the feelings that needed a much deeper grave, giving him the gift of grace to pull himself together. No one could pretend to hold that kind of agony without truly knowing its flavor on the tongue. I believed him.

Despite it all, I couldn't deny how deeply my heart hurt for him, his loss as acutely felt within my soul as it was in his. We'd both lost women we loved to brutal men who stole innocence as easily as they breathed air. The parallels were... uncomfortable.

Was it possible Lucky wasn't actually the bad guy?

"So, you're here to avenge her?" I asked gently, needing to hear it from his own lips. Desperate to hear more truths instead of the charming, cocky bullshit he normally spewed.

I needed this moment of vulnerability to last just a second longer, to know this side of Lucky was actually real.

Steely determination entered his gaze.

"Something like that. Vengeance for her. For me. For Da. Opportunity presented itself and I seized it."

Opportunity. Interesting word choice. Was I the chicken, or the egg in this scenario? Which *opportunity* came first? Did it matter? Could I ever trust him regardless of the running order of events?

"I see." Setting down my coffee mug on the glass table in front of me, I stood from my space on the chair opposite and moved beside him on the settee. I was careful not to touch him. Comforting him wasn't an option, not with the boundaries of subterfuge between us, but I could offer my presence.

"And what is your plan for Alvarez?"

His body tensed beside me and his hands fisted into his sides. For the first time, I saw true, powerful anger in Lucky—his usual restraint by the wayside.

"Access to everything he holds dear to his black heart. I'm halfway into his system now. When I get full control, I'm going to expose all the shyte he's been up to—the lives he's ruined. And I'm bleeding him of every cent he's got."

Pausing, I thought through several scenarios simultaneously. If I brought Blackbird in to speed up the process—

Could I trust Lucky enough to even make that offer? Had we considered all the avenues to make this possible, or were we relying too heavily on Kellan's ties to make our strongest play?

I'd have to sit on that one for now.

"Okay."

I stood and smoothed the creases out of my skirt, turning around to face my house guest.

"I'll help you with this. *We'll* help you with this," I amended and folded my arms across my chest, staring down my nose at his brooding presence. "But don't for a second think you have the upper hand here, Lucky. Fuck me over, and I'll fuck you twice as hard."

An impish glint entered his eye, the Lucky I knew depositing himself back into his body.

"Kellan said the same thing, Blondie, but he proved it. Care to do the same?"

A thick eyebrow rose to taunt me as he leaned back casually into my couch once again, his confession all but forgotten as he openly gawked at me.

"You're impossible." I grumbled. Leaving the living room, I grabbed my purse from the kitchen counter. "Don't mess up my house while I'm gone."

"I work, too, you know," he shot back, his warm presence close behind me as he followed me to the front foyer. "I'll see you tonight, honey."

The irritating man leaned down and kissed my forehead like we were long-time lovers. Then he tossed me a roguish wink, as if he'd get away with that shit now he'd sobbed on my shoulder.

I elbowed him in the ribs—hard enough to mark him with a tidy little bruise. He grunted and clutched his side, then let out a booming belly laugh that echoed through the metal box, its sound light and infectious. My lips quirked up before I could firmly press them into a neutral frown. Avoiding his gaze, I pressed the elevator button to go our separate ways.

We rode down in silence; him scrolling through his phone while I contemplated the details of his story.

His crusade was surprising, yet useful. The more I considered his connections and the power position I had over him, even without knowing his true agenda for me, I could use him to get Alvarez where I wanted him.

He waved as we got off the elevator and walked out the front glass doors. I waited for Josephine to arrive to take me to the office. I stared at his retreating form that grew more confident with each passing step.

Lauchlan may have a heart, but I didn't have time to see him as anything but a piece on the board. His trauma and vendetta didn't have to mean anything to me—he could still be a useful pawn. I was going to move him wherever I damn well pleased.

Why did that thought make me feel so shitty?

Cora Flynn

CHAPTER 6

Kellan

Jediah Waldorf's home was a monstrous monument to tiny-dick syndrome. I hated attending the little mixer events he used as bargaining chips to cozy up to people with actual power, and I hated being here today even more.

I sat alone on the antique chaise lounge in one of his many living rooms, the ancient furniture groaning under my considerable bulk. I shifted in irritation at the man ballsy enough to make me wait for him.

The man was all pomp and circumstance, but he was afraid of the Cartel, even if his little digs, singsong voice, and grating laughter masked it. Today, I wanted to make him terrified.

Cora Flynn

Trish was breathing down my neck—the team hadn't come up with a solid lead in the past two weeks since I'd been shut down by The Six, and I desperately needed to get the fuck away from Carlisle as soon as possible.

Even though I knew as long as Hillary Lane lived here I'd be inevitably tied to this godforsaken place. Aaron Rodriguez's life in my hands and the annoying Irish imp getting too close to our secrets meant I'd be here for a lot longer than planned.

Killing Lauchlan still wasn't off the table, no matter what Hillary wanted. He'd gotten her guard down enough to track her. That didn't sit well—my gut roiled with sour acid every time I considered if it had been somebody else who'd gotten under her skin.

Lauchlan was manipulative and smarter than he looked, but he wasn't dangerous; not in the ways I worried about. I was good at reading intent—the body was full of signs if you knew where to look—and nothing about the annoying man's energy said 'rapist' or 'serial killer.'

Since he'd slipped under Hillary's radar, though, I needed to up my protective measures.

He was trained to withstand torture. That wasn't something someone just learned off the street. He was a career criminal of some kind; I just didn't know what—and I was going to find out.

I shook my head to rid myself of the creeping memories. Memories of ramming my cock into his ass so hard I'd seen stars. The vision of him squirming and so desperate for me —he would have done just about anything for me to fuck him fast and hard.

One word—that was all I got out of him. Impressive and disappointing. I'd need to try again. *Then* I could kill him.

In thirty-eight years, no one had been my undoing. No one. Now, I found myself completely beholden to a woman who held my balls and my heart, and a man who I'd just as easily kill as I would fuck, but my curiosity was pushing me to make bad decisions.

Dangerous decisions.

"Kellan, doll! So lovely to see you!"

Jediah graced me with his presence by flouncing down the stairs in a magenta silk robe, open to reveal tiger print satin boxers and nothing else.

Four gold chains of varying lengths hung around his neck; the entire ensemble looked like he was the Cirque du Soleil version of Hugh Hefner.

Standing to greet him, the smaller man attempted to pull me in to kiss my cheeks, but I refused to budge. His smile faltered as he took in my angry stare.

"Come, come, Kellan. You know I'm not an early riser. So sorry to keep you waiting." He dipped his head in apology and motioned for me to follow him, leading me into a secondary, smaller parlor off the first room. He waved me in and gestured for me to sit in a much larger, more comfortable leather chair.

I said nothing as I held eye contact and slowly lowered, then leaned forward and rested my elbows on my knees. Interlacing my fingers, I prominently displayed the tattooed knuckles of 'hell' and 'hope' in his direction. He visibly gulped, pushing himself into a chair opposite me.

"How can I help you?"

"I contacted The Six to set up a target." I started slowly. "Thank you for their information. Through some *investigation*"—my lips curled at the word. I'd much rather be at the maiming stage than the sitting through bullshit interviews stage—"I discovered that someone has a contract out on someone close to me. I want it canceled."

"Impossible." To his credit, Jediah sat up straight, all business now, and looked me dead in the eye. "A contract can't be canceled once it's initiated. They will follow through unless they can't complete the mission, but I believe that's only happened once or twice in the organization's history. It's already a done deal."

"I need a better contact, then." I growled as my skin heated beneath the confines of my suit. "They won't be getting my money if they continue their contract against— my friend."

Jediah's normally drug-glazed eyes were now lit up with curiosity.

"They aren't killers, Kellan. I'm sure your 'friend' isn't in any danger. Surely, if they are in your circles, this person can afford whatever contract has been taken out on them?"

Harsh laughter bubbled up in my chest. Hillary was always in danger; the woman was a magnet for mayhem. I almost felt for the poor fucker who'd been handed the assignment to screw her over. When she figured out who it was—definitely a matter of when, not if, because I would find them and deliver them to her on a platter—her revenge would be far bloodier than mine ever could.

"'Danger' isn't what concerns me. The Carlos Cartel doesn't like it when someone fucks around with what's ours."

"I see." Jediah's face contorted into a frown—or what would have been a frown if he hadn't been heavily injected with Botox. "Well, if I had to guess, I would say it's an item. I've heard rumors that a few of our wealthy elite have some artwork that our European counterparts would like to get their hands on. It's certainly in line with The Six's reputation."

The Six were renowned for the theft of high-value items —I groaned inwardly as I considered all the paintings and expensive jewelry my billionaire woman might have all over the state. Shit I had never paid attention to, so now I was heavily behind the eight ball.

I shifted my position in the seat and relaxed my posture as if this conversation wasn't annoying the shit out of me.

"All of this for some artwork?"

"Ahhhh, I know it isn't the dangerous drugs and weapons you are used to peddling, my dear friend." Jediah's tone brokered the line of mocking and respectful. "But stolen artwork and dealings of said artwork is a billion-dollar black market industry. Quite lucrative in the right hands. Whatever the contract is, it will be for something truly sensational."

Sensational. Hillary probably had *seven* 'sensational' things, if not seventy. I shifted gears.

"Could I take out a contract on the person who took out the contract on—them?"

Jediah smirked, his knowing eyes seeing more than I wanted.

"You could. In theory." He cocked his head. "You would need to know what you are after, though. The Six only fulfill contracts for something specifically stated—a tangible. They are not 'hitmen for hire.'"

"I know plenty of those already." I waved a hand dismissively, ready to get out of this house and away from Jediah's simpering energy. I stood abruptly, taking two steps forward to loom over the man in question.

"I trust you'll use your discretion over this conversation, Jediah. Antonio doesn't take kindly to breaches in trust. Neither do I." I stepped in closer and lowered my head to peer into the whites of his widened eyes.

"I won't hesitate to cut off your pipeline, or slip a little something extra into your own personal supply, if I hear otherwise."

Nodding, he swallowed his tongue before sputtering, "Yes, of course, Kellan!"

I strode out of the parlor and out to the driveway without another word. Leaning against the headrest in my Jeep, I contemplated the next steps.

I was still investigating the fake HR complaint against Hillary; I needed to report back to Antonio on Aaron's fake death, and somehow figure out how Lauchlan could be useful in taking down Marco before I was forced into managing the horrific realities of human trafficking. January was only a month and a half away, and each second ticked by like there was a live bomb hovering above my ear.

Somehow, every aspect of my life now revolved around my Killer's orbit, and it was getting more impossible by the day to get out of her gravitational pull.

She wasn't a star—she was a gaping black hole of variables I couldn't control and decisions I couldn't protect her from. A hole I couldn't escape—I wouldn't escape, no matter how hard I tried to resist.

I was well and truly fucked.

"Load up boys, we're killing *cabrons* tonight!"

Mical rubbed his hands gleefully at the anticipation of a killing spree The scar across his cheek had healed, but his smile caused his skin to pull in a grimacing twist; the Joker-like rictus suited his darkness perfectly.

I couldn't deny the statement. We would kill tonight. My brothers, idiots that they were, had successfully discovered Alvarez's base of operations for their weapons dealings—deals they'd been stealing from us, and Antonio had ordered we take them down by whatever means necessary.

Normally, I would issue the orders, but the Cartel head decided that we needed a firmer hand. Antonio didn't care if all of Carlisle became a war zone—he didn't care about its people or its children. Just revenge, power, and more money to be made.

So, I bit my tongue and would channel my rage into the gangbangers who deserved it—the men who preyed on the weak. My body count might double tonight, depending on the blood bath awaiting us, but I wouldn't lose sleep over it.

Jonah nodded lazily beside him, fueled with whatever drug he'd taken before arriving at the family compound nestled in the hidden pass between Carlisle and Cascade Falls.

The three of us stood at the warehouse entrance, the open doors letting in frigid mountain air and freezing my skin. Several men and a few women were arming themselves with weapons, ammunition, and protective gear, awaiting their orders to move out.

My orders.

Before I could holler to the swelling crowd, the glaring headlights of a vehicle flooded the space behind us. Despite all the activity, the three us spun on our heels, weapons raised to take out the intruder.

I relaxed only slightly when I saw the familiar black SUV—our father had graced us with his presence tonight. A rarity.

His men stepped out first, the same three as last time with the bald man as his driver. Then Antonio climbed out of the vehicle dressed in black combat fatigues and armed to the teeth.

"*El Companeros!*" he cried, his breaths causing billows of steam in the chilly night air. "Tonight, we fight!"

Jonah and I exchanged a wary glance as Mical let out a bellowing war cry, as if our father showing up wasn't an issue.

For him, it probably wasn't. He thrived on chaos and this development only added to it. I clearly was losing my father's trust, a dangerous position to be in, heir or not. I'd have to prove myself tonight or risk the consequences.

I counted to ten backwards in my mind as I made my way over to Antonio's hired help.

"Getting bored at the palace?" I teased lightly as I shook his hand over the din of whoops and hollers behind me.

"I didn't want to miss the takedown of our enemies," he replied with a casual smile— his most dangerous. He gripped my wrist and pulled me closer, his steaming breath hot on my cheek. "What is the status of our other enemy? Is he buried yet?"

If he was asking, he already knew. I shook my head gruffly, as if his question annoyed me instead of terrified me.

"I have everything set up to take the heat away from us. This piece"—I nodded around us—"will be the perfect diversion. Billionaires can't just go missing."

He tutted a condescending *tsk* under his breath while he continued to stare me down. "You plan too much, *hijo*. Sometimes, we must simply be men of action, yes?" He bared his teeth, the casual smile molding into a vicious sneer. "Be a man of action tonight, Kellan. I am tired of you disappointing me."

I pulled out of his grasp, swallowed my hatred for the man, and turned to face the waiting crowd. "GPS coordinates are set," I barked, my fury at my father filtering through my face as if for our enemies. "We hit them hard and fast. Kill shots for anyone about to kill you. We need a few alive, so incapacitate where possible."

"Cut off their hands!" Mical shouted maniacally in the background to a myriad of hoots and enthusiastic screams. I ignored him and continued.

"Once everyone is incapacitated, get out of there. No witnesses, no stragglers. Get the fuck out of dodge, and do not come back here until one of us"—I nodded to my brothers, leaving out our latest Carlos guest—"reaches out to you. Drop the vehicles to the Cascade Falls black site and then get home as soon as possible. *Capisce?*"

Our trained soldiers immediately piled into the waiting black Jeeps, Mical and Jonah joining them. I stayed back until all the other vehicles were driving down the dirt road before turning to my father. "Are you driving with me?"

"I'll drive on my own, but I want the prisoners brought to my site." His hard stare was non-negotiable. He waved a hand toward the three stoic bodyguards still standing silently beside us. "My men will do the interrogating this time around."

Dipping my head in acknowledgment, I headed to my own Jeep and took off down the road, determined to get to the site before everyone else, using the alternate route I'd programmed into my GPS. It should shave off five minutes or so. I needed to be there first to see what we were dealing with, and give Trish a head's up we were taking out the trash tonight.

She was going to be pissed I'd given her so little notice, but our twenty-something year history would grant me some slack.

I arrived as I'd predicted and parked the vehicle off to the side of the road between two brick buildings at just the right distance. I staked out the scene before sending off a cryptic text to my mentor.

The building was nondescript at first glance—just a regular, metal-clad square box with a single light post outside to light up the front garage bay. We'd already scoped out the building using drone footage and two foot soldiers, so I knew where the four hidden security cameras were installed above the entry points and cover behind the building.

I hadn't told Mical or Jonah about my secret weapon; a powerful signal jammer Hillary's hacker had built for me. I'd hired her to do the job as a one-off, but now I knew the scope of her skill set, I'd be hiring her for more, but I didn't need my brothers getting their hands on another tool to make them more dangerous.

I always used a security jammer when I had to show up to take-downs in person—but nothing as good as Blackbird's hardware. It was the only way I could minimize the evidence of my involvement with Cartel business to keep tiptoeing on the FBI's tightrope.

Cora Flynn

Hearing the rumble of our entourage in the distance, I set up the jammer and hit the red button. Climbing out of the vehicle, I pulled on my face mask and tightened my gun belt.

Black-clad trained killers nodded as they marched past me to the building beyond. Exhaling my unrelenting sense of foreboding, I followed our makeshift army into the fray.

The next hour flew by in a flurry of bloodshed. My brothers led the charge with me close behind, covering for their recklessness while they ripped through the building of trained killers like unbridled cowboys.

One quick fucker, a heavily scarred man with a shaved head, got through their formation and shoved a sawed-off shotgun into my face. My knife ripped through his spleen before he pulled the trigger, and he fell to the ground with a piercing scream of agony.

The Alvarez men were vicious in their delivery and hungry to kill; our element of surprise only gave us so much of an advantage. Our crew lambasted through the cohort; gunpowder and the metallic stench of blood enriched the air as each member of Alvarez's crew was wiped from existence.

I fired the last bullet into the last sorry fuck who'd made the wrong choice in showing up for work tonight. Warm flecks of blood spattered my cheek as his skull shattered three paces away from me.

I felt nothing as his corpse collapsed to the dirt at my feet.

It wasn't just their supply warehouse as we had originally suspected, but their clubhouse; the back of the building contained a pool hall, kitchen, and several bedrooms, even windows looking out into the garage.

They heard and saw us coming, frantically grabbing their own weapons and calling to the others for backup, but once we'd taken control of the outward operation, the inside group didn't have a chance.

I searched the bedrooms one by one as Jonah and Mical secured a few prisoners and killed the rest. The remainder of our group loaded up weapons and moved out the cargo into waiting transport trucks as quickly as possible.

I blasted open a locked bedroom door with a single shot, surprised to find a bulging man laying in bed with several women chained to the bedposts, their naked bodies shivering from fear as wide eyes peered at me through the dim light of the lamp by the bedside.

Their heads lolled lazily despite their panic, and I knew with certainty they'd been drugged.

In the fraction of a second it took to assess the situation, the man whipped out a pistol, cocking it quickly. Quick reflexes and years of training kicked in, and I shot the gun out of his hand before he could lift his finger from the trigger.

He screamed in agony and fell back to the mattress, holding his bleeding hand to his chest, rocking back and forth in shock from the pain.

I yanked the greasy black hair off his scalp, pulling him up to face me. "Where is the key?" I nodded to the cuffs on the women's wrists and used my other gloved hand to force my finger into his gaping wound. I immediately removed the pressure, needing to know its location before the man passed out on me.

"T-t-there," he sputtered, pointing his uninjured hand into the bedside drawer. Keeping my grip on his scalp, I tore open the drawer, disgusted by the pile of used needles and bags of powder alongside the single silver key. I carefully picked it up and let go of my captive, quickly uncuffing the women.

"Get out!" I shouted, shoving them through the doorway toward safety downstairs. I didn't wait to watch them skitter down the hallway—I turned my attention back to my next victim.

"You like drugging women for fun?"

Cora Flynn

A sheen of stinking sweat dripped from the man's brow as he cowered in fear, shrinking further into the bedsheets as he cradled his bloody hand. Small whimpers filtered through his lips, but he said nothing.

"There is no excuse for men like you." Climbing on top of him, I restricted all of his movements between my thighs, ignoring the little blood that seeped into my clothes. There was about to be so much more. "Let me show you what it feels like to have something taken from you."

I took out my favorite sharpened blade from my pocket and held it against the flesh of his stomach. Sobs escaped him as I cut a deep line from the hair of his belly-button up to his sternum. Then I gripped both sides of his abdomen and pried the cut apart, exposing the soft internal flesh beneath.

A darkness took over me, desperate to be fed. Without hesitation, I pushed my hand through the opening, gripped the slippery tubing of his intestine, and pulled it through his skin.

His sobs waned to deafening silence as his body succumbed to shock, going limp as he passed out.

A slew of gunshots tore me from my task. Leaving the man to die slowly in his own filth, I took the steps two at a time and raced back down to the warehouse floor.

My stomach twisted into my throat at the three women with holes where their hearts used to be, bloody and naked on the earthen warehouse floor, their eyes no longer seeing this world.

Antonio's calculating, emotionless gaze stared back at me. "Drugged girls have no value to us." He calmly placed his gun back into his belt and turned on his heel towards his waiting men.

"Move out," he called to the echoing chamber, and the remaining members of our crew scattered at his command.

I stared hard at the bodies before me, allowing their image to harden my resolve, their blank stares and lifeless forms cementing my path forward.

My allegiance to this family had frayed to the point of no salvation. Whatever Hillary needed from me to fulfill her vendetta, I would do it.

Alvarez and Antonio were going to die by my hand, and it wouldn't come soon enough.

Cora Flynn

CHAPTER 7

Hillary

I shot daggers at the man who'd shown up here today; the audacity of my enemy pricked me like a thousand tiny needles under my skin.

Marco Alvarez stared snidely back, a satisfied little smirk on his face. He sat on the plastic chair of the charitable foundation's auditorium like a king on a throne, though he was worth nothing more than a toddler on a toilet. I turned to face the speaker; a brief reprieve from having to watch his smug, ugly face.

"Thanks to your generous donations today, you've given the gift of hope to so many young girls like Layla."

The foundation I supported—the one that helped hundreds of women and children escape sexual predators—was hosting their annual Christmas appreciation event. An audience of several dozen attendees—mostly municipal counselors and government representatives, but a handful of wealthy donors who valued the cause—burst into applause. My stomach soured, though, when Marco clapped just as enthusiastically, like he wasn't single-handedly causing the very problem this organization worked so hard to solve.

I stood and shook hands with many of the donors as the crowd dispersed. Alvarez strode over to me, sticking out his hand for a shake of his own.

"Marco." I smiled coolly in greeting, steadying myself and appraising him like a viper assessing their next meal. "I wasn't aware you were a donor."

"I'm not." His tone belied none of the malice he was capable of, no doubt to hide his true agenda from the eavesdropping ears all around us. "But what a great cause. Alvarez International intends to make a large donation today. It's the least we can do."

Over my dead body.

I would make sure the foundation didn't take one penny of his blood money. I'd double my donation this year to oust him from that farce of philanthropy.

"How wonderful." My smile turned from casual cool to bitter ice. "It's about time you started contributing to this community."

"Oh, we certainly do a lot for this community," he said loudly. Then he stepped closer and lowered his voice. "I heard your business partner is in a bit of trouble. Have you found his replacement yet?"

How in the fuck did Alvarez know anything about Aaron? As soon as I considered the question, I knew the answer. Veronica and Vicente would have let Marco in on their little sacrificial lamb plan—how they jumped ship by throwing their son to Antonio's wolf. It would be so satisfying when we burned their empire to the ground and killed three birds with the same stone.

Before I could respond, though, a high-pitched titter interrupted our glare-off.

"Ms. Lane, we are just *thrilled* to have you here!"

Marco hastily stepped back, apparently satisfied with his mediocre assertion of dominance, and melted into the crowd; the speaker, an enthusiastic middle-aged brunette by the name of Roberta shook my hand so aggressively the ligaments in my wrist groaned their frustration.

I gently removed my hand from her grip and offered a smile instead. "It's lovely to be here, Roberta. Thank you for all you do."

I meant it. Roberta and this foundation had provided shelter, education, and new opportunities for thousands of girls in Sequoia and its surrounding states. Girls as young as five years old were swept away from dangerous situations, their legal hearings expedited, and then they were protected within a network of heavily vetted goodhearted people.

"Thank you for all that *you've* done, Miss Lane." Roberta stepped back, her slight frame wavering like a reed, tears shining in her eyes. "Have you seen the latest numbers? Four hundred girls this year—*four* hundred!" Hands flew up for emphasis as tears flowed freely down her cheeks, now. "Where would they be without this organization? Who would protect them?"

Heat flushed through my cheeks. The answer to that question had haunted me every day for nine years.

"Thankfully, that's not our reality." I swallowed past the painful memories and smiled warmly, nodding toward Marty, who broke the somber moment by handing Roberta an envelope.

"This gift is from a new backer—a business partner of mine. I trust you will put it to good use."

I shook her hand once more in goodbye before heading to the long hallway to the back of the room.

Aaron had generously donated a quarter of a million dollars as a part of our partnership agreement—a clause he insisted be included. Even though he had no connection to the cause, he knew it meant something to me.

I was realizing—uncomfortably so—how much I meant to the man I'd called a friend since we were children. Many times he'd handed his feelings to me on a platter through his actions, not his words, and I was too stubborn to taste them.

They now felt pungent on my tongue, the palatable flavor laced with bitter regret. The opportunity to have a person in my court—one who'd give me the world if I'd let him—was in reach, yet the damaged part of me kept pushing him away.

I didn't want him to go away.

I needed to properly thank him once he was safely holed up at the Palace, out of Antonio's sights.

I'd wanted to whisk him away from Club 7 immediately, but he'd reasoned with me to give him one more day of "cleaning up." Whatever that entailed. As much as I didn't want to leave him to his own devices while he stood at the very center of Antonio's bullseye, I had important obligations to attend; I had to trust that he could hold his own for just twenty-four hours longer.

Kellan's list had a particularly interesting name on it— one that luck and circumstance of today's activities brought me directly to them, no additional planning required.

The culprit herself stood a mere ten feet away, chatting animatedly to Marco, a large phony smile plastered to her surgically plastic face as she charmed him. I kept my blood to a roiling simmer, disgusted that her brand of poison had sneaked into the haven Roberta created.

It was very rare that a woman's name appeared across my desk. While I'd be the first to admit my crusade was primarily against the depraved men of society, women had the same capacity for evil—it simply came out in different ways.

Sandra Owens, medical director of the foundation, was abusing her position of power, delivering young children directly back into the hands of new abusers. Now that I saw the two of them together, it was such an obvious connection; I don't know how I missed it in her background check.

Lauchlan had generously provided one of his custom micro-GPS tracking devices—the same one he'd used to track me—after I threatened to force-feed him my green smoothies for a week. I planned to fasten one to the inside of her purse and send her coordinates to the team.

She wouldn't get the opportunity to go back to her daily routine, sans genitals, after a run-in with me—not when she continued to work with the vulnerable.

I hadn't yet decided what to do with her. I could admit I didn't like the thought of killing another woman—but genital mutilation wasn't the answer either. Women had experienced enough of that in our history.

At her closed office door, I paused. My window was brief at best. Giving the handle an experimental wiggle, I pushed inward with enough pressure on the knob to unlock the cheap latch.

The part of the building where the kids were cared could rival *The Truman Show*—every angle and crevice of the facility was captured via closed circuit camera. This section didn't have nearly the same features. I'd use it to my advantage today, but would wire the funds to Roberta to up their office security immediately *after* I finished my task.

On quick feet, I located Sandra's purse—a Prada bag— behind her desk. The tracker was attached to a small square of blot paper in my jacket pocket—trust Lauchlan to make state-of-the-art tracking technology look like an LSD drop—and carefully removed its sticky backing to place it directly on the silk fabric lining closer to the bottom.

I closed the door softly behind me and confidently strode back down the hallway to the dispersing crowd. Marty waved me down from the entrance, ready to escort us to our next meeting.

Whether it was justice by night, or business by day, time stood for no man—or woman.

"Let's take a detour," I suggested to Marty as we stepped out of our final meeting of the afternoon into the chilled December air. "I have a small stop I'd like to make."

Marty eyed me, frosted gray eyes twinkling knowingly against the dull palette of grayer sky. "Kellan again?" he teased, opening the car door for me before Joey could get the chance. Closing the door behind me, he got in on the other side.

"No, not Kellan again," I huffed in annoyance, buckling my seat belt and nodding at Joey to drive. "But someone equally exhausting." I sunk back into the buttery leather of the headrest and closed my eyes. I opened one and peered over to see him staring at me expectantly.

"My father." My lips twitched down in a grimace. "I've been summoned again, and I'd like to get it over with. If you're with me, I can make sure it's a quick visit."

Marty nodded and faced forward, scrolling his phone. I peered out the window at the mountainous landscape, my mind too scattered to properly enjoy the view.

I'd denied Daddy's request for leave last time, under the guise of not wanting to request a ridiculous favor from Kellan, but mostly, I'd done so out of pure spite. I'd lied and told him that Kellan wouldn't grant it. Georgio Carlos had been my father's best friend, and his brother, the one who'd put a bullet into his brain, wasn't likely to grant him a pass, anyway. It wasn't worth the trade, if he'd be willing to trade at all.

Naturally, Camden directed the fury over the very bed he'd made himself at me. I'd ignored it for as long as I could.

"Would you like me to come in with you?" Marty asked as Joey parked in the ornate circular driveway at the front entrance to the family grand manor.

"Actually... yes." I dipped my head in thanks before abandoning my warm vehicle for the frigid air of my father's castle.

I strode into the home without knocking and ran right into the suited penguin that was Alaric.

"Miss Lane." He sniffed the air as if I carried a foul smell. "I must insist you ring the doorbell when you arrive, I—"

"I won't be ringing the doorbell to *my* home, Alaric." I arched a single challenging eyebrow in his direction, then beckoned Marty to follow me through the house, ignoring the dignified 'hmmmf' the stuffy butler tossed in my direction.

Making my way to Daddy's study, I noticed many of the paintings I'd hung were missing—rectangle shadows of dust collecting in their places.

Marty trailed a few feet behind me, his brows raising at the elaborate trim details and ornate light fixtures dotting the main hall. Likely, he was surprised I'd opted to spend money on Daddy, given the circumstances.

It was sheer familial guilt, through and through. Even I wasn't immune to the power of a narcissist.

I found the man in question seated on the leather sofa in his study as expected, but I wasn't expecting the woman sidled up next to him.

"Marcie?"

What was Marcie Davidson doing here?

"Hello, Hillary!" The blond, blue-eyed woman in her fifties beamed up at me like we were old friends. "So nice to see you again!"

Cora Flynn

I hadn't seen Marcie in years; she and her husband were in the tech sphere in Carlisle for years, so she'd attended many of the same galas. She'd also had a fling with Winter's father before he was sentenced to prison, but we'd had no personal connection otherwise.

I scanned the scene—Marcie comfortably nestled into the seat, her knees resting against Daddy's thighs, his hand resting on her calf—the cozy picture of a relationship.

"Why am I being summoned again?" I asked brusquely, more irritated than I probably should allow him to see by this sudden revelation.

"I wanted to know your Christmas plans."

Daddy's statement was simple, but the expectation in his eyes was not. Despite my reservations, I'd spent Christmas Day with him every year since his house arrest; a painful twelve hours of time-honored traditions, none of which carried any meaning, pretending our family valued our blooded bond. I'd decided months ago I wouldn't be keeping up the charade this year, and I'd told him so.

Before I could respond, Marcie jumped in.

"This isn't the way I would have wanted you to find out, but your father and I have been seeing each other for a few months now, and I was hoping you'd consider spending Christmas with me and my son this year."

An incredulous snort erupted before I could stifle it.

"I'm sorry... excuse me?"

Her sunny smile faltered as the pure hatred for my father bled through my normally controlled mask of indifference.

Narcissists truly thought the world revolved around them and every person in their orbit was to bend to their will. Daddy's audacity to think that he could control my actions through Marcie via some 'family dinner' gimmick would have been hilarious—if it wasn't so revolting.

In all my thirty-one years, Daddy had never spoken of Helen Lane. Every shred of information I had about her was from my own research—the desperation of a little girl looking to connect with another woman. He only ever mentioned my mother when he wanted to control me.

When 'my mother' would have been disappointed by my actions. When 'my mother' would have wanted me to take on a particular client or business deal. He used my mother's memory—the memory of a woman I didn't have—as a weapon wielded whenever he wanted me to do something I wasn't willing to do, instead of telling me she would have been proud, that she had wanted me.

I hadn't recognized the tactic until I was well into my twenties, and now that I refused to bend to the thinly veiled pretense of disappointing her, he was using another woman to bend my will.

Pathetic.

His days of veiled control behind closed curtains were ending; he would soon bow at *my* feet and bend to *my* will, before my gravity crushed him like the meaningless pest he was.

I heard Marty leave quietly through the open study door; I would be close behind.

"Marcie, if you're seeing my father, you should know that there is no love here." I waved in the empty space that felt so unbearably heavy between us. "I won't be spending Christmas Day with him, let alone a woman I really don't know and her offspring. I'd say it's not you, it's me, but it's definitely you." I glowered at my father. "And him."

"Hillary, control yourself," Daddy growled through gritted teeth. "You're embarrassing me."

"Your whole life is an embarrassment," I snapped, gesturing at the surrounding room. "You're on house arrest in a home your daughter had to buy for you because you lost everything betting on the wrong horse. I've done more than enough, and I'm done."

Turning on my heel, I stalked down the hallway of this house of horrors, and stomped through the snow to the waiting SUV. Marty already sat buckled up, staring out the window.

I fumed in silence on the ride back into Carlisle.

Fuck that insipid little man. After all these years to dare to pretend he had been a father, rather than a gold-sucking cockroach. He would trade me in for my empire in a second if given the chance, then slit my throat for the reward without a thought. I came by my ruthlessness honestly.

I sent off a message to Sammy, encouraging him to capture our next little lesson as soon as possible. I needed an outlet, and Sandra Owens was the perfect victim.

CHAPTER 8

Aaron

"**I**s the blindfold necessary, *Mi Reina*? Should I not know where I am being taken?"

I tugged in amusement at the silk scarf Hillary had tied around my face as her driver drove us to her secret apartment. She'd picked me up from the lowest level of my office tower's parking garage. The dull gray concrete walls were my last view before I welcomed the darkness of the eye covering.

How appropriate I would enter my new life as a blinded man. Perhaps I would be granted the gift of new sight—a revised lens to regard my empire from atop my crumbled throne.

"It's just a precaution, Aaron." Her tone was blunt, laced with exasperation. "We need to keep this location contained."

I didn't point out the fallacy of this plan, when Kellan and inevitably our Irish tagalong would likely end up within the confines of the building as well. The two men were magnets to my beautiful companion; wherever she was, they would follow.

As I followed now.

Nodding absently and entertaining the mediocre attempts at subterfuge, my thoughts turned to the many plans we'd already put into play.

Our paperwork was signed and sealed. I'd relinquished full control of the assets in my name and the decision-making power of my companies to Lane Enterprises, specifically Hillary Lane, thanks to her lawyer's expedient delivery.

I had packed nothing but the few pieces of casual clothing I owned, some trinkets of value, and a selection of books that had long lived on my nightstand with the best of intentions. There was nothing more I wanted.

Kellan was to bring me an untraceable replacement phone and laptop, but it wouldn't be today. The annoying Irishman was also helping my cause, securing a new identity and passport from a series of his contacts.

I was about to wipe my existence from this earth, and the only three people who knew my heart still beat were the woman who made it so, the man who had been supposed to halt it from pumping, and the meddling irritant somehow providing the illegal documents to keep me hidden.

I had my own connections to provide such a thing—my family's counterfeiting side of the business ranged from government documents to famous artwork, but dead men had no allies, and to be clear, I was very much a dead man.

Kellan was going to fake my demise in a car accident off a gorge outside of Cascade Falls, under the guise that my body disappeared down the river, never to be found. When I'd handed over the keys to my Mercedes for the ruse, regret swirled in the recesses of my heart. Jacques loved that car, and it had been my intention to gift it to him. I'd opted to leave him a different one in my will.

My newly renovated building had also been left to Hillary, for whatever purpose she deemed fit. I'd had so many plans for my empire with that space. Another pain to my heart.

The timing of these changes was questionable. Sebastien was instructed to manipulate the will notes to thwart any suspicion my death was faked or planned. I could only hope client confidentiality would hold and he wouldn't betray my confidence. Under Kellan's watchful eyes, perhaps he wouldn't.

The Cartel man's loyalty to me was surprising, and yet, I trusted him entirely. He'd spared my life. Then he had revealed a damning secret I hadn't earned, and was now taking serious risks to protect me.

It was not me he was ultimately trying to serve, though; every glimpse of *Mi Reina* in his gaze told me he was as besotted by her as I was. His motivations were not my concern; his actions kept me under a powerful shield until I could sharpen my sword—the least I could do was offer the man my trust in return.

Once the new laptop was in my hands, I would enlist my dark-web connections to contribute; to turn on my parents and their agenda—the online evil powers that did not know my real name or purpose.

Perhaps in that regard, the techy Irishman could offer something useful.

"Aaron?" Hillary's soft voice and touch brushed against the back of my hand.

"Apologies." I groped for her hand, threading her delicate fingers through my own and squeezing for good measure. "My mind is elsewhere."

She clicked her tongue but remained silent, her smooth skin growing warm beneath my palm. It was a new sensation, holding her hand with no other motive; her comfort soothed the collection of thoughts and I tucked them away for examination later.

I traced the lines of her palm with the pad of my thumb, the lack of sight heightening the sensation of her touch. Pinpricks of awareness tiptoed up my spine; I longed to touch her like this everywhere—to explore her body in ways I'd never appreciated before.

Dead men were romantics, it would seem.

"We're here." Hillary tore her hand from mine before I could think of another damning thought. The vehicle came to an abrupt halt, jolting me forward. A blast of chilled air hit the uncovered parts of my face before slender, deft fingers gently removed my blindfold.

Twilight colored the dark square building in front of me a coppery gold. The air was dead quiet. Hulking mountains surrounded all sides of the nondescript outpost. A dusting of snow crunched underfoot as she led me to the side door. Her driver hovered behind us as an eye scanner and thumb print released the mechanism on the metal door to open.

She and Hillary shared a look full of significance before the driver walked in ahead of us and proceeded down a dark hallway on the main floor. We didn't follow; instead, my escort took an immediate left and led me down a sterile stairwell to the level below.

We passed through a ballroom-sized space full of metal shelving, most of it empty, save for a few paper boxes and what appeared to be a lifetime supply of bottled water, toilet paper, and protein bars.

Another thumbprint opened access to a series of shelves along what appeared to be a concrete wall. Beyond was a small foyer with coat hooks and a welcome mat. She flicked a switch beside me, and the door swung closed behind us, leaving us in complete darkness.

"Sorry," she said thickly, her voice muffled in the cramped space. Another flick of plastic, and the electronic hum of tube lighting, then brilliant white flooded the interior.

She pulled me through the opening while I blinked rapidly, dazed by spots of tiny fireworks filling my vision at the abrupt change.

When my body finally shook off the assault to my senses, I took stock of my new home. It was... pleasantly surprising.

The open concept kitchen and living room area looked like any other modern apartment; warm, marble-tiled floors and white kitchen cabinets with a black quartz island made up the primary cooking area—not all that different from her setup at home. I eyed the small espresso machine sitting innocently on the counter and couldn't stifle my chuckle. My Queen would still get her perfect coffee, even through an apocalypse.

Comfortable-looking leather furniture in creams and champagne pink filled the smaller living space on the opposite side of the room. A wall of filled bookshelves along the back held enough reading material for a two-year shut-in.

Most impressive were the beams of what appeared to be natural light coming from strategic cutouts on the ceiling and walls, as if sunlight were breaking through the thick concrete.

"Have you been preparing for the end of days, *Mi Reina*? It would seem this was not designed for my comfort." I raised an eyebrow at the coffee machine, and she smiled sweetly.

"I'm prepared, Aaron. With Daddy's enemies and my own, you never know when you're going to need your own little home away from home." Her voice held a light tone, but the forced smile faltered. Her blue gaze peered into my own. "I know it's not your home, and I know this is going to be an adjustment, but I—"

I pulled her body toward me, not allowing her to finish apologizing for offering me shelter and safety. My lips crashed down into hers, forcefully removing the words from her tongue with my own as I demanded entrance. Small hands gripped my wrists as I pushed her forward and pressed my muscles against her smaller form until her thighs hit the couch cushion behind her.

Her body melted into mine, our kiss scorching into a frantic melee of sucks and nips as my hands crept into her hair to hold her in place; I was determined to dismantle her before fucking her properly.

I pulled away only far enough to whisper as I licked a trail of fevered kisses down the column of her neck.

"I am going to fuck you, *Mi Reina*. I will fuck every thought out of your head until you can no longer speak such silly things. The only words on your pretty tongue are to be 'please', 'yes', and gasping my name. Tell me you understand."

This wispy waif of a woman moved mountains and battled bears, with no hesitation—ruthless, bold, cunning, and brave. The violent need to unravel her coiled springs, to loosen every tightly wound fiber of her control, overtook all my senses. I couldn't let her leave until I had her.

Gripping the base of her skull harder, I tilted her head upward to peer into her soul through the shades of her blue eyes, awaiting my answer.

"Yes," she breathed. The light tone hardened my dick with its gentle caress. Tears collected in the corners of her eyes as I continued to pull on the roots of her hair, but my gaze never wavered from the beauty of her surrender. "*Please*, Aaron."

This woman used me, choked me, tortured my body into submission, but never had she begged me. Her pleading moan dissolved all manner of my control and my body succumbed to vicious, urgent *need*.

Releasing my hold, I let my hands fall to the zipper of her jacket and tugged it down to its base. I yanked it off her shoulders while my aching cock demanded to see her bare before me.

My hands gripped the hem of her cashmere sweater and pulled it swiftly over her head. She wore black delicate eyelet lace barely covering the erect pink of her nipples. Dropping to my knees, I buried my face between her breasts and mouthed the dainty fabric to suck on the flushed skin beneath.

She writhed, her body so responsive to my every ministration. I continued to lavish her nipples with my mouth as my hands roamed downward to remove her tight jeans. Following the heat of her skin once the pants were properly settled on the floor, I skated my hands across her calves, her thighs, and directly to the sticky heat of her cunt. Slick desire coated my fingers when I slipped them through her folds and I relished her whimpers as she bucked against my touch.

I would never be the only one to touch her this way, but I would ensure my brand on her skin, between her thighs, inside the deepest parts of her, could never be removed by another. *Mi Reina* would forever carry my imprint. She was *mine*.

"I will taste you before I fuck you."

The declaration made her eyes roll to the back of the head before I abandoned her nipples for the flavor of her clit. I nuzzled her swollen nub with little licks before latching my entire mouth over her cunt. She let out a ragged cry, breathlessly moaning my name while my top lip vibrated against her clit and my tongue delved in to suck every drop of her desire.

Her sweetness enveloped me, a scent and taste I would never be rid of, her ownership a proud reminder of the woman I coveted as my forever. Let the other men in her life smell her on my flesh and know they would never be rid of me.

Grabbing the plump flesh of her ass, I held her in place, her body desperately trying to let go as I continued my punishing pace. Within moments, her legs trembled and a flood of sweet cum coated my tongue—the delicious sounds of her orgasm caused my trapped cock a wealth of pain.

I stood and wrapped my arms around her before she could fall to the floor. Carrying her to a large circular reading chair on the other side of the room, I nestled her into the cushions. She looked up at me, dazed satisfaction relaxing her features.

I loved seeing *Mi Reina* like this—unencumbered, filled with pleasure, and free from her pain.

I needed her to be filled with my cum, myself free of the pain of loving her from afar.

The winter jacket I wore dropped to the floor, my shirt unbuttoned and trousers shucked in quick movements, before my honed body was on full display.

Dazed and beautiful storm blue eyes appraised me, her stare lingering on my swollen cock leaking pre-cum, ready to impale her.

The unfiltered trust shining through her gaze nearly broke me—my love for this woman swelled from deep within the bowels of my damaged heart.

"I will not hurt you, *Mi Reina*—but I am a desperate man." I stepped closer. "I will tear you in two with my cock and glue you back together with my cum."

She bit her lip, the pouty pink flesh taunting me at the promise. Pulling her up by her chin, I bit the taunting skin, sucked it back into my mouth to soothe it, forcing her taste onto her tongue.

Then I fucked her into two pieces.

I pulled her hips forward and thrust in without warning. Her welcoming heat held me hostage as I forced myself as deeply as she'd allow, relishing the stretch of her around my cock. Drawing back, I pounded into her again, forcing her thighs open to take more of me with every slap of skin.

The symphony of our bodies in motion was tempestuous music; haunted and soothing, possessed and depraved. I would record the sound of it next time—to remind me of the beautiful notes when the rest of our world lay in ruin.

She clung to my shoulders, nails scraping across my skin and drawing blood.

I relished her marks on my skin as I tattooed myself on her walls, claiming her just as she claimed me, our fates intertwined as if written in the stars themselves.

I was a believer in nothing—there were no gods to guide us or prophecies to provide—but I believed in her, as she believed in me.

I slowed my pace and drew her closer to my body, cradling her against my chest as I thrust in long, torturous strokes.

"I love you, *Mi Reina.*" I kissed the apples of her cheeks, her eyelids, and settled one final kiss to her forehead before cupping her jaw and seeking the truth in her own eyes. "You do not need to say it back, but it is the truth of my heart."

Glazed, lustful eyes widened, but she did not shrink from my pronouncement. A silence settled between us—I continued to move languidly into her body, gently caressing her walls with my cock as her thighs wrapped around my waist to keep me there.

We fucked like this for minutes, the tension building as our gazes held, a staring contest for lovers desperate to stay in the moment. Her muscles tensed against me, seconds from her release, when she finally broke eye contact.

"Aaron, I"—she closed her eyes and drew in a shaky breath, her flushed cheeks flooding to crimson—"I...love you, too, *mi caballero oscuro.*"

Cora Flynn

Her Dark Knight. I would cherish the endearment for the remainder of my short life.

She sobbed through her orgasm and clung to me as we bore the relief of our confessions. Grinding my hips for one last stroke, I released into her, the sweetest satisfaction of her words and her body unleashing a potent euphoria from deep within my soul.

Mi Reina. My Queen. My love.

CHAPTER 9

Lauchlan

*E*enie, *meanie, minie, mo.*

I quietly roamed Hillary's apartment being the good little captive I was, taking my time to browse through her things.

I wasn't even trying to be discreet about it.

It was what she'd be expecting of me, and I wanted nothing more than to deliver on her expectations. I picked up a polished trinket that looked like it came from India—from a visit to the countryside, not a sweatshop—and placed it back down on the bookshelf, wiggling my fingers in a wave at the security camera watching me from the corner.

Cora Flynn

This place must be cleaned by house-elves—I'd never seen a cleaner come in and yet, it was damned spotless every morning. Tomorrow, I was gonna leave crushed Cocoa Pebbles on the quartz countertop to bait them—see how many little Irish sprites she'd convinced to work for her.

She was pretty convincing, my Blondie.

In my search, I'd come up with nothing—well, I'd come up with lots of things, expensive bits and bobbles and a tasty little pair of black lace panties with the arsehole cut out of them. I'd held those up to the camera before stuffing them into my pocket—but nothing I had been actually hoping to find.

The hidden door in her closet was an interesting revelation, though. Wouldn't put it past her to house her own little torture chamber for wayward souls—or a kink dungeon to work out some of that tasty dominatrix energy.

One and the same, really.

Maybe if I was really bad, she'd drag me within its walls before dragging me through her walls.

I palmed the chub forming in my trousers and gave it a light squeeze. Between the barbarian and my Blondie, I was a horny teenager desperate for his next taste of a hot hole.

I couldn't say this was the ideal set of circumstances, but I'd be lying if I said I was sad about it. Ma's place had been getting old, and I'd needed to get closer to Hillary to fulfill my mission. Despite the wee tracker in my arm, this really was a goldmine of opportunity.

Ma had been thrilled to hear I'd been 'invited to stay' at the best billionaire lodge in town. Her nagging about my slow pace on this had been getting to me—she'd even suggested she get in on the con, to make sure I "fulfilled the assignment"—as if I was some amateur. Thankfully, my forced roomie status and new assignment as "baddie lackey" had pleased her enough to let me be, even if I knew the reprieve was temporary.

It struck me I didn't know why Hillary was so fixated on Alvarez. What had the man ever done to her? He was a world-class git, and I knew the dark secrets he'd kept under his bonnet. But did she? Who'd hurt her?

Hillary kept her cards so close to her chest. I'd be more likely to get a blow job from a nun than have her tell me, but it didn't really matter. We were all in the same bed, and I was happy to sleep in it if I got what I wanted.

My cards on the table? Their resources could take Alvarez down, and I cared more about his end than I did my own. And if I could work my way under my new Killer's Club's skins a bit more, they wouldn't harm a hair on my head.

Probably.

Sure, I was a bit mental, but things often had a way of working out for me. Why question the goddess now?

I was getting closer to my goal, anyway. I was practically tethered to my billionaire buddy—her doing, not mine—and I was eliminating all areas where it wasn't; all part of the pickpocket process.

Giving up on my quest, I flopped down on my favorite chaise in her living room and slid an arm over my head to take a quick nap before I had to go into the Devil's lair.

The git who'd hired me needed me on "special assignment," and I was getting the details this afternoon. I was good at keeping up appearances, but the double life on all fronts these days was getting old.

Not like anyone truly knew what I did for a living. It was a lonely life, being a master "acquisition agent"—not even my best mate back home had a clue what I did outside of my "tech" hours—and sometimes a man just wanted to go home and vent to his family about the hard day he'd had trying to scam people out of their millions.

I snorted into the elbow covering my face. Might as well be smoking ayahuasca with that pipe dream.

When the elevator dinged, I turned my body expectantly toward the entrance foyer off the left of the kitchen.

My expectations for Blondie were only disappointed for a fraction of a second when I saw Conan come through the alcove, his head ducking on the other side of the trim.

Unimpressed navy eyes stared back at me. "Find what you were looking for?"

"No house elves to be found, so I'll have to try again tomorrow," I quipped, flashing him a lazy smile, not bothering to get up from my perch. "Wait—are yeh spying on Blondie, now? Do you have access to her cameras?"

He grunted, the masculine caveman growl like sweet, cock-stiffening music to my ears. "Always have. Haven't needed to use them in a while."

Not until me. What a cute giant stalker he was.

He crossed beefy arms across his barrelled chest, and the black pea-coat bunched around his biceps. Even *Big & Tall* didn't have clothes that could properly fit this man.

"That's too bad." I leaned back into the seat cushion, spreading my arms across the back of the couch as I challenged his grumpy stare. "Would've gotten quite a show when Blondie shoved a toy up my arse, but that's old hat to you, in't it? When you've seen it once..."

His bushy blond brows didn't move an inch at my teasing, and I'll admit I was a little disappointed. Ribbing Kellan was quickly becoming my favorite pastime—besides fucking him, of course.

Snatching up my jacket from the back of the kitchen stool, he tossed it at me. Then my angry captor retreated toward the elevator.

"Come on," he barked in that same boxer-bunching growly voice. "I'm your keeper for this afternoon. Hillary sent me your schedule. Get a fucking move on."

Jumping up from the couch, I hastily threw on my coat and followed him to the waiting elevator. "I wasn't under the impression I needed an escort—I'm already branded, remember?" I held up my arm, pointing to the fleshy part of my forearm that held my tracking chip.

He ignored me, marched into the metal box, and resumed his murder-y stance; I stepped in after him.

I mimed speaking into my hand like it was a Dictaphone. "Low IQ and memory issues—subject shows shocking similarities to Moose Mason."

An eye twitch and a flex of the hand and... was that a lip twitch? Did this man *actually* have a sense of humor beneath all those muscles?

Still no response, though—so he was probably warding off a minor stroke instead. The man was a feckin' stone.

He "escorted" me—a snug grasp of my upper arm—out to his blue Jeep, the same one where he'd taken my microchip-virginity. He nodded to me to sit up front, but kept up the silent treatment for another few minutes down the road before finally breaking.

"I trust you as much as I trust Marco Alvarez."

Well, duh. Mafia machines like Kellan trusted no one. I wasn't after the man's trust; that was a fool's errand. I needed him to like me.

Blackmail was only one way to get someone to do what you wanted. Get them to like you, and the world became a giant oyster farm.

Kellan didn't like cocky assholes—well, he didn't like *dominant* cocky assholes. But bratty subbies who could dish it as well as take it? I could win an Oscar for that act— mostly because it wasn't an act at all.

"For a second, I thought you forgot how to talk there." I flashed my cheekiest smile and turned to face him, leaning my back against the passenger window glass. "So, you don't trust my motives, but you trust me not to have syphilis? That's twice now you've taken my virgin hole, Conan."

Shaking my head, I tutted my fake disapproval. "Taking lots of risks for a big, scary brute, aren't yeh? Let me guess"—I mimed air quotes and bobbled my head—"You don't 'condom'."

Eyes narrowing into a glare, he rubbed a heavy palm over his face. The word "hope" stared back at me. It was an odd tattoo for a scary cartel baddie, but the "hell" on his other hand balanced the scales a bit.

"I've been tested both times," he muttered, tone *almost* apologetic. "No syphilis."

"Me, too!" I singsonged cheerfully. "See, big guy? *Trust.*"

I turned back in my seat to face forward, waiting out his next bout of stoic silence. Good thing con men were patient fucks, or this one-sided conversation would be one hell of a party.

Two minutes... three minutes... four—

"I find you fuckable. End of story."

Bingo.

"Obvious one there, mate. Does that mean you're going to dig for another pot of gold at the end of my rainbow, or have you given up on the luck of the Irish now that Blondie might give you a taste?"

Pulling into the parking lot of Alvarez's building, my special friend's gargantuan body shifted and he faced me, eyes darkened to dangerous, murderous slits. Fucking beautiful.

"You will *not* talk about her that way. Keep saying shit like that, and I'll remove your fingers the next time we have a chat."

Soooooooo in love. Kinda cute—Barbarian falling for Barbie. Stuff of movies, that.

My hands rose in mock surrender. "Aye, mate. Lips are sealed."

Opening the car door, I stepped out onto a slippery patch of ice and almost kissed it with my tongue before catching my balance.

Dublin was temperate for the most part—barely cold enough to get snow throughout the winter, let alone parking

lot skating rinks. America—this part of America, at least—
was a frigid wasteland in December modern man shouldn't
touch. Miserable.

"Will you be waiting for me, Jeeves?"

Another sexy grunt that I interpreted in Neanderthal to
mean "yes."

I delicately traipsed across the parking lot, fighting for
my life on the makeshift ice rink in my Tom Fords, to deal
with the next Neanderthal on my list.

Gertie greeted me when I walked into the office. Her
warm smile and sunny disposition were an instant balm to
my chapped face.

"Hey Gert!" I pulled her in for a hug, a definite HR faux
pas. But given Marco's private dealings with women, he
could fuck right off. It was purely platonic, anyway. Gertie
had quickly become my lesbian little sister, even if she was
at least five years older.

Her smile waned as she pulled away from me, dainty
eyebrows knitted into a worried frown. "He's very crabby
today, Lauchlan. Tread carefully in there." She gestured
toward the open doorway where loud, terse voices emptied
into the hall.

"Aye, thanks for the warnin'." Winking reassuringly, I
waited for her to announce my arrival. I was in no mood to
waltz right into a madhouse of pissed off gangbangers
posing as upstanding businessmen.

There were to be no secrets between us according to
Hillary—bollocks, because there were definitely *plenty* of
secrets between us—but Kellan had let Hillary know, who
let Aaron and I know, about the raid Antonio had ordered
on the Alvarez clubhouse. Right bloodbath with mass
casualties apparently, but mostly on Alvarez's end.

Couldn't say I knew much about running a billion-dollar
criminal empire, but I imagined Marky Marco had quite the
gory mess on his hands. I looked forward to serving him the
tech equivalent of on a platter. I was *so close.*

Gertie pressed the button on her center console and muttered into the receiver. "Lauchlan is here, sir."

The indiscernible voices stopped abruptly. Drawing in a cleansing breath of bullshit-scented air, I sauntered into the room.

Three oversized gits stared back at me, with Marco, the king git, at the center of the lot, his watery shark eyes roving over me like I was the next meal.

"Welcome, Lauchlan. Please, take a seat."

Unbuttoning my suit jacket, I sat in the uncomfortable glass chair facing the 'roided-out penguin crew; there was an obvious leader—the slimmest of the three men looked to be about sixty, with silver hair and wrinkly skin with a sallow sheen like he smoked three packs an hour. The other two were poorly disguised bodyguards and looked so out of place they might as well've been strippers.

Marco dipped his head to the men in introduction

"Lauchlan, this is Xander Analo, one of our top clients."

"Pleasure to meet you, sir." I stuck out a hand in offering. Top Client sniffed in the way that only Daddy Warbucks people could, raising his eyebrows in disgust as if I'd shit on it; I hastily brought it back to my thigh and turned my attention back to Marco. "What is this about, sir?"

"I was singing your praises to Xander at a recent event —we're considerably impressed with your team's progress on several projects, and it's quite clear you have other skills we can better use. I've offered to lend you to Mr. Analo for a specialized project for the remainder of the year."

Fuck. The next three weeks was shitty timing. It'd be suspicious—if I actually thought Marco had any inkling what I was doing. If he did, though, I'd already be dead.

Nope, this was a demonstration of that fun little clause he'd snuck in when he hired me. "Special duties as needed." *What a crock of—*

"You will come to my facility starting tomorrow." Top Client's voice sounded freakishly like *Voldemort's*—all wheezy and high pitched, like he was choking on a lozenge. "Security is very high—you may not take in your phone or computer. One will be provided for you while on site."

He cleared his throat and continued. "We will require your expertise on penetration testing—specifically of the security measures we've designed for a new application."

So, they were hiring me to hack them. Interesting.

So much for my freedom and flexibility. Tethered to creepy Top Client by the day, and the scary squad by night. I wasn't a man who liked to be tied down, unless I was *actually* being tied down.

By the look on Alvarez's face, there was absolutely no way I was saying no, though. Fucking HR clauses.

"Alright, then." Forcing a practiced, charming smile, I dipped my head in acceptance. "Looking forward to working with yeh, Mr. Manalo."

His mouth puckered like he'd just sucked a pint full of salt. "You can call me 'sir'."

Oh boy.

"Yes, sir." I repeated, rolling my internal eyes a thousand times. Just what I needed; *another* narcissist calling the shots.

Marco excused me from the farce of the meeting, and Gertie wasn't at her desk when I left his office. I made a beeline for the front entrance, needing to think through this recent development in peace.

I was getting closer to my goal—months of slow movement into his system had allowed me to penetrate his firewalls and create the necessary backdoors to get out. It was painstaking work, but the only way to get by undetected. The next three weeks weren't mine anymore, so I'd have to come up with another way to continue my progress... and figure out how to shake my new beefy bodyguard.

Cora Flynn

As much as I liked him around to fuck, I worked alone. And speaking of alone, my arsehole escort wasn't waiting for me when I walked out into the parking lot.

Calling an Uber, I vowed to get the Barbarian back as soon as I found the time. Maybe with a little torture session of my own.

CHAPTER 10

Hillary

"*Aaron Rodriguez, billionaire business mogul and recent partner of Lane Enterprises, is missing and presumed dead after evidence of a gruesome car crash off the gorge of Cascade Falls was discovered late yesterday afternoon. Sources say the gray Mercedes registered in his name was last seen leaving the parking lot of his central office in Carlisle, and no one can attest to his whereabouts since. The investigation is ongoing, but foul play is not suspected at this time.*"

I scrolled through the online news story the minute it landed on my phone. I sat in his very office chair, having spent the day overseeing a myriad of business decisions on his behalf. The last time I'd been in here, I'd pinned him to the floor and rode him until my body couldn't possibly come anymore. Today, I was keeping up the façade life was continuing on without the man who'd changed everything.

The news he was missing had leaked the previous afternoon, so I was heavily immersed in damage control. Now that the 'presumed dead' status was circulating in the media, I'd have to manage the shit storm for the next several weeks to keep operations running and suspicions diverted.

As a saving grace, everything was reported as we'd expected, but it didn't stop the shiver that swept up my spine at an image of Aaron's lifeless body at the bottom of the gorge, as if it had actually happened.

Especially now I'd finally admitted how much the man meant to me.

I hadn't uttered those three fateful words to anyone romantically in a long, *long* time. I'd expected them to taste rancid when he dragged them from my throat post-orgasm. Instead, they'd tasted like a pure sugar hit; overindulgent, potent, and all-consuming, for the brief period it took to dissolve on my tongue.

The ambrosial flavor still coated my mouth, a delicious memory I couldn't wait to treat myself to again.

I loved Aaron Rodriguez. The admission made my tainted heart flutter at the possibility of something real, but the flutters instantly sunk to the earth when I admitted another truth:

My love for him wasn't enough.

I'd always known it. Perhaps that was why I'd always kept him at arm's length—somewhere I could always grab hold of him when I needed his touch, but push him away when the touch became too real.

His declaration hadn't come as a surprise. From the first time we'd fucked in the limousine more than ten years ago, I'd held his heart in a vise, and squeezed it whenever the mood suited me. Now that I'd finally given him what he wanted, I was going to have to take it away—or wrap it in a series of caveats that might make him want to take everything back.

The thought sliced viciously through my chest, the stabbing pain saying all the words I wasn't willing to.

I didn't want to lose him, but I couldn't keep him if I could only have him.

I was a wishy-washy bitch at best; a cruel heartbreaker at worst.

The stress of it all: this monumental realization, the race to get to Alvarez, my unwanted roommate, and the serious lack of sleep from my nightmares, had wormed its way under my skin. My veins crawled with the insatiable need to *hurt* something. We were sitting on the precipice of losing control, and I did not lose control.

People died when I lost control.

Scanning to the bottom of the article, I closed my browser and let those depressing thoughts slide from my mind before getting back to my very busy day. I was the Queen of Compartmentalization, and our list of ends to tie up was currently infinite.

Drawing in a deep breath to bury the anxious ball in my chest, I blew it all out in a forceful rush, then turned my attention to the task in front of me: running Aaron's company.

Thankfully, it was close to Christmas, and the company would shut down for a week to allow employees to enjoy their holidays. I just had to hold down the fort for a few days before the break, enough time to come up with a better game plan than impromptu office visits.

Our legal operations were very similar, so it wasn't hard to fill his shoes from that perspective. Aaron had more fans than he'd realized, because the tone in the building was considerably reserved and downright distraught.

Gabby was distraught, anyway. The poor woman had sobbed continuously at her desk, but she refused to go home when I offered her the rest of the day off with pay.

"He would want me here," she'd sniffed. Her watery eyes and puffy face pulled at my heartstrings. "He'd want me here, making sure you were taken care of."

Her attempt at a smile brought on another fit of crying; I gently patted her shoulder and carefully tiptoed back to the office.

While many employees would be more concerned about their job security, Gabby had a good heart and cared more for the man for his existence, not his signature on her checks. She would quietly get a sizable raise this year for her loyalty. At Lane Enterprises, loyalty mattered.

The board could fight me on that one, but I'd win.

I was doing my best to balance the line of heartbroken business partner and fierce boss-babe, but I struggled with the job. Thankfully, my reputation proceeded me; after years of honing a ruthless but fair persona, the business world wouldn't expect Hillary Lane to crumble when her business partner died.

The piles of paper in front of me slowly grew smaller. When my eyeballs became sandpaper, it was time to pack in for the day. I looked down at my messages I'd ignored for a good hour.

Kellan ViKing: I'm not playing babysitter tomorrow.

A girlish snort escaped me as I imagined all sorts of hell Lucky would put Kellan through. Watching the big man squirm under Lucky's pestering was a primary source of amusement these days. Especially knowing Lucky was a particular weakness for the man who had none. I was still figuring Lucky out and how best to use him, so it was convenient to have someone else on the receiving end of Lucky being, well… Lucky.

I was my own brand of con man if I said picturing Kellan and Lucky fucking didn't set my insides on fire and disintegrate my panties. To have been a fly on that wall...

I flicked through my other messages to save my current pair of panties until I got home.

Sammy: Packaged secured.

A violent smile filled my features at the message. The incessant need to dig my nails into something and bring it pain had hounded me for days while I waited for my team to find the right moment to capture Sandra.

She was a trickier person to get my hands on than I'd anticipated. Her husband was a military officer home on leave, and Sammy had struggled to get her alone over the course of the last two weeks.

We didn't torture innocents; I'd found no evidence of her husband's involvement in any of the obtained footage or documentation, so he wasn't a part of the equation. I wouldn't risk him in the process of nabbing her.

Sandra, however, was unequivocally guilty.

As a precaution, all employees of the foundation were closely monitored via not-so-legal exterior cameras and discreet trackers hidden within their security badge—I was the only one who received the information. Blackbird glanced through the data every so often throughout the month and updated me if she found anything out of the ordinary.

Naturally, something had come up. I'd rewatched the video Blackbird had sent me. The damning evidence of Sandra's duplicity was all over the screen.

The new families she'd brought in weren't there to give a new life to a suffering child—they were a new wave of demons with direct access now to their prey; Sandra pocketed a hefty sum in an offshore account for her delivery service.

She'd sold four children back to Alvarez this way. Today, she would pay the price for her greed.

Cora Flynn

I messaged Joey to meet me at the front doors of the office in five, quickly assembled my things, and sent off a text to Marty to close off the rest of my afternoon.

I was tired of the restless desperation, and my body ached for the sweet release that only came from delivering justice. Everything else on my agenda could wait.

Anita and Sammy were instructed to secure Sandra within a cell at the Palace—Sammy was the only other person on earth with his own access code. Other than sedation, they weren't to touch her.

I asked Gabby to lock up before racing down the hallway to the elevators, eager to get to my prey before the day was done.

I'd wanted to drive myself today, but Kellan insisted I go nowhere alone, like a big grumbly, overprotective bear. I'd been in no mood to fight him, so I relented. Joey silently drove us to the Palace in record time, understanding my sense of urgency with no need to be told.

Sandra would get her comeuppance from two well-trained pissed off women with a thirst for vicious vengeance.

She didn't know what she was in for. But today was introductory. A simple lesson. We'd work up to the torture part.

When we arrived, I changed the settings on her cell glass, turning the entire transparent wall into a frosted translucent screen, shielding our identities until I revealed them. I could watch her on the monitor outside her cell, which could see her from all angles, except for one corner underneath the panoramic viewer.

"Hello, Sandra," I intoned. My voice stayed calm and level with only a slight edge of threat to it. "Welcome to your new home."

The woman cowered in the far corner of her cell, her round form still in the rumpled clothes she'd been wearing when Sammy pulled her out of her car at the gas station.

Mauve pants and teal blue shirt shone brilliantly in the bright light, but her skin was tight and pale—and a real flicker of fear shined through her dull complexion.

"Where am I?" Her hesitant voice trembled, and her hands clenched into fists by her side as her gaze flitted around the room, looking for the source of the sound.

"I call it... The Palace." I cocked my head as she shook in her cage like a snared mouse. "It's quite luxurious, isn't it? Three square meals a day, water, and indoor plumbing. Quite an offering, considering what you're in here for."

Her wide eyes frantically scanned the room before she crumpled into a ball against the wall and slid down it into a heap on the tiled floor.

"I'm not who you're looking for," she blubbered, bringing her fisted hands to her forehead. "I'm innocent, I swear, I—"

"Oh, no, no, no, Sandra," I cooed and nodded to Joey to unlock the door, giving her permission to step inside. "That's not the truth, is it?"

Joey smirked at me. Her gray eyes went flat, though, when she wrenched open the door and stalked toward our guest. Grabbing Sandra by the hair, Joey hauled her up by her roots. Sandra screamed, the sound absorbed by the padding lining the walls.

"Meet Josephine," I introduced. My smile widened at the wet spot growing at Sandra's crotch. "Josephine *hates* women who prey on the vulnerable. Don't you, J?" I tossed the question out casually, and Joey tightened her grip on Sandra's matted bottle-blonde hair, causing another rich cry to sputter forth. "Show her how much you hate it," I commanded. my velvety tone freezing into icy shards.

Joey flipped out a switchblade in her other hand and held it to Sandra's jugular with a firm grip. She shifted the weapon suddenly and sliced the seams of Sandra's clothing, ripping the material off her body. A moment later, Sandra was completely naked, tatters of urine-soaked fabric in a loose pile on the floor.

Joey immediately brought the blade back to Sandra's exposed throat, and the woman whimpered in distress.

"It's quite scary to be vulnerable against your will, isn't it, Sandra?" I mused. Joey's blade traveled southward and nicked the delicate skin of Sandra's sternum between her fleshy breasts. A small bead of blood trailed behind it. "When strangers hold you hostage and take your body as their own ..."

I let the statement hang in the air as the woman shook violently in Joey's hold. She choked out stuttered sobs between gasping breaths. Joey simply held her there, waiting for my next set of instructions.

"If you were a man, I'd cut off your cock." The declaration brought another wave of wails. "I haven't decided just how to punish you yet. But you'll be staying here indefinitely, so I suggest you get comfortable."

Joey yanked on the chunk of hair in her grasp, then abruptly let it go. A large clump fell to the floor along with the flailing body of our naked prisoner. Sandra scrambled away from her and huddled in the cell's corner once again.

Joey stalked back to the door and joined me on the other side. The panel shut behind her, leaving Sandra alone with only a pile of ribbons to keep her company.

I'd throw her a potato sack or something just as demeaning in the coming days. For now, she could enjoy the 50-degree temperature without the comfort of clothing, and reflect on her life choices.

"Welcome to hell." I shut off the sound feed to cut the symphony of agonized screams. Joey and I shared a violent look of satisfaction.

Beating Sandra was not the play today—as much as I wanted to decorate my body with her blood, the adrenaline for violence was on pause as I considered the long play.

This woman needed to be terrified first. Stripped, threatened, and driven mad with all the possibilities of what we *could* do to her. She'd either crack or double down.

I'd give her that opportunity first. Judging by her current position, though, we wouldn't have to wait long.

I gestured for Joey to follow me to Alec's cell a few blocks down the hall. I had found no incriminating evidence why he'd been limping the last time I'd interrogated him, so I needed the reassurance he wasn't getting any misguided ideas.

Joey opened the cell for me. With her gun at the ready, she entered first to secure Alec so I could investigate the space.

He was seated on the toilet when we barged in; the murderous outrage on his face laughable given his defenseless position.

Joey cuffed his hands behind his back, leaving his naked ass perched on the bowl while I conducted a thorough sweep of the ten-by-ten cell.

Alec liked to tuck himself away beneath the camera's blind spot, but that corner was spotless, save for a greasy stain on the padding where he must rest his head.

He spewed a flurry of curses, each more colorful than the last, while I investigated the other corners, under his bed, and around his sink, but I found nothing. Nothing implied an escape plan or even the slightest bit of tampering.

Satisfied, I nodded to Joey to release the shitting man.

As I exited the cell, I waved my fingers at him with a malicious smile. The sight of his wasted body and tortured eyes was almost enough to soothe the rip in my heart he'd caused all those years ago.

Alvarez was going to wish he was dead by my hand soon enough. Then maybe, just maybe, after I rid the world of that demon, I could finally find it in my heart to kill Alec, too.

CHAPTER 11

Kellan

"It is done."

I stood in front of Antonio's monstrosity of a desk in the private office tucked away in his Californian mansion. I'd traveled to deliver the news in person, determined to keep the trail of information as closed as possible.

Too many lips sunk ships, and our ship was barely treading water.

I was to deliver the message, return to Sequoia in one piece, and join Hillary for Christmas celebrations since she'd left Camden to his own devices for the holidays.

Apparently, leaving him to own devices meant cajoling Aaron and me into a Christmas dinner—with our redheaded pest in tow. It was going to be a disaster, but I'd take it over another Christmas with my brother and nephew, where everyone was excessively happy and in love. The stark reminder how different our lives were always put me in a sour mood, despite the fact my sister-in-law was an incredible woman who deserved them all.

Antonio's dark eyes flashed with interest as his gaze roved over me, as if he could catch the lie from the position of my fingertips against my thigh. Perhaps he could. He was far more astute than most of my trained agents, seeing truths where others could not.

It was a good thing he was the one who trained me all those years ago; my senses were almost as honed as his, almost as thorough. He didn't fully believe me, in the way that he was naturally suspicious of any breathing man, but my answer had satisfied him for now.

"I heard the news," he responded in Spanish, his brow furrowing in irritation. "I wanted to send a message, not hand him an adoring funeral procession."

"It is the best way," I replied, also in Spanish, my tone even and confident. "The message has been sent to the people who needed to hear it. To the rest of the world, he is an unfortunate sap who lost everything for a joyride. We don't need any more heat right now."

My father's frown deepened, the wrinkles on his forehead splitting his face in two. He didn't like it when I spoke to him this way, but he couldn't dispute the logic of my plan, and it annoyed him.

"Yes, well." Antonio cleared his throat and beckoned to me to take a seat. "Now that this is over, we have other matters that need discussing."

My heart sank to my stomach, but I sat down in the offered leather chair, its stubby legs creaking under my weight. Shifting to get comfortable, I settled in for the conversation I'd been dreading for months.

"January is a week away, and we had a bargain." Antonio raised a carefully crafted brow in my direction, as if in challenge. "I am looking forward to you bringing a more lucrative market of girls back into the state."

"Alvarez still has the market share," I countered, attempting to look casually at my nails while my insides felt like lava. "It would be more effective to remove him from the picture first, then try to compete with him, yes?"

"You are stalling, *hijo*." The sinister smile that stretched across the his face would give children nightmares. It gave me nightmares. "This transition is happening whether or not you embrace it. And you will take it."

He stood from his chair and looked down at me, as if I were the terrified teenager he'd long since broken and remolded. "I have other plans for Alvarez. That is now in your brother's hands. You will start importing our goods and overseeing the trade routes immediately."

"No." I stood slowly and intentionally, swallowing the bile in my throat and the bitter anger in my stomach, maintaining the calm tone with every ounce of control in my body. "You gave me until January. I have some loose ends to wrap up with work before then. You know I won't be able to work on both sides with this transition. Trish will never allow it."

Antonio stared through me, his eyes hard and unyielding. A twitch of his left eye told me he was considering my words.

"We will put someone else in power—Trish has outlived her usefulness, anyway."

Panic raced through my veins; Trish could handle her own, but not when the leading criminal lord in the country put a bullseye on her back—I couldn't let that happen. I had to appeal to his sense of reason, not his lust for bloodshed.

Folding my arms across my chest, I matched his hard stare in an Alpha male standoff.

"Again, we don't need any more heat. Let me handle my resignation. I'll give them six months' notice for some bullshit reason. Don't tank the business before it's even started."

Unfiltered rage flitted across my father's face before the well-practiced mask of neutrality fell back into place.

"Get it done," he said, tone clipped, then he waved his hands toward the entrance alcove on the other side of the room. "Don't come back until you've made progress."

Spinning on my heel, I left without another word, stalking out of the exorbitant compound like a bat out of hell—ferocious and furious.

I wouldn't be coming back ever again if I had a choice. What I would give to trade places with Aaron and fake my death, then cozy up with Hillary in her private bunker and fuck her until she told *me* she loved me.

I'd hacked into her security feeds the day she'd set them up; monitoring her little terrorist operation and the private apartment she kept below ground. I checked in rarely— mostly to see how many bodies she was keeping in her dungeon, but I'd been compelled to check in more often since our resident fugitive had moved in.

Aaron fucking my killer on the couch was a vision I'd never be able to erase from my mind. The camera angle in the living room gave me the perfect view of the private show. Watching Hillary become submissive to another man, watching Aaron dominate her in a sweeter way than I would, but no less effective...

The swell of her breasts under his touch, his molded ass muscles tightening as he pounded into her hot pussy—the scene had forced me to jerk myself off to the sound of her panting and his grunts until I came just as hard.

But the words she'd said to him ... I never realized how much I ached for her to say them to me, too.

Even if I could never say them back. Even if I could never let her get that close. Even if a future for us was damn impossible.

Once I had boarded the private plane to take me home, I sent off a message, determined to ease the ache in my heart and my balls. If she'd still see me. If I was still hers, even if she loved Aaron Rodriguez.

Kellan: I need you. Meet me at your hotel. Usual room.

It was selfish of me, but I didn't care. I couldn't care. The need to plunder and pillage was threaded into the fabric of my being. I would steal her if I couldn't share her. I'd be reduced to a Neanderthal claiming his mate; as long as it worked, I wouldn't lose sleep over it.

My heart pounded in my throat as I waited for her response. If she rejected me tonight, I'd be reduced to the caveman hindbrain and would probably resort to killing someone.

I couldn't afford to bury another body right now.

Killer Lane: I'll be there for 9. Bring wine.

The wash of relief that came over me felt like a wave of cool, soothing air. Three hours—three hours until I could disappear into her body.

I could hold off breaking something until then.

My delicious release was waiting for me, her sultry form laid out on the king bed like an erotic buffet, her body barely covered with a black lace and satin teddy.

Black was my favorite color on her. She'd tied her silky blonde hair up into a high ponytail on top of her head, the perfect thickness to hold her in any position I wanted.

I wasn't wasting any time on introductions or pleasantries. I toed off my shoes and tossed my suit jacket onto the chair as I stalked toward her. I wrapped my hands around her hair and yanked her upright. Her body went limp in my arms, pliant and ready for a command as the stormy blue of her eyes caught me through lustful lidded lashes.

So, I issued our command.

"Submit."

The starting word told her what I needed from her, and if she agreed, she simply did it. Submitted to me, wholly and entirely, for the duration of our session. I released my demons into every yielding hole of her body while she released her worries by following my every order.

A mutual give-and-take of erotic desecration. I'd never come so hard as I did when Hillary allowed me such control over her, so sweetly and willingly, all pretense of our power struggles in the real world forgotten.

Her shoulders relaxed further and the blue irises darkened to navy. "I submit," she murmured. Her breath hitched when I cupped her pussy in my other palm.

The soaked fabric was hot against my skin, her swollen lips aching to be touched. I tore the black fabric with one forceful pull and pressed two fingers into her, relishing the glide of my fingers through her needy heat.

Thoughts of Aaron pounding into this pussy broke through my distorted haze of lust and violence.

"Have you been thinking of me, Killer?" I brushed my lips over the shell of her ear as I tightened my grip on her ponytail. "Are you soaked from thoughts of me destroying this pussy?"

I brought my thumb up to her clit and massaged the sensitive nub gently, stretching my fingers inside of her and stroking her walls with rhythmic curls of my knuckles.

"Or"—I pulled her against my chest, and moved my hand down to grip the back of her neck, squeezing with enough pressure to hold her in place—"Were your thoughts of Rodriguez fucking you with his massive cock?"

She froze and her eyes widened. I could see the calculation behind those intelligent blue screens. I saw the moment she concluded correctly that I'd watched her little tryst with our captive, and was choosing to fuck her, anyway. A single brow cocked in defiance and I wasn't disappointed when she took my bait.

Her smile was sweet and poisonous, like oleander; her response stilted with shudders with every pass of my fingers inside of her.

"I was thinking of his massive cock fucking me from behind—*ahhh*—while you drove your massive cock into me from the front. I was—*ohhhh*—imagining you driving into Aaron as hard as you fucked Lucky—*fuuuuck*—while I watch from my little perch with a dildo."

Fuck, the mouth on her. My Killer could only stay compliant for so long.

So, truly no secrets between us, then. The four of us were caught in some weird fuck fest, and no one seemed to have an issue with it.

I ignored my dick as it swelled even further at the thought of Aaron's ass pulling my cock inside him. I had enough problems to worry about.

Jerking my fingers out of her, I shoved her down off the bed and onto the floor, lifting her head up to face my swollen crotch.

"You're going to pay for that one, little Killer." Unzipping my pants, I shucked them down my thighs, freeing my cock from their confines. She was so close, the stiff head slapped her cheek, leaving a pearl of pre-cum along her chin.

"Take your fingers and stuff them into your cunt," I commanded, reaching for my cock and pushing the head against the seam of her lips. "I'm going to fuck your face while you fuck yourself, and I'm not stopping until you've creamed all over the floor."

That sweet smile came again when I shoved into her mouth, the heat enveloping me with the most satisfying suction. Gripping both sides of her face, I held her there, pushing as deeply into her throat as I could get. She hollowed her cheeks for me, dribbles of saliva dripping down her chin, waiting for permission to breathe.

I didn't need to control another human being to feel like a man—but Hillary relinquishing her tightly held composure to me gave me a thrill nothing in this world could compare to.

The billionaire heiress who took no prisoners allowed me the briefest moment to take her prisoner, trusting me to satisfy both of our needs. I'd taken out gang leaders, killed in cold blood, faced down some of the shittiest scum of the earth, but this—this was the ultimate feeling of power.

Without warning, I pulled back, giving her one solitary second for air, before shoving back in just as forcefully. I looked down to watch her delicate fingers enter her cunt and circle her clit with the moisture, the bottom half of her writhing in pleasure while the top half of her braced to take my cock.

A harsh growl escaped me before I could contain it, unleashing the beast inside desperate for an escape. I claimed her mouth without mercy, thrusting hard and fast, jolting her body against the bedframe behind her. Tears streamed down her cheeks; her skin blushed from flushed pink to fiery red as she came closer and closer to orgasm. When her body snapped, I quickly pulled out, lifted her from the floor and onto the bed, and tossed her into the cushions.

One orgasm from my beautiful little queen and already I felt better. Coaxing two more releases from her body ought to rid me of my demons for one night.

"Good girl," I purred, stroking the smooth skin of her calves as she came down from her high. "Did that feel good, Killer?" I nipped the inside of her thigh as I crawled up her body, then licked it with the pad of my tongue to soothe the sting. "I'm going to give you some more; can you handle that?"

She nodded weakly, but the fire in her eyes sparked back to life when I held myself above her on my knees. I unbuttoned my dress shirt and shrugged it off my shoulders, then tossed it to the end of the bed. Her hands trailed across the bare skin of my chest, my ribs, over the trail of intricate ink and the scars.

I didn't like to be touched there. She was the only one who'd ever gotten the chance.

Grabbing her wrists, I lifted her hands above her head and held them there between one of mine, reaching down for my cock with the other to line up with her entrance. I moved to grip her hip as I entered and gave her a moment to adjust to my size. Squeezing her flesh between the pads of my fingers firmly enough to bruise, I unleashed every pent-up frustration I'd held onto for weeks—months—since I'd last entered her body.

I entered that state of nirvana only she could give me; the escape that took away the rough edges and smoothed everything into soft lines. Her body bent and bowed to my will. She met every thrust with her hips, every pulse with one in return, responsive to every need my body expressed without either of us saying a word.

A ragged cry ripped from her throat and she arched upward as her second orgasm snuck up on us both. I relished the sweet music of her panting, determined to pull a third from her sweet lips.

"That's my good girl." I crooned the words against her flesh before picking up my pace. My desperation leaked through every pore of my body and into her skin. "You're so beautiful when you break for me."

I bit the slender line of her throat, her breasts, arching her back as I held my weight above her. I filled her up over and over until she was a writhing mess of need beneath me. I ground my hips, brutally rubbed my pelvis up against her clit as the tip of my cock continued to hit her G spot, and counted down the moments until she came all over me.

Within seconds, her wanton scream triggered my orgasm, hot jets of my cum flooding her in all the places my cock couldn't reach. Her arms fell to her sides as her body melted into the sheets, completely spent.

I withdrew, fixing my gaze on the point where our bodies met, where cum seeped out of her pussy in little white dew drops. I bent down and sucked our combined arousal into my mouth, held the sweet, salty taste on my tongue before hovering over her to deposit the mixture into hers.

"Open."

She did so willingly, the devious smirk on her lips telling me just how much she enjoyed it. Her tongue drove into my mouth, sucking every drip of our flavor, savoring it.

I was a complete masochist to continuously deny myself the pleasure of this woman. Yet, I'd never be able to be enough, to give enough. I'd always leave her wanting and hate myself for it.

No matter how much I tried to build something concrete, there wasn't a permanent place for me. I was a pawn masquerading as a king.

The dirty kiss became light and tender, our bodies making promises neither of us could keep. I pulled her into my side and drew the feather duvet over us, settling her within the cradle of my arms. We could clean up later. The beast within me was satisfied; now I needed to take care of her.

She wouldn't stay the night, anyway. She never did— she'd let me hold her until I fell asleep—then she slipped away in the night, her perfume lingering in the air and her scent on my skin the only reminders she'd been here at all.

Her fingertips danced along the skin of my biceps as our hearts pounded out a similar rhythm against each other's chest.

"Does this mean you're sticking around?"

I didn't know what the fuck to do with that question. I couldn't guarantee I'd be here in a year—with the way things were going, it was looking more and more unlikely by the day. Yet, I wouldn't—*couldn't* leave her.

"Yeah. I'm going nowhere, Killer."

She interlaced our fingers and fell silent. The two of us lay in the comfort of each other's warmth, the most basic of human connections taking hold. She gave me enough grace to relax before asking the inevitable.

"What happened?"

I scrubbed a palm down my face and through my beard, unwilling to keep anything from her anymore. If our lives were to be inextricably intertwined, she might as well know the entirety of how fucked up my life was.

I recapped my meeting with my father; his expectations, the threats to Trish, and the need to remove myself from both of the lives I was faking my way through, but having nowhere to turn.

She stroked my hand through all of it, remaining silent. Her eyes widened at some parts with concern, slitting in others in rage. She listened without judgment, and I was surprised how relieving it was to *confide* in someone. To trust them enough to see my fucked-up situation and ask them to stay.

Was that what I was doing? Asking her to stay?

"I'm going to get Blackbird to combine forces with Lucky," she said once I had finished. "Lucky thinks he's close to hacking into Alvarez's personal accounts, and that will give us everything we need to ruin him. I'm not willing to delay this any longer with Aaron stuck in hiding and a price on your head."

She didn't coddle me with false platitudes or apologies. Instead, she'd pounced on the opportunity for a solution. I would expect nothing less.

"You're not getting into the fucking flesh trade." The vehemence in her tone made the hairs on the back of my neck stand on end. "We'll tackle Alvarez first and then work on Antonio. I've been building out a slow play for him, and the board is almost ready."

That was news to me. I couldn't tamp down my protective instincts, learning she had been preparing to take on the devil that was my father. Whatever she was planning, I was bound to help her—I couldn't walk away and I couldn't risk her failing.

Her fate was now mine, even if I could never give her what she needed. I swallowed the fear burgeoning in my belly. The thought of losing her was more painful than any considerations of my death.

Remaining close to her was going to be much harder than keeping my distance. But my fear would not be enough to break the magnetic hold she had on me, so I was well and truly stuck.

A steely resolve filled her features, dangerous intent flashing in her eyes. "I've got you, Viking. And no one is going to fuck with what's mine."

What's hers. I liked those words on her lips. A lot.

A growl rumbled from within my chest; throaty and possessive. I rolled her toward me to take her body once more, but this time, it wasn't for an escape into her.

I would escape *with* her. Maybe that would make all the difference in the world.

CHAPTER 12

Hillary

"I've never had Christmas in a secret dungeon before."

Lucky's cheerful declaration was met with an irritated grunt from the bearded Viking seated beside him.

We were driving to the Palace—Joey in the driver's seat, as usual, with me in the passenger seat alongside her, despite vehement protests from her and Kellan.

We needed to take one vehicle to the safe house for safety's sake, and Kellan couldn't sit up front in case anyone with interest spotted us. Sure, it was unorthodox for me to be up there, but certainly less obvious than either of them.

So, my two companions sat side by side in the rear seat, one a giddy bundle of energy like an untrained puppy, the other a broody ogre who apparently worshipped the Grinch.

The Grinch and Max. That's who they were. I almost snorted into my coffee mug. Joey cocked a questioning eye in my direction, but I waved her off, choosing to keep that little observation to myself.

I'd blindfolded Lucky, like Aaron had been. He had willingly allowed me to tie the black silk around his face with sly mutters of, "You and Conan have the same kinks, eh, Blondie?"

Kellan, since he'd set up the facility, didn't need it. Four people in the universe knowing the location of this place was enough.

After deciding I wasn't spending one second with my father for the holiday and not wanting Aaron to be alone or Kellan to waste the day away working, I'd come up with the insane plan to spend Christmas together. In an apocalypse-proof safe house.

Naturally, our captive had to come with us. I knew nothing about Lucky's private life, other than he had been staying with his mother—if that cover story even held—so I had no idea if, had we not shoved a tracker into his arm and held him in flexible captivity, he even had someone to spend Christmas with in America.

I'd felt guilty about that for the briefest of moments, before remembering he was actually trying to play me for a payout, and then the guilt of forcing an Alpha male Christmas on him dissipated immediately.

He certainly didn't seem upset by it—he was outright excited to glimpse what he called my "Armageddon Barbie House."

Biting my lip, I took another swallow of coffee to hide my growing amusement. Lucky's wit was a secret indulgence I allowed myself. That he annoyed the shit out of Kellan was just a side bonus.

Kellan. I snuck a glance in the rearview mirror to catch the blond God unapologetically staring at me, as if conducting a rare jewelry appraisal. Dark blue eyes stared intensely through mine, the range of emotions passing in a flash I couldn't pick out a single one.

Our last 'session' had changed something between us. The bullshit he regularly spewed about protecting me or not protecting me was absent, but I couldn't help the niggling feeling that he had been staking a claim for Aaron's sake; like I was a prize between them he needed to covet.

Admittedly, knowing he'd watched Aaron and I fucking like rabbits by hacking my private feeds was a massive red flag, but also incredibly hot. The timing felt too coincidental, though—like he was afraid he'd lose all of me to Aaron, so he needed to remind me he could give me what I needed, too.

He'd proven that over and over in the bedroom—but in real life?

I was waiting for him to turn back into the sullen, self-destructive Viking again, where he pushed me out the door with my ass on the pavement, while watching through his security cameras to make sure I got home safely.

Aaron had painstakingly proven over our entire lives I could trust him with my heart. It took years for me to wake up, but I finally could see the hold he had on me—and my hold on him.

Kellan hadn't earned that trust. He would protect me in the ways *he* thought appropriate, even if it meant running away. I wasn't willing to hand him my heart on a platter for a slew of hollow promises.

Lucky I barely trusted, but it was a finicky line. Sure, I'd taken all necessary precautions; a tracker, several cameras, and a beefy Viking bodyguard to keep him in check, but he was an integral part of our plan, so now I was bringing him to my secure facility.

Cora Flynn

If I was being really honest with myself, our chemistry was undeniable; even now, blindfolded and a sitting duck, the smooth line of his jaw, pouty lips set into a permanent smirk, and the way he filled out his jacket... Lucky was undeniably hot.

Fine and fuckable, and his inability to treat me like a scary billionaire princess was refreshing and attractive. He was trying to steal from me—what he was after, I still didn't know—but he could have taken a very different approach. He could have been sniveling and simpering; worse, he could have had tiny dick syndrome, where he attempted to "put me in my place" with bravado and fake Big Dick Energy.

Lucky had done none of these things. I could never be sure this personality he was presenting was genuine, but... I did believe... Somehow. Risking a lobotomy, I could admit he was growing on me, but I couldn't see a way through this without someone killing him.

Probably Aaron, since apparently Lucky was becoming Kellan's other sex toy. Aaron had made no secret he'd squash Lucky like an insignificant bug if I'd let him.

Perhaps I would. If he betrayed us, I'd use the fly swatter myself.

But today, we were *not* killing each other. We were going to eat the catered turkey dinner sitting in the warming dishes in the trunk and pretend we could all get along for a few hours before heading back to our real, fucked up lives.

So... just like my usual family Christmas dinners. How depressing.

When we arrived, snow was falling in huge flakes, a romantic setting for a day tainted with false hopes and forced friendships.

We exited the vehicle, Lauchlan surefooted despite the lack of sight, and circled the car to grab our things.

I turned to my most trusted hired help.

"Joey, head home for the rest of the day. I'll take the emergency vehicle back to the condo. You deserve Christmas with your family."

"Hill—"Kellan started.

"I'm a trained killer." I interrupted, pointing to my chest. I pointed at him. "You are a trained killer." I pointed at Lucky. "He's bait." I ignored the sputters of indignant protest and continued. "Do you really think we're safer with Joey?"

It was a test—would he relent, or would he snarl and rave about all the ways I needed protection?

After a mute stare down of exchanged eye daggers, he rolled his eyes, grabbed the box of takeout containers from the trunk, and stomped through the snow toward the rear door.

Lauchlan cocked his head as if heavily focusing on something, and then moved to follow the sound of Kellan's footsteps, heading in almost the exact direction.

Huh. So, the man was also trained in sensory deprivation. We needed to delve deeper into his skill sets, because swindling rich people seemed to be only the tip of the iceberg.

I grabbed his elbow to guide him to the door, unlocking it with my eye scan and thumbprint. Then I led them both down the steep concrete steps into the bowels of the basement.

Lucky's cherry cola and cedar scent clung to me as I steered him in the right direction. His soothing cologne eased my growing nerves at what I'd gotten myself into.

Despite it all, I found the con man's presence reassuring. A therapist would have a field day.

I let him go so I could open the secure door to the apartment. Ushering the two men inside the entrance alcove, I closed the door behind us.

My thoughts drifted to Sandra and Alec upstairs. Did they know today was Christmas Day? Had the lunacy of sitting under bright lights twenty-four hours a day made Sandra lose all sense of time yet?

I hoped she still held a semblance of her sanity to understand her family was sick with worry while she slowly succumbed to her fate.

Her husband had filed a missing persons report and was making a stink on local news channels, begging the public for information. She wouldn't be coming home. She could slip away into madness for a few months before I gave her what she needed to end her life herself. It was the only mercy I would give her.

I removed Lucky's blindfold with quick fingers, the heat of his skin making me intimately aware of his touch. His sea-glass green eyes twinkled, curiosity dancing in them as he stared back at me.

"And the Lord said, 'let there be light,' and she was truly feckin' stunning."

He winked lasciviously after that nonsensical sentence. Then his impish grin widened as he kicked off his boots and waltzed through the door without another word.

Kellan huffed an irritated sigh and followed him, boots, coat and all.

"Hey! Take your boots off!" I called, trailing behind him after removing mine. "This is a home, you barbarian!"

"Oy, I call him that, too!" Lucky exclaimed gleefully as his gaze swept around the apartment. He whistled appreciatively. "Nicest dungeon I've ever been to." He promptly plopped himself on my couch, assuming his usual position with his feet up and head back, like he was back in my condo in Carlisle.

Before I could scold him properly, Aaron walked out of the little hall leading to the bathroom, his dark hair slicked back and tucked behind the ears from a fresh shower. A tight, black, long-sleeve athletic tee stretched across the muscles of his chest in the most delicious way. Black, athletic track pants, the kind made from moisture-wicking material that molded around a man's ass and thighs, made everything about his strong body stand out.

In all the years I'd known him, Aaron wore a suit to almost every occasion; seeing him look like a regular man was a treat—although truthfully, Aaron could never look like a regular anything.

Lucky had gone casual today, too. He removed his jacket to reveal a form-fitting olive green Henley with waffle stitching, the cut of the casual clothing expensive and showing off every smooth line of his defined shoulders and arms. Dark, fitted jeans stretched across his hips, accentuating a biteable bubble butt.

His bright green Grinch socks betrayed his manly persona, and I nearly choked on my earlier comparison. A teenage boy trapped in an elaborate, eye-catching portrait of the perfectly masculine form.

"*Mi Reina*." Aaron pulled me into his arms, wrapping me into his embrace, vanilla and sandalwood enveloping me in a comforting cocoon. I settled against his chest for a brief moment, before leaning back to catch sight of his depthless caramel eyes.

Before I could breathe a word, his lips were on mine, a forceful crash of teeth and tongues as he devoured me. He cupped my cheeks and pinned me in place until he had finished his exploration.

"Aye, well, that's new." Lucky's voice broke me from my lustful fog; I turned to see two men watching us with hunger in their eyes; a dangerous simmer in Kellan's, a wicked glimmer in Lauchlan's.

Right—this is just one of the many reasons this was a bad idea.

"It is." Aaron agreed, releasing me to turn me around to face the men. My back settled into his chest as he banded his arms around my front. "And it is not. Perhaps you should have tried the choking, yes?"

Lucky's burst of laughter broke the growing tension in the room, the well of chuckles bringing tears to his eyes. "You made a joke! I didn't know you had it in you, Mr. Roboto." He wiped his face with his palm, the enormous grin bursting at the seams. "Good for you."

My Viking protector was beside me in an instant, having set down the dishes and removed his coat. The tight white dress shirt he wore stretched across his gigantic frame; every colorful tattoo was a bold shadow beneath the thin layer of fabric. Tight navy trousers stuck to his thick thighs like a second skin, the outline of a well-endowed man on full display. His blond hair hung down to his shoulders, tousled from the wind and snow.

The man was the epitome of rugged masculinity and perfectly crafted workmanship, a rough gemstone pulled from the earth, too perfect in its raw form to be tampered with by a jeweler's touch.

He took my chin between his fingers, but his intense stare was unreadable when he sandwiched my compact frame between his and Aaron's large, domineering bodies.

He brought his mouth to mine in a demanding kiss, parting my lips and searing my skin with his hot tongue and controlling presence. His body pushed me deeper into Aaron's, the rigid outline of his hardening length digging into my back.

When the commanding Alpha-hole was satisfied he'd properly staked his claim, I pushed out from between them, wriggling my way into my own personal space.

"As much as I'm all about group activities"—I looked down my nose at the pair of them with a pointed frown—"I refuse to be the pawn of some caveman chess match, okay?"

Lucky's hand wrapped around my biceps, gently pulling me between his arms in a loose hold. When I blinked up at him in surprise, he smirked down at me, the quirk of his lips a tempting offer.

"So, it's a bad idea to offer my lips as tribute, too, Blondie?"

"No!" came the resounding response from the two possessive men behind me. I hastily shoved out of Lucky's arms before any of them could resort to a battle for dominance.

I did *not* need to kick anyone's ass today—not on Christmas.

"Before this goes any further, let me make something clear. You"—I pointed to Lauchlan and threw him my sternest glare, the one used to make businessmen quiver; he didn't even bat an eye—"are our captive, not a member of the club."

I spun on my heel to face the others, desperately hoping this admission wouldn't change the course of our day. My voice stayed strong, but my gaze pleaded for understanding. "I care about both of you and I'm not choosing between you, so let's try to work through that over turkey."

Neither man batted an eye at that statement either— *was I losing my touch?*—as if they'd expected this outcome, and they'd already made their peace with it.

That was... unexpected.

"And, if we can't work through that over turkey," Lauchlan piped up unhelpfully, "I'm a very happy voyeur. Promise you won't know I'm here." He mimed zipping his lips. He paused, then mimed *un*zipping his lips. "I can take my dick out, though, right? I mean, if I can't partake, I'd like to at least—"

"Fuck off, *Capericita Roja*," Kellan growled, his blazing eyes turning his wrath onto the lippy Irishman. "You're not a part of this."

The belly laugh that escaped through Aaron's lips was a sound I had never heard in my lifetime. It started as a rolling chuckle, then rose to a crescendo of outright guffaws.

The sheer joy on his face was beautiful; raw and enigmatic. The rarity of it made it a precious commodity.

Kellan—or rather, Kellan at Lucky's expense—had brought it out of him. My heart stuttered at the brilliance of it; his caramel eyes were backlit like he'd tasted genuine joy.

I was desperate to see more of it. I wanted to be the source of it.

"*Capericita Roja!*" My serious businessman chortled, slapping his thigh and leaning against the back of the couch to stabilize himself. "That is perfect, my friend. *Capericita Roja.*"

Lucky cocked his head in veiled confusion. "Glad we're all making jokes at my expense," he tutted lightly. "Can we eat now? I don't want Mr. Roboto having an aneurism after discovering his sense of humor."

Masculine pissing party over, Aaron and Kellan removed the takeout containers for the catering box, setting everything out on the table while I directed Lucky's help in setting out the silverware. It was an odd dance of domestic activity, and yet we all played our parts like the cogs of a well-honed machine, moving in sync to the sound of clattering dishes and Lucky unapologetically humming "The Bad Touch" by the *Bloodhound Gang.*

The meal was surprisingly hot, and I ate it with enthusiasm, realizing with every bite that despite sitting in an underground bunker beneath two tortured prisoners, despite spending it with three criminals with the most complicated web of connection we could have bargained for, and despite being estranged from the family who'd given me life, this was the most pleasant Christmas dinner I'd ever had.

Lucky ate four helpings of Yorkshire pudding. They'd been a favorite of my grandmother, so I always included them with a traditional meal, though Daddy ignored any form of carbs.

"Ma used to bake Yorkshire puddings for Christmas dinner before she came to America," he mused before he bit into his third pastry. "Dreadful cook, though. They were hard as stone." He popped it into his mouth in one bite, chewed and swallowed. "My compliments to the chef!" he declared.

They were a favorite of mine, too—one of the few English foods I enjoyed.

"*Buñuelos*," Aaron murmured thoughtfully, a tiny smile taking hold of the corners of his lips as he took another Yorkshire pudding of his own. "Colombian fritters. Our cook made them when I was a boy. They are still my favorite."

Kellan's permanent scowl lifted and a rare warmth entered his cold eyes. "I love *buñuelos*. We made *kanelbuller* before Mamma was killed. It's like a Swedish cinnamon bun," he said, glancing around at our blank looks.

His mother had been killed. How had I never thought to ask where his mother was? There was nothing online about her—no trace at all. I'd tried to find out through my sources, but we had never broached the subject. I didn't want to talk about mine, and surely, he'd know all about Helen Lane from his own stalking of me—but not once had I tried to ask him about it.

Shame flushed down my neck for a brief moment, flooding my insides with uncomfortable heat. If Kellan wanted to become something more than my would-be protector, I needed to know more about him. Would he share the darkness of his past with me, or would we be trapped in a stalemate of false dependence?

Lucky, thankfully, used his cheeky powers for good.

"I didn't know that about you, Kell-Bell. You look like you've never eaten a cinnamon bun in your life." He patted his equally flat stomach and grinned, turning his attention to me. "Happy to see you have taste buds after all, Blondie. I was afraid you'd make us eat tofu-turkey and unbuttered Brussel sprouts."

Scoffing, I grabbed another Yorkshire pudding, smothered it in a heaping serving of gravy and quirked a challenging brow in his direction.

"My body is a temple, Lucky. But unbuttered brussel sprouts? Yuck."

We continued to eat in relatively comfortable silence until the meal was done. Pushing back from the table, I gathered the empty plates and brought them to the counter, pleased when all three men rose to help.

We settled to the living room couches with glasses of wine once everything was cleaned up. Aaron unceremoniously grabbed me and placed me in his lap; Kellan and Lucky sat opposite us on the giant sectional.

As unorthodox as this day was, I was determined to bring some sense of normalcy to our lives, even for the briefest of moments before everything in our sights devolved into chaos. Normalcy on Christmas day meant presents.

"Okay, since it's Christmas, I have a little something for you."

Lucky's head perked up. "Presents?"

Kellan's semi-relaxed expression soured into a surly frown. "Killer—"

I held up two fingers to shush him.

"Fuck off, Kellan dearest," I cooed, smiling sweetly. "Gifts are my love language, so you'll take my present like a good boy."

Aaron muffled a chuckle against my neck, and I didn't miss Lucky's sly smirk. Kellan's cool gaze was unimpressed by my taunting, but he put his scowl back in his pocket for later.

Shifting in Aaron's arms, I stood to grab the small wrapped presents in the deep pockets of my coat. Handing them each a package, I retook my position in my gorgeous Colombian's lap.

"Okay, open!" I commanded, unable to stifle the wide grin creeping across my face. "Lucky, last," I amended with a giggle, his crestfallen expression pulling an outright laugh out of me.

Gifts *were* my love language. Money was a tool to be wielded most of the time. To build businesses, to build dreams, to build lifestyles and security; and to bring joy to those you loved.

I had more money than I'd ever be able to spend in twenty lifetimes. Much went to businesses building new, better products to improve people's lives—some went to charity, and, admittedly, some went to the frivolous things that I enjoyed in life. Like Louboutin shoes, Jaguars, and gifts for the people I cared about.

In this case, that meant one for Lucky, too.

When nobody moved, I elbowed Aaron in the ribs. "All right, you first."

He gently pulled me to the side, sitting me firmly on his thigh, holding me in place with one arm, while he reached around to unwrap the dainty black box in his other hand.

He untied the delicate lace bow with reverence and flicked open the lid with caressing fingers. His muscles tensed around me at the sight of my gift.

"*Mi Reina.*" His voice was barely audible as he pulled the platinum ring from its bedding and held it up to the light.

The ring was custom-made, worth a small fortune, and inlaid with a precious Mozambique ruby. The round cut gemstone was almost identical to the necklace he'd gifted me years ago.

He noticed.

"Almost a perfect match." He pulled off the elaborate gold family crest ring he wore on his right ring finger and replaced it with mine. "Perfect fit." He mused, then pulled me tighter into his arms. "Thank you."

"Rubies represent passion and protection." I wrapped my small fingers around his large hand and squeezed, smiling up into the warmth of his eyes. "Fitting, right?"

"And wealth." Lucky piped up before Aaron could respond. "You two are the wealthiest fuckers I know, so makes sense to me." He flipped me a lazy wink. I flipped him the finger.

"Your turn, Viking." While distracted by Aaron's opening, I hadn't missed the fact that Kellan hadn't taken his eyes off his present, holding it in his hands as if it were a bomb about to detonate.

He wasn't used to people being generous without an ulterior motive, and it showed. My heart ached for the man who'd learned to trust no one so young. My lessons had come much older.

When he lifted his gaze to meet mine, I glimpsed his warring emotions, but I could not separate any single one from the whole. What I would give to decipher this man's thoughts.

Would the man ever be able to let me in? Could I let *him* in?

He let out an exasperated sigh, then ripped open the package between his palms, far less delicately than the careful businessman. He held up the pendant in front of his face, scrutinizing its details.

"It's tungsten." I stood, clasped his hand and turned it over in his palm. The hand-crafted amulet was a replication of Thor's Hammer, with the engraved Viking trident symbol, *Algiz*.

"The trident symbol means protection." Taking the amulet from his hand, I reached around and secured it around his neck. The pendant fell just below his sternum between his pec muscles. Cupping his bearded cheeks in my palms, I stared deep into conflicted, navy pools. "You have always been my sword and shield, Viking. Thank you."

Gifts made him mute, apparently. He cleared his throat gruffly, acknowledged my words with a brief nod, then lightly gripped my wrists, removing my hands from his face.

"Thank you," he muttered, though fingering the amulet at his chest. The air was thick with unnamed emotion, so I hurried on to my final giftee.

"Your turn."

When I turned to Lucky, he was staring at me with unbridled curiosity. For a brief moment, his eyes carried none of the mischievous, calculating energy; instead, they held a softness, an openness I wasn't used to seeing. Maybe it was a trick of the light, but the sea-glass tone was a brilliant shade of moss green—pure and captivating.

As soon as I saw it, the window into perhaps the *true* Lucky melted back into the impish glint of a naughty boy.

Good. He would like his present, then.

He tore into the wrapping like said naughty boy and unwrapped a theater-sized bag of Skittles.

"For me?" He gasped, playing up the gift like he'd received a priceless prize, and held it to his chest. "I simply *couldn't*, Blondie. You really know the way to a man's heart."

He ripped open the bag and promptly popped an entire handful into his mouth.

"Thank you, love." He turned his attention to the other two men in the room, whose brows were furrowed into matching frowns. "Gentlemen, I'm the winner tonight. I don't care how much you can pawn your trinkets off for. Skittle?"

When he held the bag out to me with a wink, I wrinkled my nose in distaste. "No, thanks. Enjoy."

I padded back to the oversized chair to cuddle back up into Aaron's lap. We relaxed into an unsettled silence. Kellan's brooding emotions and Lucky's obnoxious candy chewing filled the void for the better part of several minutes.

Attempting to create a Christmas day with the two men I cared about and our captive probably hadn't been my greatest idea. Gifts for them likely wasn't the best play, either. But spending Christmas in a bunker, avoiding our toxic bloodlines, and removing us from the insanity of our lives for just one day had been the only move I could make on the board today.

The gnawing feeling in my gut told me our lives were about to get so much worse.

"Let's play a game," Lucky drawled, naturally the one to break the silence. His mischievous gaze flicked back and forth between the three of us. "Never have I ever? I'll start. Never have I ever... had a threesome with a man between me and a woman."

He grabbed his drink from the coffee table before a dastardly smirk split his lips in two. "No, wait. Done that. Lots, actually. What do you say, Kell-Bell? You taking a drink?"

"No," came Kellan's stilted reply, thick eyebrows raised in exasperated annoyance.

"You're telling me you've never had someone rail your arse while you're balls deep in a woman? Fuck, Conan, you're missin' out on a pure taste of Heaven."

He held out his wineglass, gesturing with it toward me before taking a long pull of the red liquid. "You can rail me while I rail her anytime. I love a quick trip to visit my pal Jesus."

Biting my lip, I held in my giggle for as long as I could. My body shook in Aaron's arms, before the girlish sound burst from my lips, evolving into a full fit of sniggering choked breaths.

Aaron held my wine as I writhed in his lap. Ab muscles clenching in fists, I laughed hard enough to fulfill an exorcism. The tension in the room, in my body, in our tiny little world broke completely.

"It wasn't that funny," Kellan muttered drily over my noise; I laughed even harder.

"I broke her." Lucky chuckled, his eyes alight with amusement, the pride in wearing me down all over his handsome, boyish face.

"She cannot be broken," Aaron deadpanned, but I caught a quirk of his lips in my periphery as I wiped away tears.

"You're right." Aaron handed me back my glass, and I drew a long swig before facing the three men, now completely entrenched in my life and my mission.

"I can't be broken, gentlemen." I raised my glass in a toast. "So don't even try."

Cora Flynn

CHAPTER 13

Lauchlan

"Bellamy, you dodgy prat, how are yeh?"

I held my cell between my shoulder and my cheek like Charlie Sheen in an eighties film as I adjusted my cufflinks, checking myself out in Blondie's guest bathroom mirror.

Beard trimmed, hair styled, devilish twinkle in the eye at the ready? Check, check, and check.

I was getting pretty comfortable in my new digs; a beautiful rich and powerful woman had kidnapped me, branded me, and was now holding me hostage between her two boyfriends and buying me Christmas presents of my favorite American candy.

Terrible life, that.

I hadn't heard from Bellamy in a few months, not since he'd handed me this assignment. I'd known him since I was a wee boy, him being one of Da's dearest friends, and the man always gave me the best jobs.

"How's the job, Locky-boy? Haven't heard a word from yeh. Been taken in by the American beauties?"

One American beauty; quite literally taken in.

"Great work takes time, Bellamy, you know I don't rush perfection."

His rough laugh bellowed out from the end of the line, years of smoking fags like a chimney barking from his lips.

"Right," he chortled, the sound suspiciously muffled by a long intake of breath–fags again–before his tone turned unnaturally serious.

"Wanted to warn yeh, son. Someone's looking into your assignment."

I stilled my primping and considered my words.

Hillary looking into me wasn't surprising–expected, really–but I was confident she didn't know my real identity. She was competent, crafty, and damn well brilliant when it came to busting balls and building empires; if she knew about me, she would have already crushed my tender babies like water balloons in her tiny fists.

My dick swelled in my trousers at the thought–fucking masochist.

But Bellamy hadn't said 'me'—he'd said 'assignment'. Which meant someone knew my real identity, or someone knew someone had targeted Hillary.

"Oh?" I managed, needing more information before I hung myself with it.

"Six got a call a while ago–man looking to target your target and was right disappointed when he couldn't get what he wanted. The odds of two contracts on the same person? Never happened before." The hissy sound of smoke blown into the speaker filled my ear.

"Now, one of our networks was hacked—our guys tell us it was by a hired third party and traced back to an FBI server. Could be nothing, but I'd watch your back."

"Can you send me all the data? I'll run it through my own channels."

Bellamy's laugh echoed back at me. "Right, all your 'techy' stuff." He emphasized tech as if it were a joke, but his tone turned solemn again.

"Ever think of leavin' this life?" Another long drag of the fag crackled into the phone. "Since your Da died, I mean. You've got some smarts behind yeh, you could start something new when this is all—"

"Bellamy, my boy, I *love* this life," I interrupted, not for the first time since this wasn't a new conversation. "When I'm sent to hell, it'll be a wall-less office in a room full of accountants. I might as well live the dream while I'm on this side of the dirt."

I meant it, too. Conning, the thrill of the chase, the subterfuge, the dance of it all? A man in his right mind with the skill sets I had would never choose to leave it for a mainstream job of listening to Barb chatter about her cats or watching Nelson trim his toenails in the break room.

The only way I'd be leaving this life was in a black body bag, and really? What a fitting end to a killer heist.

"Well," Bellamy said dubiously, "keep me posted on your progress. We're going to need to wrap this one up soon, Locky. We're getting pressure from the client for quick results. It's not like you to take a few months for this kind of job."

"It'll be done," I promised. I adjusted my tie one final time before stepping out of the bathroom to grab my overcoat. "Have faith, Bellamy. I've never let you down, yet."

"No, yeh haven't." Bellamy sighed at the admission. "Slan, Locky."

"Slan." I returned the greeting and hung up, eagerly awaiting the files to do my own investigation into whoever was looking into me.

An electric current swept up my spine at the thrill of a little unexpected game of cat-and-mouse. Another 'pro' for the old 'con man as a career' tally. Couldn't get this kind of excitement working for Deloitte or some dodgy insurance company.

Glancing at my watch, I hurried down the hall to head to my other special assignment—the bollocks 'penetration testing' for the git Xander Manalo.

What kind of name was Xander, anyway? Twat-waffling turd.

It was my last morning for the project—I'd successfully made my way into every weak point of their network, and had issued my professional advice on what to work on to minimize their risk.

Marco Alvarez was taking this shiny Audi for a test drive, and I was just waiting for the real job—the one where he asked me to use my superpowers for something shady. Little did he know, I used my superpowers for shady shyte every day. He hadn't broached the subject yet, and I was a bit disappointed—I wanted another mark on his coffin to take him down—but it would be any day now; my spidey senses were tingling.

I needed some distance from this Elon Musk wanna be, anyway. Being tied down was as miserable as a thorny dildo, and three weeks was the exact amount of patience I had for that kind of job. I was antsy to say a silent 'fuck you' to Xandy and get on to my afternoon meeting.

Blondie was finally introducing me to her hacker. We'd put our heads together, finish the botnet I'd been building. Then finally—finally—I'd crash Marco's systems and steal every piece of information I could get my greedy little hands on.

I principally wanted access to his bank accounts—the secret ones with private transfers would be best, but I'd take his personal ones and ruin him that way, too. Cut off the head, and all that.

I'd already selected every charity in the country who'd be receiving a sizable anonymous check—with a side cut for me, of course. I wasn't a bleeding heart; I was getting revenge for Shayna bringing the gobshite down, and revenge for my heartbreak by lining my pockets with his comeuppance.

Shayna. I ignored the twinge in my chest as I saw her smile in my mind; I usually pictured her pouting in some sort of teenage hissy fit to ease the ache, but it was her smile that broke me. Her smile was a brand that still burned to the touch.

Nope, not diving into that pot of piss today. Back to Blondie.

When the holy show with Alvarez was over, I'd buy my Blondie something nice with the windfall. An island, maybe? Never bought a present for a billionaire before. I'd have to think about it.

It was only fair—when I finally found that pretty little painting, it would be traded on the black market for a cool hundred million, at least—and I'd get at least five percent of that. I didn't know the going rates for tropical islands these days, but I'd see if I could cut a deal with Mr. Roboto to chip in a few million.

The man was as soft for my lass as a pot of pudding. I'd have to work on winning him over a little better. The sexy Colombian could sit on my face and I'd call him Daddy any day of the week, but he looked at me like he'd drown me in a vat of acid the moment Hillary gave him permission.

Challenge accepted, Daddy Roboto. I'm going to get under your skin, and you're going to love it.

I could drive myself today with Conan and Blondie off doing something important—small luxuries—and I took advantage of the quiet on the short commute to the pompous twit's office.

Schmoozing and charming the pants off the masses was my strongest skill, but I was mostly a solitary guy. Living in Hillary's space and having a daily escort was driving me a bit mad.

Sometimes, a man just wanted to sit on the couch in his underwear in peace.

Unbidden, thoughts of Conan, Blondie, and Daddy Roboto popped into my head; the little sandwich show in the dungeon had *definitely* piqued my interest. I'd tugged my dick in the shower as a little Christmas present to myself, imagining every way I could convince each of them to use me.

As long as I was stuck with the three of them, I needed to get in on that action, or I'd have a chapped dick and a raw fist soon.

Shutting down those thoughts, I arrived and turned on autopilot for my summary meeting with Xander. Once I was given the green light to return to my app project, I hosted a quick team meeting with my merry band of misfits before heading back to the Queen's palace for our meeting with Blackbird.

I loved the cloak and dagger of it all. "Blackbird." I wondered if they'd heard of my codename, the one I'd earned as a cocky-as-shyte college grad with a score to prove. *Madra Rua*—The Red Fox. I'd have to ask.

When I arrived at the condo, my beautiful blonde bombshell was waiting for me in the living room. She looked tempting as a goddess in her plum power suit and four-inch heels. When she rose to greet me, she was exactly my height; I stared into the baby blues I saw in my dreams and grinned like an excited schoolboy.

"Where's Blackbird?" I clapped my hands together, ready to put these final few pieces in place.

"She's not meeting us in person, Lucky." Hillary's lips twitched in amusement before she turned on her heel, leading me to her bedroom and into her massive closet.

She placed her palm on a hidden screen behind a rack of coats, and the secret sex room opened up. The panel slid open to reveal a square space, ten by ten by my reckoning, an entire wall of computer screens on one side. I followed her in, impressed by the top-notch hardware and equipment, and plopped myself into the computer chair in front of me.

"Nope." My queen chastised, popping the 'p' as she stared down at me. "That's my seat. You can stand for this conversation."

Feck me, she was a bossy brat sometimes. I was tempted to pull her down into my lap, but I thought better of it.

Wasn't wise to goad a woman in her own cage when she could kick my arse.

"Aye, aye, Captain." I mock saluted and stood, my gaze scanning around the dimly lit room as she moved into the seat and logged in to her system.

I turned to the rear wall and froze, my eyes catching on the prize.

My prize. *The* prize.

Blood pounded in my ears. The painting, encased in acrylic plexiglass to protect it from the elements. Its oil-based colors blinded me with their brilliance despite the darkness of the room.

"Reclining Nude," by Amedeo Modigliani, over a hundred years old, and one of the most celebrated Italian paintings. I could paint a nude woman with her breasts hanging out and it would be considered "lewd'" but my Blondie had purchased the artwork from a private owner after it had been a featured exhibition at the MET a few years ago—for a cool $150 million. American.

"Ah, Blondie?" I schooled my voice to a smooth, curious tone. "Why do you have a priceless painting in a broom closet?"

She spun around in her chair, and her eyes flitted between my own and the naked girl. They appraised me with indifference, like priceless artwork in secret spy closets was a normal thing. "It was an investment, Lucky. I protect my investments."

"Don't rich people hoard these things in vaults like dragons?" I joked, unable to rip my eyes away from my goldmine. After months of searching, it was really fucking here, and I was about to become a very rich man.

"I prefer to keep it close by," she responded airily, turning back to the monitor to input yet another password. "No sunlight, temperature and humidity controlled. Seeing as it's my most valuable possession—money-wise," she amended, with one last click on the keyboard before turning back to face me.

"So, you didn't pay a literal fortune to put it in a shrine in your sitting room, to show off your riches to all your friends?" I kept my voice light and mildly interested, despite the wild horses racing through my heart.

Rolling her eyes to the ceiling, she scoffed dismissively, but I saw the quirk of her lips as she hid her smile. "Lucky, everyone in the world knows I'm rich. I don't need a painting to prove it." She eyed the monitor, which was apparently still loading, before folding her arms and turning her attention back to me.

"Empires fall every day. Stock markets crash. I am one critical decision away from financial ruin—we all are. So, investing cash into an appreciating asset is an investment strategy. If I ever need to sell it quickly, I know I'll quickly double my money, which is a much better return than if I ever put the same amount in the market."

Letting out a low whistle, I had to appreciate the reasoning behind it, even if only a *billionaire* could say such things with a straight face and mean them. I couldn't even make a joke about it; before I could respond, a blurred-out face appeared on the screen, some masking software in place to hide their identity.

"Blackbird," Hillary started, apparently not in the mood for polite pleasantries today, "meet Lucky. We need your help on a project that's top priority, and he's going to explain it to you. Before we go further, though, you need to know that it's extremely under the radar and could come with some severe consequences. Are you in?"

"Fuck, yeah." Despite the voice modification software they were using to make their voice sound like Darth Vader, her enthusiasm bled through the line. Drug-like euphoria filled my limbs; every little dream of mine was about to come true.

I figured I'd be here a few more months with the way my search was going. Now, I had an elite hacker willing to finish what I'd started, and my prize was literally within reach of my fingertips.

Within a few weeks, I could be on a boat in the Mediterranean, my enemy destroyed, Shayna's body laid to rest, and one hell of a richer man.

For the first time in my fuckin' life, I felt a small tug of guilt in my gut. I wasn't the sorry sap who got tied up with feelings. Hillary Lane could afford the loss; I had a job to do. My help with Alvarez would take down her enemy, so surely, we could work out a deal where she'd forgive me—*after* I bought her that island.

While she explained the plan to Blackbird, I searched Hillary's face; the calm control and steely determination of a competent Queen in action.

I was lying to myself—she'd never forgive me. She valued loyalty more than anything else; I'd seen it in action with every action, and no amount of groveling or piña coladas would change my Blondie's mind.

I'd put off thinking about the inevitable, but now I had to face it head on. Was I willing to risk making an enemy out of Hillary Lane?

The more honest question was a wee bit harder to ask. Was I willing to walk away from my Blondie, who had captured every bit of my waking attention? Enemies I had aplenty—but beautiful, fierce, intelligent women who sat on my side of the insanity bench with the balls to follow through?

The answer made my life a hell of a lot more complicated.

My thoughts raced to Bellamy. Someone was investigating my assignment because they'd wanted to target Hillary, which brought about a bunch of loaded questions.

How many enemies did this woman have?

Who'd targeted her in the first place?

Was it personal, or was it just some horny prick who loved semi-accurate nude paintings and wasn't willing to sell all his organs on the black market for it?

And why the fuck hadn't I questioned any of this before?

Hell of a time to develop a conscience.

The room had gone silent; I looked up to see Hillary and the hacker's blobbed face staring at me expectantly.

Blowing out a breath to clear my head, I flashed my most charming smile. I had some questions I needed answers to before I could scamper off like a handsome fox, which meant I'd be sticking out the job a little while longer.

"Sorry about that." I spoke cheerfully, moving into my Blondie's personal space to face Blackbird head-on. "Here's what I'm going to need from you to destroy this fucker…"

I had some bloody decisions to make. But first… sweet, sweet revenge.

CHAPTER 14

Hillary

"What in the ever-loving feck do you have in this thing?" Lucky complained as he dragged my oversized Louis Vuitton suitcase behind him in the snow as we crossed the driveway to Winter's home.

I visited every year in January for a weekend to spend some time with my bestie and her family. This year, I had been blessed with an Irish tag-along.

I'd considered canceling, but my little adopted nephew's birthday party was tomorrow. I didn't get to be a part of his life nearly enough, and the overwhelming "aunt guilt" had made that choice an impossibility.

Kellan was away on FBI business, and he'd made it abundantly clear he would be refusing "babysitting duty" as he called it, from now on.

Aaron, of course, was indisposed at the Palace and, as much as I wanted to dump Lucky off there for the weekend and not have to deal with him, I didn't trust Aaron not to kill him. Now I knew what Lucky was after in my home, there was no way he was getting the weekend alone at my condo to thieve it from right under my nose.

The man had practically salivated when he saw the Modigliani in the panic room. I already had cursed myself for not making the connection sooner. *Of course*, he would be after my most valuable possession—Lucky was the most competent thief I'd ever met. Which was saying quite a lot. In my time at Jediah's parties, I'd met more than a few–it didn't surprise me he wasn't after some diamonds or a designer gown—he was going for the grand prize of stolen goods.

Now it was a matter of time; I was confident in my security measures, so I just had to wait until he got himself caught. Although, admittedly, I hadn't figured out what I was going to do to him when he got stuck in my web.

My dungeon was for predators only; he would not get the same torture treatment my other guests did. Blackbird had informed me, after our little business meeting, she'd been impressed by his plan and his level of knowledge. We were likely going to actually pull this off

So, like it or not, Lucky was far more valuable to me alive than dead, or alive and tortured.

Trading in grays was a daily deal in this life I'd chosen. Shady businessmen, crooked legal teams, manipulative city councils—all par for the course to walk the roads of this world. I was willing to trade Lucky's duplicity for his skill set if it meant I could take down Alvarez—and, if he did it successfully, I'd take him off my permanent chopping block.

He drove me up the wall most days, but... I liked him.

I didn't want to—it would be easier to toss him in a cell if I didn't. His Irish charm had snared me at Quintessence and despite his childish tendencies, he was cunning, intelligent, and unassuming—the perfect partner in crime if *I* wasn't the one he was trying to swindle. His sexier than sin body and captivating eyes were a bonus, but it was his exasperating sense of whimsy and wit that amplified his appeal.

I'd met thousands of people—hundreds of thousands— over the years of rubbing shoulders with Daddy's circle of influence before I built my own. Hundreds of men and women had tried to seduce me, barter favors from me, lavish me with gifts and praise with nothing of substance beyond their motives.

Maybe it was because I'd known his motives this whole time, but I struggled to see Lucky as an actual threat. He was a cocky mouse, thinking he could mimic the nature of a lion, but *I* was the lion. Jungle cats weren't afraid of rodents.

But if I was wrong, and he double-crossed us? Kellan and Aaron could have their turns with him first, then I'd finish him. A fair fight, like Aaron had been gifted, except there wouldn't be anyone coming to Lucky's rescue.

So, for now, Lucky would be stuck to my side, away from my priceless paintings and any of the countless ways he could get into trouble. That meant this weekend he was with me.

I didn't trust him with priceless artwork, but I didn't see him as a threat to the people I loved. It was a juxtaposition I wasn't able to explain. Yet.

I had to lean into my gut on this one.

I also had to come up with a cover story for his appearance. I was thankful Winter couldn't see my face when I'd explained I was bringing the man "I'm seeing." I refused to use the word 'boyfriend,' but it didn't matter; she'd obnoxiously squealed in my ear with excitement. Then she'd hollered to the guys I was bringing my boyfriend and they'd "need to behave."

I could take solace in the fact Shane and Logan were sure to *not* behave and give Lucky hell. I'd just sit back for the weekend and enjoy the show.

And speak of the devils… As we rounded the corner, the entire goddamned family was waiting at the entrance, not even bothering to hide their curious eyes and smug grins.

"Pay up!" Shane called out as we walked closer. Drew sheepishly shook his head at his husband. We stopped awkwardly in front of our welcome party.

"What was the bet this time?" I cocked an eyebrow in the direction of my least favorite of Winter's husbands; Shane just winked at me.

"I thought you were covering for Kellan," Drew admitted, running a hand through his short blond hair as his guilty hazel eyes met mine. "Shane said there was no way he'd be coming without giving the guys a heads up, but I"—his eyes darted behind me to my companion, and he dropped his voice, as if doing so would save Lucky's feelings —"thought something might have finally clicked with you two. I owe him fifty bucks."

"'Fraid Kellan still has his head stuck up his arse on that one, mate," Lucky piped up unhelpfully. He dragged my suitcase to a stop behind him and reached out to Drew to shake his hand. "I'm Lauchlan. Nice to meet you."

Winter, standing between Travis and Logan with Noble on her hip shyly peering at us from between his fingers, gave Lucky a once over and then mouthed 'he's hot,' before beckoning us into the house. Cam grabbed my suitcase and hoisted it over his shoulder like it was the weight of a pillow; I smirked at Lucky in satisfaction.

Cam was a jacked carpenter now, but he used to be one of the best boxers in the state and still trained regularly. Kellan used to spar with his half-brother, and it was as bloody and erotic as it sounded.

We piled into the front foyer, exchanging hugs and introductory handshakes while I cooed over Noble's growing form. The little bundle turned one within the week, and as his favorite auntie, I'd brought him his birthday present.

Winter handed Noble off to Travis, and I immediately yanked my best friend into my chest for a tight hug. We'd grown up in Cascade Falls most of our lives, but hadn't become friends until adulthood. Now, she was my most cherished relationship, and I hated we lived hours apart.

When we were young and dumb, we could have spent years of our time in each other's company. Now that we had our shit together, we had to relegate our girl time to rare weekends because our lives kept getting in the way. Daily memes and text messages just weren't enough.

Tears pricked my eyes like they always did when we reunited, and I quickly brushed them into her long auburn hair before pulling away to properly assess her.

Winter looked light years better than my last visit—her postpartum depression appeared finally under control with the right meds and lifestyle changes. Her blue-green eyes sparkled and the smile on her face was relaxed and genuine. I was so grateful she had five good partners taking care of her when I couldn't.

"Are you guys hungry?" Her eyes shone with love as she glanced over at Logan and Cam. "These two cooked you an authentic Southern meal, and you're going to want to eat it hot."

"Since when can you cook?" I pushed Logan's shoulder affectionately with a smile. He hadn't cooked a single meal in all the time I'd known him; before he was married—to Winter, not me—he'd lived off catered salads and gourmet takeout.

"Since everyone in this house kept giving me shit," Logan retorted. Winter ushered us into the huge eat-in kitchen at the rear of the house.

As promised, a spread fit for a queen was laid out on the harvest table, and I gladly took a seat. I rarely indulged in high-fat, salty foods, but Cam's cooking was impossible to say no to.

"So, how did you two meet?" Travis asked over dinner. Winter's most charming husband flashed one of his bright smiles; kind, curious green eyes authentically wanted the story.

Well, this one would be easy to answer, at least.

"Quintessence, funnily enough." I snuck a glance at Lucky, who had grabbed a seat at the end of the table next to the highchair, and had taken to playing with Noble—who was squishing the remains of his buttered biscuits into his hair. "He had the balls to hit on me when your uncle stood me up."

"Kellan is one brave fucker." Shane flicked his long, dark braid over his shoulder. His storm gray eyes flashed with amusement before he shoved a huge helping of potatoes into his mouth.

"Hold up." Lucky's attention turned from the miniature food fight Noble had started to Travis. "Kellan is your *uncle*?"

Travis shifted in his seat, looking uncomfortable, but he didn't dodge the question. "It's complicated, but yeah." He waved a hand toward Cam, who sat on the opposite side of the table. "We're both related to Kellan. It's a fucked up family tree."

Lucky's gaze flicked back and forth between Travis and Cam, as if searching for the family resemblance. There wasn't any; Cam was dark-skinned, with brilliant blue eyes and close-cropped hair; Travis was white, albeit nicely tanned, with wavy black hair and green eyes.

Before Lucky could ask another question, Travis quickly switched the subject. "Has Jeremy made you my latest?" he asked eagerly.

I had to smile at his enthusiasm. Travis oversaw the entire bar operation across their five locations, and the signature drinks were his creations.

"You know I only drink dirty martinis, Trav, but I'm sure it's delicious." I turned to Lucky to at least fill him in. "These guys own Quintessence and their four affiliate clubs."

"That's grand!" His sea-glass eyes lit up with interest. "Love it there. Reminds me of Artesian Bar in London."

"Really!?" Winter beamed excitedly at Logan, who returned her smile with a confident smirk of his own. "That's the restaurant we modeled it after! That's literally the *best* praise." She tossed me a wide smile; Lucky had her immediate approval.

Logan flashed an all-too-familiar cocky grin at his wife. "And whose idea was that?" He taunted cheekily, sipping his tonic water. "You know the best ones are all mine."

"Definitely not," Shane disagreed, buttering another roll idly while cocking a disbelieving brow at Logan. "Lava Cake Sundays were my idea. If you ate chocolate and had taste buds, you'd know what we're talking about."

"I cooked this meal, didn't I?" Logan shot back, pointing his fork accusingly in Shane's direction.

"*I* cooked this meal," Cam said, matching Logan's challenging stare. "You prepped the carrots and potatoes. A monkey can do that."

Drew, Cam, and Winter joined in, and the six of them were soon chattering back and forth over who in the family contributed the most brains to their operation, and what *actually* classified as cooking. Lucky and I watched on with amusement; the overwhelming feeling of having dinner in a happy home settled contentedly in my gut.

Shane broke off from the chatter and reached across the table for another helping of glazed carrots, tossing a wink at my smug companion. "You're in now, man. You've just made her day."

My heart sunk a little into my chest at the way Winter had grinned at Lucky, the lie sitting heavy in my stomach. I hated concealing yet another thing from her, but the clusterfuck that was my life was far too complicated to get into right now. One day, I hoped to confess all of my sins, knowing she would forgive me for every one of them; I would never forgive myself if her family was harmed in my crossfire.

I understood Kellan's motives for keeping his distance from his family, even when I knew how much they meant to him. But I had a seat at his table. And we drank from the same cup of poison made from the blood of our enemies. His distance from me wasn't warranted, and I wouldn't put up with that bullshit narrative much longer.

The rest of dinner continued and the usual chatter and banter of Winter's crew was a balm to my heart. They'd just gotten back from their Christmas vacation abroad—the annual gift I'd given them since they'd gotten married a few years ago. I loved hearing about their adventures in the Costa Rican jungle or in the outback of Australia; it was a treat to give Winter something where she could make lasting memories surrounded by the people she loved.

These men took such good care of her, and tonight, my beautiful best friend radiated contentment.

I swatted at the zing of jealousy that shot up my spine, wondering what being content would feel like. Would I find it pleasantly peaceful, or debilitating and boring? Would I even recognize the emotion, or would I unwittingly destroy it with more chaos, not understanding what it was?

Controlled chaos was my nature. Contented calm was as foreign to me as ancient Aramaic.

"How old is this little man this weekend?" Lucky asked, playing dumb as Travis and Shane stood to clear our plates from the table.

"Almost a year." Drew ruffled the baby's butter-crusted hair affectionately. Noble spit a drooly wad of potato at him, and giggled at the sound. The goopy slop landed with a squelching plop.

"Alright, little man," Lucky bent down to eye level in front of the highchair, risking a potato spit kiss in the eye to speak to the devil. He held up the brightly colored plastic spoon. "Now yeh see it"—with a flash of his hands, the spoon disappeared from view—"now you don't!"

Noble shrieked with glee and clapped his hands wildly at the amateur trick, a fit of giggles erupting from his little belly.

"Ah, you like that one, do yeh?" The redheaded magician caught me staring at him and flashed me a thousand-watt smile. "Looks like I impressed your auntie, too. Want to see it again?"

Snorting, I shook my head and stood to help clean the pots. Lucky continued his antics, and loud cackles erupted from the little boy's lips every few minutes.

"He's great with kids," Winter murmured as we stood side by side at the sink, her washing, me drying, satisfied to simply be in each other's company. "Is he—you know—a serious contender?"

"Are you asking if he's a contender as my second husband, or to have children with?" I snagged a sip of my wine in between dries, arching a brow at her. "Because the answer to both of them is no."

"No?" Her lips quirked up at the corners as if choking off a smirk.

"No," I repeated, downing the last gulp of Sauvignon Blanc and returning to my task. "Lucky is fun, but that's the extent of it—and I'm never having children."

"She's right, love." The heat of Lucky's chest pressed against my back as he circled his arms around me in a loose hold.

Eavesdropping bastard. The guys must have taken Noble away to get cleaned up. "I am a *lot* of fun, but that's really all I'm good for. And I had a vasectomy at 20, so I'm not champing at the bit for a redo."

Huh. That was an interesting nugget of information. When I mentioned I had no interest in being a mother, most men tried to mansplain all the reasons I'd regret it, even going so far as to tell me I'd change my mind in a few years.

I wouldn't. I loved being an Auntie, but that was where my maternal instinct ended. To hear Lucky felt the same? The acknowledgment shouldn't stir *any* reaction from me, but I felt a tug of something in my belly regardless.

Indigestion from the pound of butter I'd just consumed. The only logical explanation.

Winter's expression was curious, but she didn't push it. Lucky gently released me to nudge her out of the way from the sink, taking her place beside me.

"I'll earn my keep, love."

Rolling up his shirt sleeves, he dropped his hands into the hot soapy water and started scrubbing. Winter shot me another weighted look of approval and I made a face of exasperation before grabbing the sudsy plate from Lucky's hand.

"You never told me she had five husbands," he mused quietly while we finished our menial task. I waited for him to continue, but he just let the statement linger in the air between us.

"I didn't," I acknowledged and placed the last batch of cutlery back in the drawer. "Does it matter?"

Drying his hands on the dish towel, he turned around to lean against the sink and folded his arms across his chest. His brows arched in interest.

"Is that what you're planning with Mr. Roboto and Conan?" His tone was casual, but his eyes were alight with amusement. "Did I walk into some polyamorous support club?"

He was teasing, but the words struck a chord in me. My plan... all of my plans for years involved bringing down bad people by doing bad things and building an empire to help fund my mission. Nothing else mattered.

I didn't have a plan—I couldn't even find the words to explain what I was doing. With Aaron, with Kellan, with my attraction to him. I was taking this fucked up scenario three steps at a time, throwing a lot of money and the risk of incarceration at a problem I was desperate to solve. That was the extent of my life *plan*.

I released a long sigh; the breath left through my lips in a soft hiss. I didn't filter my response, choosing to be forthright instead of engaging in our usual dance of phony words.

"Lucky, when Alvarez is long gone, I'll figure out what I'm doing with the rest of my life. Right now, I'm just treading water, okay?"

His forehead wrinkled in concern, but no witty retort came. If I'd known a bit of honesty could make this man shut up...

Abruptly, he reached for me, pulling me by the shoulders toward him. He pressed a soft kiss to my forehead like we were seasoned lovers seeking comfort from each other.

"Roger that." When his eyes met mine, for a moment, I fell under their lulling spell. Their normally glowing radiance was a softly storming sea. Then just as quickly, he broke its magic. "Let's go find our room, ya?"

Right. Our room. We were here *together*, which meant we would share a room tonight. Luckily, the guest room— my room—had a settee. Lucky would sleep there. The king bed wasn't big enough for the two of us.

"Hill!" Winter hollered from the living room. "Stop making out and come play Balderdash."

"I fecking *love* Balderdash!" Lucky exclaimed. He dropped my hands like they were on fire and strolled toward the alcove leading to the next room. He turned expectantly. "Yeh coming, Blondie?"

Cora Flynn

I rolled my eyes at his puppy-like enthusiasm but I fell in step beside him, ready to immerse myself some more in the love and laughter of my friends.

I needed a reminder of all the good in this world before I gave my soul over to the dark.

CHAPTER 15

Hillary

*T*he earth shuddered beneath my feet as I stumbled through the darkness, raucous wind whipping my hair into vicious knots. Flashes of foreboding red light clung to my periphery, but when I turned my head to catch its glow, it disappeared; a nebulous, terrifying omen. A sticky film coated my hands, its resinous residue crawling up my skin in painful, jagged tingles. My bare feet dragged on rocky ground, sharpened stones pierced my heels, hobbling me on my path forward... Into nothingness.

Ominous chuckles broke through the whistling of the wind, the dark laughter echoing all around me in a cacophony of dizzying sound. Terrified chills skittered *across my skin. Despite the sweat on my brow, my body froze with panic.*

A broad hooded figure came into view, floating toward me shrouded in shadow, before stopping to hover in front of my marbled form.

"Hello, Hillary," the masculine voice rumbled, the demonic tone evil personified. "I've been waiting for you."

"Blondie. Blondie!"

My body writhed within the soft duvet as powerful hands pinned me in place against the mattress. An awful, ragged scream of pure terror flooded my ears as I fought to make sense of my surroundings.

My earphones had been removed, and the garbled sound of a man's Irish lilt was muffled against the shrill screams that hadn't abated—the piercing sound of them about to cause a migraine.

"Blondie! Hillary! Shyte," the man shouted, just before my sleep mask was ripped off my face. The abrupt brilliance of light blurred my vision before my eyes settled on … Lucky.

Sleep-rumpled Lucky, dressed in nothing but a pair of black boxers, had me pinned beneath him on the bed, his brows knitted into a panicked frown.

The screams—still the screams. Where were they coming from?

The bleary-eyed Irishman cursed and then leaned in, abruptly putting his mouth over mine, coaxing my tongue against his in a frantic kiss. The faint taste of mint toothpaste washed over me.

The screams abruptly stopped. Oh—they were mine. The banshee impression had come from me.

The wild horses in my heart hadn't stopped racing despite the warm body holding me hostage. Blood pounded in my ears as I leaned into his kiss, desperate for a distraction from the relentless nightmares and their torture on my mind.

He leaned away, breaking the kiss and his hold on me, searching my eyes for answers. I didn't have any I could give him; not without exposing every solemn secret that had taken sanctuary in the depths of my soul.

"I need you to fuck me," I blurted, my cheeks pink because of my moment of vulnerability, not at the frantic tone to take his cock.

For once in his life, Lucky was speechless. As soon as I said it, I knew it was exactly what I needed—sex would help me escape my mind through the use of my body. I needed to get lost in Lucky; to get swept up in his pillowy lips and molded body and thick cock—the one I'd stroked, but never had inside me.

I needed *him*.

"Please," I begged; tears pricked at my eyes, but I was desperate for them not to fall. I'd be embarrassed in the morning, but I couldn't consider it now—not with my heart still pounding and my brain still spiraling. "Please, Lucky," I pleaded softly, conveying the pain in my chest through my eyes, hoping he'd give me this one out—just this one night.

All his hesitation faded. The green of his eyes darkened to a rich olive, and a raw hunger swam in their depths. He grabbed my chin roughly and his lips descended on mine, demanding entrance.

He held me firmly in place; I was entirely at his mercy as he plundered my mouth and took what he wanted. He forced me to open up to him, as if the kiss could release every demon that ever shackled my mind. I let him whisk me away, just as I'd begged him to. I gave in to the heat of his body, the comforting sweet scent of cedar and cherries, and masculine sweat, the strength of his muscular form as he melted into me, just barely holding his full weight off of my body.

Firm lips became soft and pliable as he abruptly shifted the nature of it. Frenzied desperation dissolved into the most tender of kisses; careful caresses of delicate touches as his knuckles ran up and down the sides of my ribs, before his large thumbs settled on the outline of my nipples in the silk sleep shirt.

He rolled his thumbs in tandem. A heated electric current flicked through my chest and straight down to my pussy. His lips moved from my mouth to my jaw, his stubble scraping along my sensitive skin as he nipped a trail along the shadow of bone leading to my ear. His hard length dug into my stomach; I could feel the twitch of it every time I arched to meet him. A dark satisfaction overtook me; I affected his body with the same power he did mine.

"My beautiful Blondie," he murmured into my hair, before rising on his knees to stare down at me, the fires of potent lust burning in his gaze.

"Do you need an escape, lass? Do you need me to feed you my fingers and my cock until you can't think about anything but me, filling you up and making you scream?"

My pussy gushed at his dirty words, my body completely overtaken by animal instinct and the need to fuck—all cognitive function on the sidelines as I lay beneath him, waiting for him to fulfill his promises.

Kellan gave me an escape through submission. Aaron gave me an escape through mutual dominance. I never imagined Lucky could do the same—teasing me into a roiling mess of desire.

"Ah, ah," he tutted, the devilish smirk raking across his perfect face. "I'm gonna need an answer, lass."

He held my gaze and bent down, his toned abs rippling with the movement, until his face was situated right above my pubic bone. He grazed his teeth over my clit through the silk fabric of my shorts. The slight nip soaked my panties and my body bowed off the bed at the sharp sensation.

Normal me wouldn't play his game; I wouldn't allow him the satisfaction and I'd turn the tables in my favor; punish him with his own game for reducing me to a begging fuck-girl.

But I wasn't normal me. The nightmares, the exhaustion of this crusade, and the continuous feeling of not doing enough—I had been reduced to the begging, desperate fuck-girl simpering beneath the Irish playboy.

In this moment, I relished the freedom that came with being his toy.

"Fuck me." The words came out on a whimper, not a command, as I gave in to being his pretty little pawn for the night.

I would take back my throne by force tomorrow.

His smile rivaled the Cheshire Cat, laced with dark intent, as he yanked off my shorts and slid them down my legs. On his way back up to the bullseye, his nose traced a line up the inside of my thigh, his bristly stubble sending shivers up my spine. He stopped at the apex and inhaled deeply.

"Fuck, I love the scent of you." He quickly buried his face right into my pussy and pulled back again to look at me, dew drops of my arousal clinging to his chin. "I want you to mark me, lass. Have you ever squirt before?"

Eyes widening, I nodded mutely, although I didn't tell him I'd never squirt at a man's touch. My own, with the right toy, yes. Even a few women in college had managed the feat—but never by a man.

"I'll have to leave my mark on you too, then." Lucky winked. The routine action was downright sinful when he was hovering above my pussy. "Wouldn't want yeh thinking someone else can do it better."

Without warning, he shoved a single finger inside me, then another, the two curling together, stroking my walls. My hips bucked up to meet him, but he held me in place with his forearm banded across my middle, keeping me where he wanted me.

I wanted to say I hated it; that this act was simply one of distraction and I would have fucked any man in my vicinity to rid myself of the painful thoughts. It'd be a lie.

Somehow I had known Lucky could be this man for me; who could safely tear me up and stitch me back together with laughter and light.

"That's a good lass," he praised as he pulled his fingers free, sticky arousal thickly coating them. He sucked them into his mouth, closing his eyes with a soft groan as he licked them clean.

"So sweet," he growled, palming the rigid outline of his cock in his other hand before dropping it back to touch me again.

Three fingers twisted inside me in a methodical rhythm; I shuddered, so close to coming, before he drew one of them out, sliding it to my ass and nuzzling my entrance there with a tentative swirl.

"No lube tonight, Blondie." His wicked grin told me exactly what he would do when he had some. "But I'll be coming back to get of taste of you here when we do."

"Won't. Be. Another. Time." I panted as he eased his finger into the hole, the stretch and sting giving way to molten pleasure.

"Oh, yes, there will," he crooned, as he stretched my pussy and my asshole at the same time. His fingers worked in such a practiced motion, I realized making women squirt was likely his signature move.

"Do you know how many fantasies of mine you star in? How many times I've fucked you in my dreams? How many times my cum has filled your pussy?"

I searched for the cocky grin, but his face held nothing but serious concentration, his fingers working so well together. The crescendo of my orgasm was just a bar away in the song.

"I'm not letting you alone until I've discovered every single way I can make you come undone, lass."

His other hand moved up to my clit and his palm provided much needed friction and weight. The fingers inside me rubbed along my sensitive wall, and I could feel them almost touch through the membrane. An intense pressure built up in my abdomen, like I was going to pee.

"Let go, love." His command was a suggestive whisper, and every sensation in my body built up to the pinnacle of tension before my body snapped like an errant bow string.

Ecstasy raced through my veins like a hit of the most potent drug, toe curling tingles worked their way through every cell of my body; the purest rush of euphoria burst from my core like a supernova explosion, the heat coursing in my blood a close comparison.

Warm liquid flooded the bedsheets, and Lucky quickly ducked his head down, his mouth closing over my gushing pussy to capture what remained of it.

"Fuck, Blondie." His growl sounded territorial, an animal claiming his prey. "I'm going to rip you apart with what you do to me."

He shucked his boxers in one smooth push and his thick, veiny cock sprung free. A pearlescent drip of pre-cum seeped from the tip. He pushed my thighs open, lined up, and thrust into me without hesitation. He bottomed out, unable to get deeper.

My pussy stretched around him, thoroughly warmed up and aching for more. I wrapped my legs around his waist and my arms around his neck, meeting his gaze for a solitary moment.

Time stilled. I saw so much in his captivating eyes, though the usual lightness in them held nothing but hedonistic intent. For that single second, I caught a glimpse of the authentic man beneath—without the cocky arrogance or the sly remarks—a window to the soul of a man who needed my comfort as much as I needed his.

Was he as surprised by this connection as I was? Was this basic evolutionary chemistry, or did Lucky actually have something I needed? Something I... wanted?

"Hold on," he gritted through his teeth, before slamming into me, pushing me deeper into the mattress with hard, desperate ruts. The raw need to fuck like animals came out with each thrust.

He fucked me hard and fast, adjusting my hips to get the deepest angle, the most delicious friction between his pubic bone and my clit, sliding his hands all over my skin with each pounding movement.

My pussy was going to be a swollen, battered mess, but I didn't care. I wanted to be so thoroughly spent; I wanted to feel him for days and remember how Lucky took my pain away. How he granted me this escape.

Another round of fiery tingles swept up my spine. My body detonated around him as my orgasm pulled a ragged cry from my throat; I melted into the sheets, my limbs letting go from their stifling hold around his body.

Lucky thrust into me three more times before pulling out, jets of hot cum painting my torso and breasts. He massaged the mixture into my skin, a possessive gleam in his eye, before collapsing next to me.

"I'll get tested for you," he joked as he nuzzled into my side, stroking my hair with a gentle palm. "Then I'll paint your insides white like a Jackson Pollock painting."

A snort escaped me, then a giggle, and then an outright guffaw; the seriousness of what we'd just done and what it might mean disappearing as Lucky lightened the moment like he always did.

We laid in a mess of our own juices, collecting our breaths as we came down from our high. Eventually, he interlaced our fingers and tugged me upward.

"Let's get you cleaned up." He lifted me off the bed and, cradling me in his arms, carried me to the ensuite. "Then, sleep."

I was wrong. I hadn't been Lucky's pawn. He'd worshipped me as his Queen, and I would feel every part of that worship when we woke up in the morning.

I would come up with a solution for this problem tomorrow.

A shrill alarm sounded from my phone; all of my 'do not disturb' settings came on as soon as 11 pm hit, save for Winter calling or three specific alarms—one for my home, one for my office, and one for... The Palace.

My eyes flew open, and I was shocked to see I wasn't wearing my sleep mask. Or my earphones. A warm body curled around me; Lucky was cradling the pillow next to my ear, soft snores rumbling from between his pouty lips. His fingers were loosely interlocked with mine.

Huh. I hadn't slept without my sleep aids since... Fuck, the alarm.

I shot up out of the bed and grabbed my phone to see the warning message flash across the screen.

The Palace. The Palace was compromised.

"Lucky," I shouted, scrambling out of the duvet cocoon and racing to throw on some clothing. "Wake up!"

"Hrrummf," he mumbled as he came to; I pulled on pants and frantically scrolled through the camera footage with my other hand as I did so.

Alec's cell was empty. So was Sandra's. And we were four hours away.

"Fuck!" I grabbed a hoodie and raced into the ensuite, grabbing Lucky's clothes on the floor and tossing them at his head. "Get dressed. I'm going to need you to drive."

Whether it was the panic in my tone or the deranged killer in my eyes, Lucky didn't ask questions, just yanked on his own clothes and followed me down the stairs and out into the driveway.

I would call Winter later and make up some bogus emergency. I had no time to waste.

I tossed Lucky the keys and jumped into the passenger seat; him taking the wheel as I frantically called Aaron on my phone.

"What do you need, *Mi Reina*?" he answered calmly, as if he hadn't been in a deep sleep and was just waiting for an opportunity to serve. A short dose of relief flooded through my racing mind before panic took up once more.

"I'm going to send you a series of codes to get out of the apartment. I don't have time to explain, but there are two people who were being held captive upstairs that just escaped. I need you to grab a gun from the bedroom closet and try to lock them down. I'll explain everything later, but we're on our way."

This was the very last way I'd want to explain my vigilante vendetta, but I didn't have time to think about that right now. Not when my prisoners were out in the wild, risking my entire operation.

"Done." A muffled rustling of fabric came through the line. Then the racing of feet on the tiled floor told me he was already moving towards the closet.

"I have to call Kellan—I'm sending him as backup. We'll be there as soon as possible. Be careful, *mi caballero oscuro*."

I hung up the phone and frantically dialed Kellan, who answered on the second ring.

"The Palace is compromised."

I quickly summarized what I had told Aaron, with no need to explain. Kellan knew the purpose behind the building, and while he didn't know who I had in there, he'd known I'd intended to use the cells for this very purpose. I didn't need to tell him what the stakes were.

"On my way. Rodriguez and I will catch them, Killer. Dead or alive?"

"Whatever way you can get them."

I wasn't willing to risk everything I'd built to keep up Alec's lifelong torture. And Sandra was going to end up dead, anyway.

I hung up and immediately brought up the camera footage to review on the drive. I needed to figure out just how in the fuck one of the most secure facilities in America got compromised.

Lauchlan didn't question, didn't even make jokes as he broke every speed limit in the county on back country roads to get us home as quickly as possible.

These three men were going to help me fix this. We were going to fix this. We had to fix this.

If not, I was unbelievably, undeniably, inextricably *fucked*.

CHAPTER 16

Aaron

I stumbled through the apartment, as familiar to me in the darkness as my previous home. Pulling on pants and a sweatshirt on my way to the front entrance alcove, I clutched the burner phone Kellan had supplied me with in my right fist.

The gun hung heavy in the pocket of my pants, its weight thwacking against my thigh with every movement. Sweatpants were not designed to hold weapons.

I deftly buttoned my jacket and pulled on my boots before I punched in the code Hillary had sent into the keypad on the wall. The door swung open ominously into the cavernous bunker beyond.

When ny phone rang again, I answered without thought. My footsteps echoed against the concrete walls as I rushed through the shelving to the staircase at the opposite end of the hall.

Two people had this number. My Queen and the Cartel King. I would need both to help me with this mission tonight.

"Yes?" I answered succinctly, almost at the stairs.

"I'm ten minutes away," Kellan growled. "The prisoners are unarmed and will be weak, but don't take any chances. Shoot on sight if you need to."

"It is done." I hung up the phone and pocketed it, replacing it with the gun between my palms. The weight of the weapon was comforting as I quietly made my way up the stairs, listening for any sounds on the other side.

Hearing nothing, I rounded the corner where the stairwell met a long corridor and squinted in the inky black. I abruptly turned left when I saw no shadows. The large metal entry door had been left ajar.

The night was cool, but the universe smiled down upon me. The full moon overhead lit up the snow, giving me full sight into the still night.

Two sets of footprints marked snowy paths headed in opposing directions. By the size of them, the prisoners were escaping on bare feet; it wasn't cold enough for immediate frostbite, but they would not last long without proper clothing.

Which to follow?

I allowed the stars to guide me and selected the path to my right, following the trail eastward and down to the silhouetted track of a snowed-in driveway. It was just narrow enough to fit a single vehicle. The route veered to a sharp left where the curve of the road met a steep hill; the footprints disappeared into a roll of disturbed snow, suggesting the prisoner fell. I took my time on the icy embankment, noting the fresh drops of blood crusting the top layer of snow halfway down the hill.

So, they were hurt. From the fall? Or had an old wound re-opened? Were they prisoners in isolation only, or had they been tortured?

Stinging mountain winds bit my cheeks, embedding icy claws into my skin. Surely, the fugitives were frozen by now.

Kellan had said they were weak; what had Hillary done to them? What had they done to her? *Mi Reina* was a fierce force to be reckoned with, of sound heart and strong mind. Whatever these two sorry souls had done, any punishment would have been earned tenfold.

The disturbed snow led into the copse of trees to my left; I stood stock still, listening for any sounds beyond the greenery. A grin tugged at the corners of my mouth when I heard the soft crunching of snow several yards ahead.

Picking up my pace, I raced through the underbrush. The thick branches tore patches out of my coat as I brushed past them, leaving a plume of goose feathers behind in my wake.

The shadow of a thin figure came into view. The wisp of a human cursed softly as they scuffled through a swath of thorny plant skeletons. Soft whimpers of pain echoed through the trees as the thorns scraped through their bare skin and blood spilled onto the white blanket below.

They didn't hear me until I was upon them. A rake thin man with scruffy, shoulder-length matted hair turned at the very last second, haunted eyes widening in horror. I clamped a hand around the nape of his neck and yanked him by the roots of his hair, forcing him to the ground.

A slew of curses escaped dry, cracked lips as the man writhed in my grasp until the moment he registered it was a futile endeavor. I was far stronger, fully clothed, and determined to bring him pain. He softened in my hold and submitted, what little life he had in his limbs draining out of him.

I held the gun to his temple, tempted to force him to his knees at my feet, to pay his penance to *Mi Reina*. I could kill this man right now, cleanse him of all his sins with a forced baptism in the snow. I could leave him to gurgle his final breaths through bloody gasps of air.

Now that I saw his lifeless form, ragged and on the cusp of collapse, my curiosity was piqued. What had this man done to incite the wrath of my love?

I had not tortured a soul in a good while, but the skill set never left the body or the mind once rooted beneath the skin. I would leave him alive until Hillary returned, but first, I would uncover a few answers for myself.

Without warning, I hoisted the frail man over my shoulder, his weight barely more than Hillary's, and carried him out to the road and up the steep hill through the snow. Headlights lit up the path ahead from behind, and I turned to see Kellan's Jeep rolling effortlessly forward along the unplowed road.

He stopped at the crest of the hill and climbed out like a bull; rage and aggression emanated from him in violent currents.

I waved him off. "I have this one taken care of." I re-situated the man on my back. He'd stopped pounding on my shoulder blades, succumbing to his inevitable fate. "Follow the footsteps to the left of the entry door. That will lead you to the next one."

Kellan nodded brusquely and leaped back into the SUV, snow flicking off his tires and into my face as he took off down the remainder of the trail.

Hillary had entrusted the two of us with this task—we would not let her down.

I again continued forward, contemplating this set of circumstances. Kellan and I were once again working together to support the woman in our care. The woman we would die for. I took comfort knowing he had grown to be my *companero*; it was a natural coupling. In another life, we could have been brothers. Perhaps lovers. He was an equal opponent; the darkness in him rivaled mine. His fierce desire to claim Hillary as rabid as my own.

Tonight, we were comrades, unveiling our darkness to our queen's enemies, unleashing it to protect her light.

I slogged through, the extra weight of my captive admittedly making the trek far slower. Back at Hillary's building, I carried him down the dark corridor, curious to see where he'd been housed all this time.

The sting of this secret being held from me sat low in my heart, though more of an irritant than a stabbing wound. Two prisoners had been living above the safe house the several weeks I'd also used the building as my cage; judging by this man's appearance, unless he had been previously homeless on the streets of Carlisle, he had been held far longer.

Had *Mi Reina* been concerned at my judgment? Was this a matter of trust between us, or had she kept the secret for my protection?

My love for her knew no bounds; she held my companies, my life's work, and now my life in her hands. I needed her to understand she could lay all she held dearest in her heart at my feet. I would cherish it, protect it. Exact revenge on those who squandered it.

As I would now.

The dark corridor led to a set of metal doors locked with a keypad and a biometric scanner. I punched in the bypass code she'd texted me by memory. Then shifting the dead weight across my shoulder, I impatiently waited for the pneumatic door to slide open.

My captive had gone suspiciously limp in my hold, his chest rising and falling against my back, a cornered kitten waiting to claw.

Cora Flynn

I strode down the empty, silent hallway as the hairs at the back of my neck stood on end at the sight to the left of me. Thick glass walls looked into white, padded cells. A single cot, toilet, and protected shower head were embedded into the ceiling. The confined spaces held nothing else.

The cells were clinical. Despite their bright exterior, they exuded immeasurable darkness—the intent of such spaces only two things: the insufferable torture and isolated torment of men and women who deserved it.

Mi Reina, the angel of persecution. This revelation was a mild shock to the system, and yet, exactly what I should expect of my passionate Queen. Taking matters into her own hands—exacting justice in a prison of her own making as she did in the boardrooms of our businesses.

Pitbulls could learn from her aggressive confidence. A blessing from the stars and a curse from the bowels of hell —it would be the very thing that killed the woman I loved.

The hoard of emergency supplies sitting on the basement shelves now made practical sense. How long had Hillary owned such a building? One did not purchase a torture condo—she would have had to design it. Who had she entrusted with such a secret?

A deep discomfort settled into my bones as I answered my question. *Kellan*. He would be the only person she'd trust with this.

The figure shifted in my grip, pulling me from that line of thought. A sharp knee jabbed into my ribs. The wind knocked out of my lungs, I stumbled, the weight of his body propelling me forward and off my frame onto the concrete floor in front of me.

The waif of a man scrambled away on his hands and knees. I stalked towards him, swallowing the bitterness clawing at my throat.

I would fight for her trust in all things. She would no longer have only Kellan to protect her darkness. I would hand over my penchant for administering pain, and we could bask in the black sea of tormented souls together.

The desperation in the man's gaze was no match for the insatiable hunger for violence in mine. By the time my hands clasped onto his scrawny shoulders, he had already slumped in defeat, hanging his head with a sob. I lifted his bony body off the ground and carried him into the furthest cell down the hallway.

I threw him on the cot, the sheets and pillow yellowing with grease stains. Perhaps this had been his room.

I pulled the string of my hood out of its casing, quickly employing a quick cuff around his hands to keep him in place. The short length of the rope didn't lend itself to a more complex, more secure shibari tie, but it was all I could do under these circumstances. I removed the string from the hood of my sweater beneath my jacket, and tied the same design around his ankles. His eyes remained dormant while I worked.

Was he still coherent? Had he succumbed to the madness of confinement? Was he still responsive to a little... coercion?

Unzipping my jacket, I fingered the hidden pocket within the interior shell and unlocked the tiny metal clasp to grab the small stiletto blade of my favorite dagger.

I pulled out the military grade black matte metal; the custom design was one of my most prized possessions. The dagger had seen me through many of Vicente's training 'lessons'; had pierced the flesh of men who housed evil in their veins as if it were blood. I unleashed their evil into the drain on the floor, releasing them from their torment—only after a little torment of my own.

I was well accustomed to guns and how to use them; they were convenient weapons, but boring. They left jagged holes of instant brutality. Knives left beautiful trails of artwork on the skin—a lesson in delayed gratification.

I much preferred this method.

My captive's face turned ashen as he eyed the weapon in my palm. I delicately fingered the blade as if it were my tender lover, excited at the prospect of using my old friend once again. It had been too long.

"What is your name?"

My words were calm and measured, soothingly hypnotic as I moved closer. A thrill of electricity tingled up my spine at the raw fear emanating from every pore of his skin. The stench of animalistic terror filled my nostrils when I loomed over his cowering body; the familiar scent separated my rational brain from the thirsty hind brain of a trained killer.

The man's lips folded in on themselves, as if staying silent would spare him from my intentions.

"Your master is on her way, *ñero.*" I spun the blade in my hand and caught it nimbly between two fingers; the razored edge sliced off a thin layer of skin along the pad of my knuckle. I'd sharpened it in recent days as an activity to bide my time; now, it was perfectly primed to exact vengeance for *Mi Reina.* "And you and I are going to get to know each other in the meantime."

I advanced on him, deciding to start with the flesh of his shoulders, to peel back the layers of skin one by one until his sobs shattered the windows and his sweat slicked the floor. I knew how to keep a man alive under torture—*Mi Reina* would decide his end when she arrived.

I was the Dark Knight of a Queen, a bold title among men; I'd wield her wrath as if it were my own and punish her enemies until they were ribbons of flesh on the floor.

Starting with him.

CHAPTER 17

Kellan

Hillary Lane was truly going to be the death of me.

How many times had I covered for her ass with the Bureau when her vendetta went a little too far? How many times did I tell her this revenge mission was a bad idea? Why the fuck did I continue to protect her when she was impossible to protect from herself?

I knew the answers to these questions, but I wasn't going to waste time thinking about my feelings when I was knee deep in snow, trying to track some woman she'd deemed worthy of her mountainside prison.

A woman. It was the first time I'd ever seen a woman within these walls, and it'd surprised me when I'd watched the footage of Sammy taking her in. I trusted Sammy's judgment and knew he wouldn't harm a woman if she was innocent, so I had to trust Hillary knew what she was doing with this one.

As soon as this woman was back in her cell, Hillary was going to give me some answers. *All* the answers. We didn't have time for any more secrets between us—especially when this little midnight tryst had already put our entire mission at risk.

Luckily, the deep snow was on my side, the woman's trail easy to follow up the mountain pass; but she was surprisingly quick, given she'd only had about a twenty-minute head start.

Twenty minutes in great conditions might as well be two hours—but in the middle of the night in the middle of January? I should have found her by now. Her limbs would be frozen stiff, seeing as she wouldn't have any winter clothes on, but adrenaline was powerful. Evidently, powerful enough to get a massive jump on me.

The trail of footprints led through an icy gully and into another part of the forest before ending where the treed landscape met the main road.

Fuck. Left or right?

There weren't any notable markers out here in the mountains—it would be impossible for someone to have their bearings without the help of a phone or GPS.

My FBI tracking training kicked in; research showed that when faced with a fork in the road, the brain was more likely to choose a right turn than a left turn.

So, right it was. I sure as fuck hoped the Bureau's data was up to date, and that this woman wasn't an anomaly in her thinking.

I hunched my shoulders and lowered my body, racing along the shoulder of the road to appear smaller; the moonlight guided my way. The only vehicles driving this segment at this time of night would be long-haul truckers. A truck stop was just a few miles from here.

If she'd already hitchhiked with a well-intentioned trucker, we were fucked.

I upped my pace, determined to find my Killer's captive before she could ruin the woman I so desperately needed in my life. Instinct took over, and I abandoned every cynical thought in my head, pumping my legs as fast as they'd take me, while still scanning both sides of the road for any signs of life or disruption.

Rounding the bend in the road, I came upon the lit-up parking lot of the trucker's diner and refueling station. Luckily, it wasn't a large rest stop. If she was here, I should be able to find her easily.

Unluckily, that meant I wasn't able to hide well, either.

I slowed my pace and nonchalantly strode through the pumps, heading toward the diner itself.

A bell chimed as I entered through the glass doors. I offered a friendly smile to the attendant scrolling through their phone at the convenience counter, but she barely looked up to give me a second glance.

Good—the less anyone paid attention to me here, the better. I scanned the diner to the right of the doorway. Only two tables had patrons, and none of them were women. I was about to head back to the washrooms when the conversation of a mid-fifties trucker and the server at the front cash caught my attention.

"I'll need two cups of coffee and two of your breakfasts, Brenda." His graying brows knitted together before he added, "And a donut, too. I've got a straggler on board and she's going to need some medical attention, so I'm taking her into the city. Gave her my phone to call her family in the truck."

Fuck. I'd bet my entire cartel fortune the woman he was being a Good Samaritan for was the same woman I was after.

Cora Flynn

The man waited at the counter while Brenda got busy with the order. It was now or never. I turned on my heel and assessed the parking lot. Three long-haul trailers.

Crouching low, I ran between them, hauling myself up quickly on the step plate to peer inside each cab. The third truck, the one parked farthest away from the diner, was the ticket.

A haggard blonde woman wrapped in a blanket peered back at me, her eyes wide with fright. I held a finger to my lips, and took out my FBI badge, holding it to the glass of the window. She stared at it, her face lighting with recognition. Frantically, she opened the door to speak to me.

"Sorry to scare you, ma'am." I put the badge back in my pocket. "Your friend called the FBI, and I was already in the area tonight. Are you okay?"

Anyone with two brain cells would know the scenario was unlikely—why would an FBI agent be in the middle of nowhere in the middle of the night?—but she was scared, vulnerable, and desperate.

If there was a hell, my actions tonight would absolutely cinch my invitation.

Her teeth chattered violently, but she spoke through them.

"F-fr-fro-frozen." She shivered enough to mimic an epileptic seizure and fell into my arms when I offered her a hand.

"Come with me." I issued the command in my most soothing tone, the one used to coax confessions out of trained killers. "I'll get you somewhere safe and then we can talk."

I was running out of time. Breakfast didn't take long to cook, and if the trucker was a good guy, he'd be rushing to get back to make sure his damsel in distress was okay.

She took my hand. I guided her down the steep step of the truck, leading her to the other side of the diner building where I wouldn't be in sight of any cameras. The steep incline to our right looked like my only escape option, and I cursed at the stupidity of the plan forming in my mind. My body would be wrecked tomorrow.

Without warning, I bundled her in my arms, cradled her head, and clamped a firm hand over her mouth to muffle her scream. I threw us off the side of the hill, our bodies bouncing and rolling into the thick brush below.

Agony ripped through my right thigh where a sharp rock punctured through my pants and into the muscle tissue, but I didn't let go. I'd suffer a thousand puncture wounds to secure this woman if it meant keeping Hillary safe.

When we came to a full stop, I wrapped my hands around her neck in a sleeper hold, knocking her unconscious before she could attempt to run away. Under the blanket, she was wearing barely anything at all—a thin cotton t-shirt and pajama pants—and her toes were already turning purple with frostbite.

I bundled her into the blanket like a sausage roll and carried her over my shoulder. My thigh ached with sharp pain with every step. At six miles away from Hill's warehouse, it would take me over an hour to return in these conditions.

My companion wouldn't be unconscious for an hour. I had another few seconds, at best. I dropped her to the snow and hovered over her body, waiting for her to return to the land of the living.

The thick tree line protected us from view, so even if the friendly trucker were to look over the cliff side, he wouldn't be able to see us. I hoped he'd think she got scared off and simply disappeared.

Not my problem. *She* was my problem, and she'd presumably made a phone call. Which meant Hillary could be fucked.

If Hillary was fucked, we were all fucked.

She came to with a jolt and a startled cry as she whipped her head around in confusion. Her watery gaze landed on me, the stark reflection of betrayal in her eyes.

Before she could get out a word, I crouched beside her, my large body looming over her frail, shivering form.

"Before we go any further, I'm going to need a few answers."

I stared through her, my lips curled into a snarl of disgust like she was a piece of dog shit under an expensive shoe. She cowered beneath me, exhausted, and likely near hypothermia. Her one shot at freedom had been taken from her within seconds.

"Who did you call just now?"

A determined glint entered her eyes, and she made a show of clamping her lips shut, as if realizing there wasn't a chance in hell she was ever making it back home.

"Dying of hypothermia is a peaceful way to go." I fingered the edge of the blanket, tugging it away from her skin.

The steely resolve faltered when I took her only source of security. But it was replaced by bitter, feral hatred. I wasn't going to get anywhere with this woman.

Stubbornness in the face of death was valiant by some, stupid by others. For her, it was stupid.

Releasing a long puff of breath into the freezing air, I hauled out my phone and dialed Hillary's number. She answered on the first ring.

"Rodriguez has the man," I growled into the receiver. "I have the woman."

"Oh, thank god." The relief in her voice was palpable. Pride made its way into my heart, knowing I could give this to her. That I had kept her safe.

"I need to know what she did." I shifted the phone between my neck and shoulder as I hauled the woman up from her perch on the snow. Pushing her in front of me, I urged her on frostbitten feet forward through the trees ahead of us.

I'd never killed a woman before—not intentionally as a premeditated murder. If today was going to be the first, I needed to be damn well sure she deserved the bullet through her heart.

"She sent four children in protection back to Alvarez's people." Hillary's tone was clipped, the rage in her voice filtering through the phone line and settling deep into my belly. "And she was going to send more."

Familiar darkness ballooned in my brain, taking over all of my senses with the primal need to kill.

"Still dead or alive?" I asked, watching the woman's head snap back at the question, like a rabbit sensing the wolf right behind her. She took off— 'at a run' would be a stretch, given she hobbled over the thorny landscape—but she clearly read the writing on the wall.

"Yes." Hillary's answer was quick and fierce, the permission I needed to rid the world of another piece of filth.

I watched the limping woman run desperately away from me, practically tasting her terror on the air.

"Got it. I'll see you back at the ranch."

I hung up and stuffed the phone back into my pocket. Pulling out Old Faithful and its silencer, I screwed it on tight, watching the little rabbit get further and further away.

Throwing the blanket over my shoulder, I took off after her, gaining ground within seconds. She pushed on, tearing her t-shirt against bare branches and stumbling into the crunchy snow at her feet.

I held out the gun to aim at her skull, not needing her to turn around. I didn't need see the light leave her eyes; I took no pleasure in this kill. My only gratification from her death was to protect the woman I loved.

My finger released the trigger, and the muffled shot exited the chamber and entered the soft tissue of her brain. Her body went stiff, even as it sagged to the ground.

I pocketed the gun and drew out my knife. Slicing long cuts down her arms and torso, I let the smell of fresh blood carry on the wind. Wolves or cougars would ensure all evidence was gone by morning.

Sticky wetness coated my pant leg. I looked down to my thigh bleeding into the fabric of my jeans. Before I could bleed out into the snow and leave a trail for some wayward sap to follow, I ripped a strip from the blanket and tied it around my leg in the best makeshift tourniquet I could manage. Then I buried the rest of the blanket underneath her body.

I left the scene of the crime immediately and followed my compass back to Hillary's bunker. A full ninety minutes later, I was back at my Jeep. Hillary's Jaguar was parked haphazardly at the building's entrance.

They'd made it back in record time; I hadn't expected her for another hour at least. The sun was about to rise and we still had one more prisoner to take care of, provided Rodriguez hadn't already killed him.

It was time for some answers. I wasn't leaving until I got every single one of them.

CHAPTER 18

Hillary

Content warning: This chapter includes descriptions of sexual violence.

Breaking every speed limit in the county, Lucky arrived at the Palace in record time. His driving skills impressed me while I panicked beside him for three solid hours, even as my mind whirled with every single possibility.

I'd scrolled through the camera footage for hours in real-time, trying to get any clue how Alec did it. He'd disappeared from the corner camera for hours last night. Then, out of nowhere, all the doors to every cell sprung open.

Cora Flynn

Alec had immediately taken off down the corridor, seizing his chance to escape. Sandra had suspiciously peered around the doorways, tentatively moving down the hallway to the exterior door before racing in the opposite direction.

That was it—all the information I had. Alec must have been planning this for a while. However, I was determined to understand how before the day was out.

Now—now I had to decide the man's permanent fate. Kellan's call confirmed Sandra was no longer on this side of the dirt. No part of me was upset about it. If anything, I was relieved the decision to kill her was no longer in my hands, that the universe had taken care of that for me.

Well, the universe in the form of my broody Viking who'd scoured the woods on my behalf, then vanquished my enemy as if she was his own.

Gratitude replaced the fear in my heart for a moment. All three men had come to my rescue tonight. None of them had hesitated to leap into the fray when I came calling, and every one of them had followed through.

It appeared I had a few devils in my corner, after all.

I owed them an explanation. I eyed Lucky as we got out of the vehicle; he'd said very few words on the drive, proving he had the capability of being serious when the time called for it. As much as I didn't want to bring him into this circle of trust, it was now impossible to avoid.

He had taken care of me in my most vulnerable moment last night, and he continued to do so into daybreak. Whatever this was between us, I owed him an answer as much as the rest.

After we dealt with Alec. The man was still breathing, according to Aaron's last text, and I'd need to rid myself of his torment once and for all.

Lucky followed close behind as I moved down the dark hall and through the secure doors, abruptly stopping at Alec's cell.

Aaron had situated Alec on the toilet in the corner, binding his hands and feet with some sort of string. Deep gashes trailed down both of our captive's thighs, thick ribbons of...

Holy fuck, was that *skin*?

Lucky let out a low whistle of surprise as we both stared, mouths open, at the scene beyond the room.

I'd known Aaron since we were children; his collected quietness had never been mistaken for weakness by any of our peers. Everyone took it for the warning it was; the man was a coiled snake, calmly waiting to strike when it suited him.

I'd seen him strike in the boardroom and in the bedroom; I'd never been on the receiving end of his spoken blows, but I'd always known he harbored a vicious darkness within him. Vicente and Veronica had raised a hardened wolf in sheep's clothing; a brutal killer poised to take over a poisoned crown.

In all those years, I had never actually *seen* it, but I'd known, deep in my heart, what he was capable of. His sadistic energy called to me, like we were two parts of a whole.

I watched Aaron slice another strip of flesh, this time from Alec's shoulder blade. His screams were barely audible behind the three layers of protective glass. My Knight carefully pulled the strip with his gloved fingers and tossed it on the floor.

"Sick fuck." Lucky's voice was barely audible beside me, but he failed to hide the awe in his tone. "Didn't know Mr. Roboto had it in him. Malicious creature, in't he?"

The entrance door to the corridor banged open; I turned to see Kellan limping down the hallway, the fierce frown on his features embodying a true Viking warrior in every way.

I raced to his side and threw my arms around his waist, breathing in the overwhelming scent of fresh mountain air and the faint residue of gunpowder on his skin.

"Thank you." I pressed my cheek into his chest, not bothering to swipe away tears as they fell freely onto his jacket. Strong arms wrapped around me and pulled me deeper into his hold. The palm of his hand cupping the back of my head, he gently tilted my face upward to stare into his eyes.

I didn't get the chance to see any of the emotions swirling in the dark blue depths; his mouth descended on mine in a fierce claiming; my tears soaked into his beard as his tongue forced its way between my lips, as if trying to suck away every portion of my pain.

He stole the breath from my lungs, the thoughts from my mind, and every panicked modicum of fear from deep within my gut. His firm mouth molded into something gentler—the touch of our lips conveying far more than our words ever could.

"Good to see you, Big Guy." Lucky nodded to Kellan in a rare show of deference when I pulled away from his hold. Kellan grunted in response, but it didn't hold the typical ire usually reserved for our Irish companion.

As if an afterthought, Lucky added in a softer voice. "Thanks for protecting *Mo Mhuirin*."

The phrase was smooth as melted butter on his tongue, but I had no idea what it meant. I quirked my head in question, but he didn't indulge me, choosing instead to blow me a kiss and a wink before he gestured toward the window.

"Should we go rescue the fucker?" His brows rose as Aaron tore another, longer piece of skin from Alec's calf, exposing a layer of grisly muscle beneath. "I'm all for a little blood play every now and again, but this is next level."

The backlit green glinted with mischievous energy as he sought our Viking's gaze from the corner of his eye, the rest of his attention remained fixed on the gruesome tableau.

"Glad you didn't choose *that* method of torture, Conan. Totally different type of edging, that."

To my utter shock, Kellan let out a burst of deep, rumbling laughter; the abrupt resonance echoed off the concrete walls around us. The sound must have carried to the room beyond; Aaron's head rose from his passion project. His caramel brown eyes were almost black as he stared back at us through the windowpane.

He slowly ambled toward the door—leaving Alec screaming in writhing agony—as if this were just another Tuesday. When he stepped out into the hall, I rushed to my Dark Knight and wrapped my arms around his neck, tugging his head down to mine for a brutal kiss.

He was covered in blood and all manner of human tissue, but I didn't care. I'd bathe in every facet of filth with this man every time he brought justice to my enemies. The depravity in his method said he would burn the world down for me, without question, and punish anyone who tried to escape its raging fire.

Fuck if I didn't love him fiercely for it.

Our tongues tangled with such desperation, it was like we were kissing for the first time—teeth clashing and lips everywhere, as if we would never feel each other's bodies ever again after this moment.

"Thank you," I whispered solemnly, staring into the dark eyes that filled some of my best dreams. "Thank you for your protection, *mi caballero oscuro.*"

"It is my honor to serve you, *Mi Reina.*" He bowed his forehead to touch mine, the gesture more intimate than any form of sex we'd ever had. I brought a hand to his cheek and swiped away a streak of blood before pushing around to face the others.

"Let's go downstairs." I grabbed Aaron's bloody hand with my clean gloved one and waved the other two men to follow. "He isn't going anywhere, and it's about time I gave you an explanation for all of this."

Alec's head lolled haphazardly to his shoulders, apparently having passed out from Aaron's administration of pain. He was alive, but barely.

I'd researched the countless ways to kill a man, but "flaying alive" wasn't in my repertoire of tricks.

"Will he bleed out?" I asked casually as I moved back down the concrete stairwell into the private oasis below.

"Unlikely," came Aaron's smooth reply. "It is supposed to prolong suffering for as long as possible. He will not die until you wish it."

What a twisted, sadistic, *thoughtful* soul.

I led Aaron, Kellan, and Lucky back into the apartment and pointed for them to sit on the couches. Aaron raised a dubious brow, looking down at his sweater red-stained and flecked with what, I didn't need to know.

"We're going to have to abandon this site now anyway, Aaron." I shrugged. "I don't plan on salvaging the furniture."

"And we're going to need to get out of here as soon as possible." Kellan's gravelly tone brooked no arguments. "She made a call before I caught her, and I have no idea who she called or what she told them. We're leaving by daybreak, no matter what."

"I'll be quick, then." The smile I offered didn't reach my eyes, the anxiety in my gut roiling like bitter acid as I prepared to tell them the story I never thought I'd tell anyone again.

The three men sat on the couch cushions—the same seats they'd taken during our Christmas festivities—a much more pleasant day. Instead of sitting with one of them, I leaned back against the wall and faced them fully.

"When I was in college, I met a woman." I twisted my hands in front of me, the nervous energy in my veins leaking into my limbs. "At first she was just a friend, but over time, she became my lover."

The jagged rock in my throat was nearly impossible to swallow, but I managed it, my audience patiently waiting for the punchline. I hadn't allowed myself to think of Isabella in years, choosing to bury her memories under the load of my vendetta in her honor.

Unable to make eye contact, I cleared my throat and continued.

"Isabella was a spitfire. The most beautiful woman in the room. She came from a poor family and attended Barnard on a full scholarship, working her ass off to prove she belonged there."

The bittersweet memories turned rancid the longer I held them on my tongue. My beautiful *Cariño*. The girl who broke me.

"I was so young then, and stupid. A little rich white girl from a small town who'd never really tasted true freedom. Despite Daddy and Stanley's arrangement to marry me off to Logan, I filled my days with studying, and my nights fucking and partying with her. We eventually moved in together in an apartment off campus."

I realized in that moment that most of this information would be new to Lucky. My history wasn't recorded in newspapers the way it was for some American heiresses; subconsciously, I'd let him into my life in its entirety— something I'd have to come to terms with, and confront him with—later. I raised my head to stare directly into the sea-green foam of his eyes; he stared back, conveying nothing but rapt attention, an unusually solemn spirit filling out his posture.

It gave me the reassurance to continue.

"We weren't exclusive—we couldn't be, with my fiancé at home, and two extremely homophobic fathers. So, we both agreed that while we loved fiercely in secret, we'd continue the guise that we were just best friends in public. And one day, she met a man that wasn't just a beard—she fell for him."

Cora Flynn

My bitter tone belied my unwarranted feelings of betrayal, even after all this time. I broke Lucky's gaze and examined the creases in the floorboards, needing the distraction for what came next.

"It broke my heart, but the longevity of what we had didn't exist. She would return home to Brazil when she graduated, and I was returning to Cascade Falls to work with Daddy's companies, with plans to start my own."

I filled my lungs with stale basement air and exhaled sharply—finally getting to the meat of the story; how my prisoner upstairs had come into our lives—the person who destroyed Isabella and took my innocence along with her. The man who'd changed everything.

"Alec Turner was handsome, charming, and successful, claiming to work as a hired contractor for a DC law firm. They'd met at a party and he'd immediately swept her off her feet. He was all she could talk about, but he never came around. I'd only met him a handful of times. He started giving me red flags when he didn't want to join her and her friends, and she became more and more reclusive because of it. I'd raised it with her a few times, but every time she waved me off, thinking I was just jealous.

"I *had* been jealous. Isabella was everything I wanted in a partner—beauty, grace, poise, intelligence. Fiercely protective, and feisty as hell. But I was also right. With each passing week, she became a shell of who she once was."

My audience must have forgotten to breathe. The apartment was as silent as a tomb, save for my lonely, shaking voice. I raised my eyes again, this time focusing on Kellan. The hardest man in the room to read on a good day, but the pensive look on his face felt like he was finally seeing me—through my bullshit, through my hardheadedness; just me in my rawest form.

I couldn't delve deeper into that terrifying thought. Not now. I fixated on a point on the wall behind him instead. The slight crack in the drywall was far easier to speak to.

"Eventually, he wanted her to move in with him, and I begged and pleaded with her to stay with me. I didn't trust him, or his intentions. When he came out with us, I'd watched him go off into dark corners of clubs to speak with known high-end gang members—the ones who peddled designer drugs and designer girls. I knew if she moved out with him, I'd lose her altogether.

"One night, she called me to come pick her up from a club. She was high as a kite, her dress torn in several places. I took her back to our apartment and cleaned her up, tucked her into bed, and promised to protect her.

"The next week, she disappeared with him again, and didn't return until a few days later. I'd been ready to call the National Guard, and then she waltzed into our apartment like nothing had happened. There were faded bruises on her arms and legs, and two track marks in her arm that she insisted were bug bites."

Aaron's growl of anger broke my train of thought. My head whipped up to meet his vehement disgust, his pretty, pouty lips curled into a savage snarl.

He stared at me in challenge, as if taunting me to finish my story, so he could go upstairs to kill Alec himself; I had no doubt in my mind Aaron would strip the man's entire skinsuit off his body if it would bring me pleasure. That kind of dedication was petrifying and yet so deeply comforting.

I unflinchingly met the challenge of his stare and kept speaking.

"I changed the locks on our apartment and kept a close eye on her, but it wasn't enough. It happened again. She was flunking her classes and was clearly miserable. What I didn't know was Isabella had been a victim of sexual assault as a child. An uncle. She was the textbook perfect victim for grooming, and Alec continued to make me out as the enemy, slowly working his way under her defenses with presents and nice words, and then threats of his disappointment when she was reluctant to do what he asked of her."

Blistering heat crept up the back of my neck, and my throat tightened as I fought back the burning ache of tears. The shame had buried me under its weight all these years, yet still suffocated me as if it had been yesterday when I lost her.

How much hope I had in my heart that...

I swallowed the thorny vine that had crept its way up my throat and blinked back the haze of tears hovering on my eyelids waiting for gravity to take them.

"She was getting ready one night, and somehow, I convinced her to stay home and watch a movie with me. We drank two bottles of wine, laughed until our sides hurt, and passed out in our bed—the one we hadn't slept together in in months—and I remembered feeling like I'd finally had my best friend back, even if we'd never be lovers again."

Bile raged in my gut, the acid churning and biting viciously at my insides at what was coming; the strength of these memories was enough to knock me over with the lasting effects of disgrace, guilt, and scathing doubt.

Their expectant eyes on me, each man waiting for the terrible punchline to become their chant for vengeance in my honor. It would never be for my honor—I needed to honor Isabella. And all the women who'd fallen victim to scum like Alec. Like Alvarez.

"I woke up in the middle of the night with a man hovering over the bed, his hands wrapped around Isabella's neck, strangling the life out of her. She barely fought back, her eyes glossed over with whatever drug he'd given her, and I struggled to move, incapacitated with whatever he'd given me, too. I was helpless, trapped in my body, as he raped her beside me, and then squeezed her throat until she couldn't breathe anymore. Until she never breathed ever again."

The ravenous edge of that night's terror trickled through me again at the memory. Terror of being helpless, of being useless. Terror I'd never hear her voice again.

The frantic need to control my limbs as he laughed at me, as he forced himself inside her, as we both lay helpless to stop him. How he'd angled me to my side, so I could watch the whole thing, how I saw the single tear escape down her face before all life left her tiny body.

My breath stuttered in my chest, the agony of that one life-altering night forcing its ugly head back into my heart. Isabella was the one person I'd ever loved—the one person I had allowed myself to love; without pretense, without an agenda—the most beautiful woman to ever cross my path. The last woman I'd ever allowed myself to touch; preserving her honor in some warped sense of duty. I couldn't preserve her life, so I'd preserve who she was to me in death.

My will to defy gravity dissolved, and my tears slid down my cheeks in hot, angry rivulets of pain.

"A tox screen showed that he'd injected us with a paralytic used for anesthesia, but he left no trace behind, literally disappearing into the night. Daddy paid off the news outlets to keep any of this from the press, and her parents were told that she'd died from a drug overdose at a party. A fucking insult."

Blind rage still overtook my senses every time I recalled her obituary. The most beautiful woman in the world never even had a proper burial service. Her parents couldn't come to America for the funeral, so I had the body preserved and shipped to Brazil with my own savings. I paid for her burial plot, but I was a coward—in all the years after, I couldn't bring myself to visit it. I couldn't tell her buried bones I'd failed her.

Maybe one day I'd find it in myself to make the trek. Once she was properly avenged, and her memory was more than a solemn tale that filled my nightmares and walking daydreams.

I raised my wet eyes, braving their gazes for the faintest fraction of a moment before staring through the floor again: concern, anger, love.

They made no move to come to my rescue, knowing me well enough to understand my need for space to share this. If one of them held me right now, I'd shatter into millions of shards, and not one of them could glue me back together.

"He should have killed me that night, too. I don't know why he didn't—he's never fessed up to it. Maybe because Daddy would have hunted him to the ends of the earth, and Isabella's family would never have the resources to."

I swiped my wet chin, angry I couldn't hold off the tears. Angry the world was so deeply unbalanced, where the rich little white girl had the world in her pocket, when the equally talented, supremely intelligent Portuguese girl had been left to rot. Angry, despite how far I'd come, how many scales I'd tipped, these women and children still drowned in an ocean of inequity. I was a drop in the bucket, yet I had hung my life on the line on ill-advised hope that many drops would make the bucket overflow and eventually, I would win.

Eventually, she'd forgive me.

A deep, painful breath expanded my lungs and gave me the strength to finish the story—I wasn't allowed to suffer a mental breakdown until the work was done. And the work would *never* be done.

"For weeks, I wished I was dead, too. I drowned myself in alcohol, locked myself away from the world. And then, I smartened up, and made it my mission to find him.

"When I did, he confirmed my suspicions. He was a trafficker. He located beautiful, exotic women on this side of American soil, groomed them, and then sold them to the highest bidder. Through my research, I fell into the darkest rabbit hole of sins. America had a mass network of women and children being coerced into sexual slavery. I needed to do something about it—to honor her. To atone for thinking I could handle it on my own—for not taking it seriously enough."

I heard rustling from the couch. Then three masculine, looming presences got closer to me. I still couldn't look at them. Not yet. They made no move to touch me, respecting the unspoken boundary as I let go of my heaviest secret. Another punch of gratitude hit my heart, warring with the immeasurable hole of loss.

"I built this place to hold anyone of Alec's caliber, if I ever got my hands on them. I hired a network of mercenaries who could exact justice on the men and women who paid for the services of sex slaves. I invested in the system to protect the victims we could save.

"We've castrated over 100 men and saved over 500 children. And we've barely made a dent. I'm so tired of running around, pretending to play Batman, while these men continue to play God."

A low whistle broke through my stilted declaration; Lucky. There. He finally knew who he was dealing with. The woman he'd been trying to steal from was actually a murderous avenger with a survivor's guilt complex.

"I found out recently that Alvarez was running the girls back then. Alec reported to him. So, my nemesis of today is also the nemesis of my past. The universe is one hell of a bitch sometimes."

My poor attempt at a joke fell flat. She *was* one hell of a bitch. This vendetta had become a life sentence, a torturous taunt of my worst nightmare on repeat—except it was no longer me trapped in my body, watching the woman I loved being raped and killed—it was the crescendo of silent screams of the many women being taken from their homes, forced to succumb to the same fate.

Cora Flynn

Children who became victims long before they experienced their first kiss, only to become perfectly groomed dolls, molded to meet evil expectations.

I finally found the strength to raise my eyes; terrified to see the cruel pricks of judgment or the simpering softness of sympathy. But when I searched the three men's troubled gazes, I found neither; rich caramels lined with wrathful concern, dark navy icicles filled with brutal fury, and sea-glass greens with nothing but open compassion.

How different these men were, and yet—here they were. For me.

Salty drops slid down into my mouth as I pursed my lips and made my last plea. "This is deeply personal for me, and I need your help. I need you to help me kill him. For her."

My eyes became the pathways to waterfalls now. Tears tumbled over my eyelids in rivers of pain I had never allowed myself to feel; the dam had finally cracked after too many makeshift repairs to salvage my sanity.

I sobbed and collapsed into a puddle on the floor; my resolve to keep my walls strong and impenetrable crumbled. Strong arms lifted me and carried me to the couch—the hard chest of citrus and amber let me know Kellan held me.

"I'm so sorry, Killer," he soothed, stroking calloused palms down my back as he rocked me back and forth against him. "I'm so sorry."

Gentle hands lifted my hair off my shoulders and moved to the base of my skull, massaging the scalp at the top of my spine. Lucky had moved behind the couch to offer his own version of comfort; I basked in his touch like a preening cat desperate for their warmth. A hand gripped my chin, tilting my head toward them; Aaron knelt at Kellan's feet, leaning over both our bodies, his gaze held me securely.

"We will help you, *Mi Reina*. We will rid you of your first demon and then take over hell together. Yes?"

I hiccuped, the puff of air escaping in an embarrassingly girlish squeak before I burrowed back into Kellan's chest.

Lucky chuckled softly and placed a light kiss atop my head before standing, rounding the couch, and holding out a hand for me to take.

"Come on, Blondie. It's time to let that peckerhead go. Roboto is going to lend you his little toy to take your pound of flesh, and then we'll burn this dungeon to the ground."

I leaned over to place a light kiss on Aaron's lips, then let Lucky pull me out of Kellan's arms. I stood awkwardly in their midst, feeling uncomfortable and exposed, my power draining from me with each admission of my most deplorable failures.

Aaron held out his hand and slipped the cool metal of a sharpened dagger into my grip.

"For Isabella," he said firmly, then wordlessly he turned on his heel, leading us out into the cavernous basement.

Lucky wrapped an arm around my shoulder and steered me upstairs, Kellan on our heels, his commanding Viking presence protecting us at the rear. When we arrived at the last cell, Aaron held open the door and beckoned me in.

Alec lay on the floor shivering with shock, and a silky sheen of sweat beaded across the remaining skin of his body.

He was useless to me now—incoherent and bleeding out. Despite what Aaron thought, I was sure he'd die from shock within hours. I refused to let the luck of fate pull him from this world, not when I could take it from him.

I stood over his body, acknowledging it was truly time to let him go. Holding him in captivity to make him suffer had continued to make me suffer. I understood now that no amount of extended torture would bring back Isabella.

"For Isabella!" The words were a bitter declaration to lay my beautiful *Cariño* to rest.

Without mercy, I drew back and thrust the knife with power into Alec's chest, then twisted it sharply into his heart, exactly as he had done to mine. Blood poured from the wound; Alec convulsed on the floor, twitching chest at odds with his frozen limbs.

I removed the dagger, then punctured his lung with another strategic stab, fascinated for a moment by the blood flooding into his throat and sputtering out of his mouth.

I withdrew the blade and cleaned it on the wool sleeve of my jacket. My gaze, though, never wavered from Alec's eyes as life left them.

The grisly satisfaction I was waiting for did not arrive.

Not while Marco Alvarez still conducted the orchestra of unwilling women and children in our state.

Not while Antonio remained ready and willing to replace every aspect of Alvarez's business with his own.

Not when there were more victims to avenge.

Nodding once, I spun on my heel and tossed the dagger to Aaron. He caught it deftly, spinning it on his finger. He bent down to Alec's lifeless body and stabbed the knife into the man's stomach.

"For Isabella," he said solemnly, then handed the bloodied knife to Lucky.

The Irishman's gaze was as severe as I'd ever seen it, and he didn't break eye contact with me as he stabbed Alec's corpse in the dick, wrenching it deep into the flesh before withdrawing the blade.

"For Isabella," he said, then passed the weapon into Kellan's waiting palm.

Kellan knelt over Alec's face and plunged the stiletto into Alec's eye. "*Som man bäddar får man ligga.*" He spat, then yanked the grisly knife out of the man's skull and wiped it on the blanket tourniquet across his thigh.

I grimaced at what was left of Alec's body. The mangled, bloodied mess a scene out of *Dexter* against the stark white floor. I stared at it, cataloging every gruesome detail, determined to bring out this imagery every time my brain wanted to work against me with another nightmare.

It was sadistic and twisted and yet, the exact comfort I needed.

Alec was dead, and the burden of keeping him alive was no longer mine to carry. It was time to move forward with the rest of our mission. Sandra had made a call, and we needed to get moving.

Walking over to the corner of the room, I was determined to relieve myself of one more burden before we left.

How had he escaped?

Under the camera's corner blind spot, I peeled back the padded framework to see a jagged hole cut out in the grouted tile, a series of electrical wires pulled down and sliced through the uneven edges—likely from sharp shards of the ceramic tile itself. It would have been painstaking work, and Alec wouldn't have known necessarily *what* he was cutting into, but his persistence had paid off.

Until it hadn't. Instead of being a captive in a warm cell with food and water every day, he was now dead. Served him fucking right.

"We're going to need a fire."

Back to bitch mode. There were plenty of villains still in this town, and we needed to get our asses moving if we were going to make every sorry fuck bleed through their eyeballs.

"Aye, that's where I come in." Lucky's gaze strayed from the bleeding corpse on the floor to mine, a renewed light and purpose shining in his eyes. A little—well, a *lot*—of blood and bone didn't affect him, apparently. "I'm a very skilled arsonist, Blondie. Leave that part to me."

"Do what you need to do. You have ten minutes." Direction delivered, I turned to my other two soldiers as Lucky scurried off with an excited whoop.

"Kellan, I need all records of this building destroyed. It's registered under a shell corporation and won't be easily traced, but just in case."

He nodded and pulled out his phone, dialing a number quickly and moving to the corner of the room to murmur into the receiver.

Aaron stood in front of me, calmly awaiting my instructions. His once raging face was placid, as if he had already accepted this new direction of the plan, and was ready and willing to carry it out at a moment's notice.

His loyalty and dedication to me pierced my heart like my dagger had pierced Alec's, but I put the intensity of those feelings on pause for the sake of the mission.

"Aaron, grab whatever you need to bring with you from the basement. You're going to stay with me. We'll bring you into the building through my hidden entrance, and you'll be on house arrest there for a little while. But you'll have fresh air and lots of natural light, which is a little better than here."

Guilt pricked the back of my neck that Aaron was exchanging one cage for another, but it was all we could do for the moment.

I made a vow to the universe I would get my Knight his life back. He would return to the company he'd built, the home he cherished, and the mantle he had been born and bred to lead.

We just had to kill Alvarez, destroy his parents, and go after Antonio, and then everything in our lives would go back to normal.

But most urgent—that call. Someone, somewhere, knew Sandra had been taken, and we had to find them before they found us. Or everything I'd worked so hard for to avenge Isabella's death, the sacrifices I've made, the stains on my soul...

Would all have been for nothing.

CHAPTER 19

Lauchlan

What a feckin' day.

Working for Marco Alvarez, even fake-working for him, was a soul-sucking lot of drivel. After successfully completing the app assignment, he'd sold me to Xandy Analo, and now he wanted to send me off on another special assignment to California for a few weeks.

Blondie's Blackbird had almost completed the final steps to break into Marco's most incriminating files—or at least, what we suspected were his most incriminating files—so I was just twiddling my thumbs waiting for the last shoe to drop to unleash chaos into little Marky Mark's world.

Cora Flynn

I was working on the FBI angle, too. My software couldn't unravel the e-signature, so I took a different approach. Something ludicrous, with a two percent chance of coming through, but it was worth a shot. I was trolling the FBI employee database; siphoning through all active agents in Sequoia and the ones who were on assignment within 200 miles of Carlisle. It was a complete goose chase —there wasn't a clear connection that the FBI had requested Hillary as their target, and the likelihood the request came through someone local? Almost batshit crazy.

Been called worse, and it was a good excuse to use my latest creation. The software was so illegal I'd be sent to prison for a much harder sentence than I would for stealing Hillary's naked chick, so I was taking a risk to use it. But I was a dog with a T-bone with loose ends, and this one was one puzzle I was determined to chew the marrow out of.

Especially since the whole nature of my assignment was giving me heartburn.

Younger me had loved the chase of a good con. Pulling the wool over arseholes' eyes, taking something from right out under their noses—the game was a good bit of fun and I always walked away with a pile of loot for my troubles.

I wasn't used to this odd crisis of conscience. After Hillary Lane's monumental confession in the dungeon, I could admit I was feeling a little... hesitant about stealing her painting and never seeing her again.

Fat chance of that happening, really. She'd hunt me down to the ends of the earth; I was sure of it. Theft surely wasn't up there on the same scale as raping and murdering your best friend right in front of you, but I'd just witnessed what lengths the woman would go to get revenge on the men who'd wronged her; I wasn't eager to stick my neck out just so she could plunge a knife into it.

Still, I had a job to do—The Six had spared Ma for failing her con with the Cascade Falls bloke because of extenuating circumstances, but they wouldn't spare me if I fucked this one up. Too much lay on the line—for the pot of cash at the end of the rainbow, and for the high-value client who'd hired us. Reputation was all one had in this business; I wouldn't be getting a free pass on account of my feelings.

Wasn't sure what those were exactly. My dick knew it liked her, and my head enjoyed that snappy wit and sharp mind even more. She was fucking terrifying in an exhilarating sort of way, and now I knew she was capable of murder—well, I was a lot less afraid and a whole lot more intrigued by my Billionaire Blondie.

As long as I wasn't the one she was murdering, of course. Stealing a painting might put me in that category, though...

My life was a hell of a lot easier without an angel on my shoulder. My pal, the Devil, seemed to have disappeared from his comfortable perch, leaving me with annoying chatter from the 'good guy.'

And I was about to get more annoying chatter; Ma was insistent she needed to see me—Today.

I flashed the electronic card on the keypad and the elevator took me up to her suite. "Family chat", she said, always code for 'we need to talk.'

What about, I hadn't a clue. My job was progressing. She was working an angle with some rich guy in town, since she no longer did any work for The Six, and we still had dinner once a week to check in. I hadn't lived most of my life near my mother, so she was still a bit of a mystery.

When I walked into the apartment, she stood in front of the floor to ceiling windows, looking down, sipping on a glass of wine.

"Oy, Ma," I said in greeting, and leaned in to kiss her cheek before settling myself on the couch. "I can't stay long. I've got a few meetings today with the cover job. What's the craic?"

She shifted her weight and slowly turned around to face me, a pinched look of distaste on her lips.

"How are you getting on with the Lane assignment?"

Okay, no preamble. I stared up at her, furrowing my brows. "Good, Ma. You know this. I've found the painting and—"

Her eyes—blue, not green like mine—lit up, and I didn't miss the greedy glint in them.

"You found it!" she screeched. A drop of wine sloshed out of the goblet and onto my cheek, she was so giddy. "Locke, when are you taking it?"

I shrugged a disinterested shoulder, but I was, in fact, very interested in the level of interest this woman was giving off.

"Dunno. The time isn't right yet. I don't have my exit plan in place, and I'm going to need—"

"I have a proposal for you." She slid onto the couch cushion beside mine, and I realized the cup of wine in her hand was not her first. Or her fourth, by the thick smell of booze coming off her lips.

Christ, it was just after noon. Had my mother become a drunk when I wasn't looking?

I looked at her expectantly, waiting for another cloud of booze-soaked air to hit my face when she spoke.

"Don't bring it back to The Six," she said, her voice barely audible. An almost maniacal look crouched in her eyes. "Bring it to me. I have a contact on the black market ready to sell it—and I'll give you forty percent of the cut."

"Forty percent to swindle The Six? Are you mad?" I leaped up from the couch and spun on my heel to stare down at my insane mother. "That's a death sentence, and you know it."

"It doesn't have to be." Ma pouted, biting her lower lip in feigned thought; she was clearly trying to swindle me into this idea. "Forty million would set you up for the rest of your life. Go disappear to Thailand, or Costa Rica. Find a girl and live out the rest of your days."

"So, you can live out the rest of yours." I scoffed bitterly. "This is to line your pockets, not mine."

Her gaze hardened for one tiny second, betraying her true feelings, before watering. Like my words had mortally wounded her. My Ma was attempting to con me into conning The Six, from a con I'd already been hired to con.

This was the stuff of a *Monty Python* movie.

"I want a better life for you than what your Da and I gave you." She sniffled like the master manipulator she was and stared up at me through mascara-clumped eyelashes. "Is that so hard to believe?"

Ah, yes, yes it was. Ma's interests in me were limited, at best, ever since she took off to America when I was a boy. But I'd play her game.

"Nah, it isn't." I settled back into the couch beside her and drew her hand into mine. "I'm gonna need more information, Ma. Who's your contact? What's your exit plan? I don't want you out in the world alone, either."

"I won't be alone, Locke." She reached for a tissue on the end table and delicately wiped her nose, then folded her hands into her lap; I waited for her to carry on with it. "I met a man I'm going to take with me. We'll live out our days in a little Tahitian hut on the beach and I'll never look back."

Fitting—she'd just confirmed *I* was not a part of the exit plan—as I'd have guessed. This assignment was her ticket away from the disgrace she'd earned in our world, and she expected me to throw away *my* life to hand it to her.

"Let me think about it," I said eventually. I rose and offered her an impish grin—as if this were just another exciting challenge I was considering. Then I headed to the door.

"Give me a week, yah? I'll have my own exit figured out by then."

"Okay, Locke." She followed me to the entryway and pecked my cheek. The soft smile on her features told me she well and truly thought this was in the bag for her.

Even my mother would drive a knife into my back if given the chance. Didn't matter if it was metaphorical. I took the stairs this go around, tramping down them two and three at a time, my footfalls bouncing around the concrete stairwell like the thoughts in my head.

No way was I considering it. I wasn't about to add The Six to the list of enemies who wanted me dead—I was a ballsy git, but I wasn't stupid.

But Ma was no damsel, and if this was what she was after, she was going to move every mountain in Sequoia to get it. I was going to have to move fast.

Instead of blaring music through my car speakers on my drive back to Hillary's condo, I rode in silence, sorting through all the strings I'd laid out in a line.

Marco's servers. Soon, I'd have access to every file and be able to leak all of his wrongdoings into the world. I wanted him dead, but I wanted him dead by shank in a prison cell. I wanted him to suffer for months with anxiety, knowing he was going to be sent to some maximum security filled with murders and rapists, and then I wanted the same to happen to him in the coldness of an eight-by-eight windowless room.

Hillary's painting was more complicated. I knew where it was and had direct access to her apartment. Now I just needed the code to her secret room, and I'd be able to take off with it. But Kellan and Aaron had never been a part of my plan, and those fuckers would sooner cut off my head than let me get away with hurting her.

I shivered as I considered Mr. Roboto's preferred method of torture. Was I willing to be shredded into ribbons for some crappy piece of 20th century art?

Her ogre companions aside—was I willing to face her rage head-on? I liked Blondie. A lot. She challenged me and made it seem like she saw through me, even if I haven't been telling her the truth half of the time. She'd be one hell of an enemy, but she could be one hell of a friend.

A man could always make use of a beautiful billionaire ready and willing to cut off heads in vengeance for him.

I snorted at the picture of Hillary doing just that in a *Wonder Woman*-type costume, except this one was black and bright pink, tight along her torso with a pleated pink skirt and thigh-high black boots, and a Batwoman helmet, showing off sexy pink lips beneath the mask. It was this man's hottest wet dream.

What was my alternative? We weren't all going to take on Alvarez and then become one big dysfunctional family. A Cartel son, a banished billionaire, and me? Even the worst jokes didn't have that kind of punchline.

A secure message pinged through my phone and disrupted my disjointed inner monologue. My heart pounded like I'd dropped a hit of ecstasy as I read it.

Blackbird's work was complete. A tasty little bug was working its way through every encrypted file on Marco's personal server. Within three days, we'd have everything we needed to take the fucker down.

I had three days to make some monumental, life-changing decisions.

Fuck.

I sat in my Blondie's condo underground car park several hours later. Waiting for her to show up, I scrolled through my phone to pass the time.

Aaron was already up there, completing his house arrest like a dutiful little boyfriend. After seeing his side of psycho, I wasn't exactly eager to spend some one-on-one time with him.

Cora Flynn

It was bad enough I'd had to give up my bed. Hillary hadn't invited either of us into her bed on account of the seventeen different things she needed to sleep, so I was now sleeping on the couch.

As much as I loved that couch for lazy napping when the mood struck, it was shyte for an eight-hour snooze, and when I woke this morning, my back felt like my sexy Barbarian had used it as his own personal punching bag.

Maybe I could convince the robot to convince Hillary to let him sleep with her—he'd have better luck with it, given they were obviously moon-eyed for each other; Then I could have *my* bed back.

Win-win.

My software had done its job, and I was sifting through the fifty-odd photos of known FBI agents working in the Carlisle area. Apparently, this city was a hotbed of white-collar crime in America; the FBI loved hanging out to capture the big, bad billionaires in action.

My brows furrowed as I examined each person, wracking my brain if I had seen any of them anywhere. Facial recognition was a skill I'd honed—one couldn't be a good con man if you forgot a name or a face—but not a single one of them looked remotely familiar.

Until number 37. My jaw practically dislocated at what could have been the broody Viking's LinkedIn profile picture. His hair was shorter, just above his ears, and a suit jacket and tie covered up the badass tattoos on his arms and torso. But that was Kellan Carlos, all right.

How in the ever-loving *fuck* was that possible?

The man I'd fucked—multiple times—was a double agent? Was the American justice system truly so corrupt they'd knowingly hired a cartel felon, or was this some kind of power play the cartel paid for? I didn't know nearly enough about gang politics to care, other than I'd been spending my time with *an FBI agent* while trying to complete a very high-profile con job.

I pushed rewind on every interaction we'd had from start to finish—from the first fuck, to Jediah's party, the fight I walked into—everything leading up to now. If Hillary didn't know about this, I'd eat my shirt. I was new on the scene, but these guys had a history; if Kellan had kept this from Hillary, I'd invite him to my next con, because he was truly an expert swindler to pull that one off.

I stared dumbly at the photo for a few more minutes. Would Kellan kill me as a cartel man who was in love with Hillary, or would he bring me in as a perp for the FBI? Would he lock me up and then arrange for someone else to pull my guts out of my arsehole from the inside, so he could kill two birds with one stone?

Fear wasn't a familiar emotion, but the sharp sting in my belly was most definitely fear. I was no longer one hundred percent confident I could work my way out of this one without some severe consequences to my health.

I had to move; fast. I got out of the car and took the private elevator up to Blondie's suite. I needed to take another look at the keypad—see if there was some way I could bypass it or hack it or—

When I strode through Hillary's entryway and into her kitchen, I halted in my tracks.

Blondie and Mr. Roboto were seated on the couches in grim silence, as if waiting for me.

Sharp tingles pricked the back of my neck as I looked back and forth between them, my eyes settling on the artwork laid out on the coffee table.

The painting. My painting. The nude girl worth $150 million just laying about like it was a toddler's drawing.

"Lauchlan," Hillary cooed, using my full name; I was really in trouble. She beckoned me over to the couch cushion beside her, her blue eyes flashing with dark challenge. "Take a seat."

Not the first time I'd heard that command from her lips. Probably wasn't the time for that joke.

Cora Flynn

Wordlessly, I bit my tongue and did as she asked, plopping down on the couch cushion and leaving a bit of space between us. If the viper was going to strike me today, I wasn't just going to *give* it my jugular.

Aaron stared back at me from the opposing furniture, his dark eyes staring emotionlessly, like the robot he was. Better than vicious hate, I s'posed, but—

"Take it."

Hillary waved her wine glass toward the painting on the table in front of us. Her cool stare gave nothing away, like she and Aaron had attended the same Robotic School for Billionaires.

I stirred uncomfortably in my seat, trying to grab hold of the charming mask of indifference I always kept in my back pocket, but I couldn't seem to find it.

"Not sure what you mean, Blondie." I tutted lightly, using every bit of training I ever had to keep myself together. "I don't need any more nude women in my life, if that's what you're after."

"Cut the shit, Lauchlan." That beautiful blue gaze glazed into a frosty polar vortex. "No more secrets. That's what you're after, so take it." She gestured again to the priceless painting still encased in its protective glass condom.

From the first moment I'd watched her at the bar over a whiskey, I'd considered Hillary a smart woman; a cunning woman; fucking beautiful and sinful... and a *force*. I never thought I could best her because she was weak and gullible. I thought I could best her because I was the *best*.

It was a hard lesson to swallow that she'd figured me out long before I'd done the same for her.

The jig was up. How I played this would determine if I walked out of the apartment as a human man, or as a slew of ribbons for Bellatrix's dress.

What did I want? I realized I couldn't answer that question without including her in it. I wanted to complete my assignment and have her in my life. I wanted to seek revenge on Marco, and be by her side to see him carted off to prison.

I wanted a life with people who understood me and chose me, anyway. I didn't want an island hut all alone with all the riches in the world.

I'd been envious as all hell as I watched her friend's family as an outsider. An entire group of misfits had found something in each other and made a home. And damn it if that seed hadn't been planted in my pretty little head.

"What if I don't want it anymore, Blondie? What if I found something I want more, instead?"

No amount of torture training could keep my heart from beating out of my chest as I held her gaze. Aaron stayed motionless outside of our fixated little bubble, but I'd no sooner trust him not to stab me within seconds if Hillary gave him the nod.

"And what would that be?" Still no emotion, still no insight into her devious mind. The truth might set me free, but it might also get me killed.

"Well, I want the job done," I replied smoothly, staring into those turbulent seas as I let the honest words roll off my tongue. "I want Marco Alvarez to rot in hell, and you and I be the overlords of his dungeon. I want to complete my assignment, so I don't get myself murdered by some pretty powerful baddies, and then I want to figure out what the rest of my life looks like—but I know this, Blondie. I'd like to keep you in it."

"And how do you propose you do that?"

I drew in a breath and held it in my lungs, contemplating that answer. I repeated the phrase she'd said to me not so many days ago.

"Blondie, I'm just treading water here while I'm tethered to you lot. Once Alvarez was taken out, I was going to figure it out then."

Still nothing in those icy depths of hers. Did she get the same training I had? This woman was hard as stone.

"I see."

She said the words as if she really saw me; I didn't know what to make of it. I didn't want to read into it too heavily and find myself headless, but—

"I've known all along you were after something from me, Lucky." Her words interrupted my melting brain spiral. "So, this isn't some kind of 'epic betrayal' where my heart is broken and you've left me in pieces. I played you like you played me."

My brows rose, and my heart stuttered in my chest. A con man being played by a mark? It was a testament to how fucked up I was. Knowing Hillary Lane had one upped me this whole time turned me on more than the hardest hit of Viagra. My dick ached in my pants despite the circumstances.

Had I finally met my match?

And why did that statement bring me this overwhelming sense of relief?

"I don't have it in me to play you anymore. There's too much at stake. So, decide—are you in or out? And if you're out, Aaron is going to make sure you're *really* out, if you catch my meaning."

I finally grew my balls back with that threat. If we were moving forward based on any equal footing, this direction wasn't it.

"I don't know if being blackmailed with my life proves my allegiance to you, Blondie. Do yeh want me to stay because you want me to, or because you're forcing my hand? Which is it?"

She cocked her head at Aaron, and they seemed to have a private conversation in ones and zeros across the room. I didn't make any move to look at him. He would do whatever she told him to—she was the one I needed to convince.

"Tell me something real, then. Something that will fuck you over just as hard. Then, we'll be even." I posed my challenge, watching as she put the wineglass down on the coffee table, awfully close to the priceless artifact, and folded her arms across her chest.

"You want to *start* a relationship built on trust?" The words were edged in jagged defiance. "I knew you were trying to con me, and yet, I still brought you into my deepest, darkest hell, and presented you with the poison to kill me. What's yours?"

So, a little less blackmail, but still material to use as blackmail. Blondie had a funny way of sealing the deal, but really, what else was there? Other than signing our promises in blood—wouldn't put it past the gruesome tailor over there—I couldn't see any other way forward.

Tilting my head to look up at the ceiling, I blew out all the breath in my lungs and scrubbed my hands over my face.

Now or never, then.

"I was handpicked for this job. Didn't question it, because I'd been wanting to come to America for years to get close to Alvarez, and I wasn't gonna look a gift horse in the mouth. Ma already lived here. You were just a beautiful mark, and acquiring high-valued items is my specialty. Everything came together easily.

"Today, I visited my Ma's place. She's a part of this life, too, but forcibly retired. Had a job go south years ago, and now she's champing at the bit to get back in the game. She wants me to double-cross my employer and sell it to her black-market contact, and give me four times what I'd get for it otherwise. She wants to retire with her new beau and disappear."

I waved a hand at the innocent little fortune resting between us.

"I'm not doing it. I don't con for the money; I've made my little nest egg already. I con for the thrill. You were the ultimate thrill, Blondie. Never expected for anything to come out of it. I'm two months behind on this job because I don't want it to end. I don't want *you* to end."

Her smooth mask creased into a series of crumpled wrinkles, like a cute, little—but dangerous—puppy dog.

"Who's your mother, Lucky? Give me that, and I'll find a reason to trust you."

Betray my mother to a vengeful billionaire to save my skin. Was I that callous? I was a lot of deplorable adjectives, but handing over my Ma to be butchered was a line I couldn't cross.

"I can't do that, Blondie." I met her hawkish stare with a sorrowful one of my own. "I'd have to be a sorry sack of shyte to sell out my mother. I'm not all keen on the woman, but I don't want her dead, either."

Was that respect in her eyes, or indigestion? Impossible to tell with the furrowed brow and pursed lips and narrowed eyes—her poker face wasn't neutral; it looked like she'd swallowed a lemon. But she hadn't sicced Aaron's blade on me yet, so that had to mean something.

Her sexy little killer body stood from the couch and faced me, a ferocious warrior in a pretty blue dress and pink lipstick.

"Here's the deal. I'm having this painting shipped today. It's going on a boat to a secure facility where you will never find it. So, you've lost this contract."

She pointed a delicate finger at the doorway behind me.

"I'll let you leave right now. You can disappear forever. Take that little nest egg and find somewhere to bury it on the other side of the world. No questions asked. You have no evidence of anything you've seen here, and knowing your history, you won't risk going to any authorities, anyway. Leave now, and you can be scott-free."

Blackbird had already confirmed everything with Alvarez was already in motion. I could walk away knowing even without my involvement from here on out, he would get what was coming to him. And yet...

The offer was far more generous than I would have expected. I mulled it over briefly before asking the obvious question.

"And if I stay?"

"No more secrets," she repeated. In rapid Spanish, she exchanged a few words with Aaron, who agreed with what she was saying, nodding with deference before turning a hard, murderous stare on me.

"You've proven yourself to be valuable to all of us. No more secrets, and you can be part of the team. After Alvarez is off the board, we need to take out Antonio. After Antonio, I don't know what the agenda is, but it's going to be arduous and brutal and bloody. Are you in, or are you a free man?"

What a hell of a question. But an easy one to answer.

I hung all of my bullshit training on the proverbial coat hook and spoke with all the sincerity I could muster, swiveling my head to make the promise to both of them.

"I'm in."

Cora Flynn

CHAPTER 20

Hillary

"If you have any news on our son's whereabouts, please reach out to our hotline."

Veronica's simpering appeal blared through my phone speaker, interrupted by Vicente's soothing baritone. "A reward will be offered to anyone bringing forth accurate information. We just want our son back."

The two of them stood at the mayor's podium, the public plea for their only son's return the biggest farce I'd heard this year. Veronica wore a long, fitted black dress, a netted covering over her face like a 1930s damsel in mourning, and Vicente completed the picture with a tailored black suit and red-rimmed eyes.

I choked on a bitter scoff as I shut off my phone, shifting my gaze to the missing man in question.

"Laying it on thick, aren't they?"

I caught Aaron's eye across the living room; he was splayed out on the couch opposite me, laying on his back with his nose in an art history book. I hadn't even known he liked art.

He snapped the book shut and shifted in his seat. Rolling his long body to the side to face me, his dark eyes seared into mine.

"They are dutiful parents, yes?" he deadpanned, his emotionless stare betraying nothing, as if we were discussing something as demure as the weather. "Ensuring I am fully dead before planning my funeral."

"They're vile humans," I spat, my wrath at the Rodriguez pair no longer hidden. "The only good thing to come from them is you."

"Oh?" His lips quirked up the tiniest fraction. "Is *Mi Reina* plotting revenge on my behalf? I believe your torture palace is no longer an option."

He was teasing me. Maybe Lucky was right; despite the chaos surrounding us at every turn, Aaron was discovering his sense of humor.

I liked it.

"One day, Aaron, I will show your parents *exactly* what I think of them," I declared vehemently, the words now a solemn pact between us. "Although your methods seem to be far more effective than mine."

I quirked a challenging eyebrow, calling him out on his Sweeney Todd impersonation for the first time. His eyes blazed at the mention of it, a tempting mix of power and pleasure.

"It is unfortunate that I learned that method from my father. Unfortunate for him, since that will be the way he enters his coffin."

The words sent a toe-curling shiver down my spine, but not out of fear.

Fuck, had Aaron always been this sexy? He'd always been devastatingly handsome—tall, dark, and dreamy in fitted suits with fantastic hair—but something about the dangerous demon within him made me wetter than his sweet words ever could.

I wasn't going to spend any time analyzing *that* realization right now. I had enough problems to worry about if I had a sociopath fetish.

"Your hate for them is personal, *Mi Reina*. I am flattered to think you are protecting me, but there is more. What is it?"

Well, that took a ninety-degree turn. My face flushed hot at the memory; a silly insignificant moment that shouldn't have any bearing over my adult feelings, but it did.

"There are many reasons to hate your parents without any personal feelings whatsoever, Aaron." I waved dismissively, as if him bringing up the possibility of more hadn't caused a visible reaction on my cheeks. "Their involvement in the flesh trade, for one."

"This is true." His stare penetrated through me like a caramel laser beam. "But then you would hate Antonio with the same passion, yes? Why?"

"I do hate Antonio with the same passion," I insisted and crossed my arms like a petulant child as he pinned me to the couch with his words.

A chestnut eyebrow rose as a tendril of matching hair fell into Aaron's face, but he did nothing to swipe it away. His gaze fixated on me like a target.

"Remember when we shared our first moment—in that closet when we were teens?"

Why was I blushing right now? I was a goddamned successful, empowered woman. That Veronica could still make me feel this way all these years later was a testament to the power of that single moment, and I hated it.

Aaron nodded thoughtfully. "You didn't speak to me for months afterwards. I had thought I embarrassed you."

"I was embarrassed," I admitted, staring down at my cream skirt and smoothing the non-existent wrinkles. "But not for the reasons you might think.

"I was a fourteen-year-old without a mother and an absent father, Aaron. Fucking lost and impressionable, with a backbone made from super-glued paperclips and papier-mâché. I know I looked cultured and mature, but I was just this lost little girl who wanted someone to care about her. You made me feel that way that night."

His impenetrable stare softened, and it made me feel less self-conscious about what I was about to share, even if only slightly.

"Veronica cornered me afterwards. She told me she forced you to do those things to me so that she had something to blackmail me with, given that Logan and I were already in an arranged relationship at that point. She told me I was a stupid, gullible girl, and how ashamed Daddy would be of his little whore. She held it over me for a solid year until I'd hardened enough to know the difference —and knew you well enough to know you would never hurt me that way."

Energy crackled between us as Aaron's fury bled out from his body into the surrounding air. It was so potent I could breathe it in and taste its fiery sting.

"That was just the start of a long stint of punitive power plays." I shrugged, as if an incident sixteen years ago really wasn't of any consequence, when I had castrated men and stabbed real rapists to death in the time since, but it was a lie.

The scathing words of other women when they weaponized morality against the innocent sexual exploration of youth were scarring; the mottled tissue embedded in an adolescent's vision of themselves. It was no different for me—Veronica's words had made me believe I was someone dirty, only worthy of one thing. She was wrong.

It was toxic, manipulative, and intentional; words she had used to control my definition of my own power and body. A man could call me a whore at fourteen or at forty, and I'd laugh it off every time—but Veronica choosing the same words? Veronica choosing those words to an impressionable teenage girl, who at the time was falling deeply in love with her son?

The scar had never healed.

Aaron didn't buy what I was selling. He rose from his spot on the couch as quickly as a striking snake, lifted me from my seat and resumed my place, pulling me down into his lap, banding his arms tightly around my waist.

"I am sorry, *Mi Reina*. She is a terrible woman who was jealous of you even then."

He pressed a gentle kiss to the top of my head and I snuggled into his warmth, no longer interested in pretending I was too strong to have my feelings hurt once upon a time.

A soothing palm stroked down my back and upward into the base of my neck, over and over until I was a melted puddle within his grip.

For the last several years, I'd deprived myself of a real romantic connection with anyone, mistaking the need to have someone as a weakness instead of a strength, determined to never have my chest ripped out of my body ever again.

My stupidity was a shining light now; I drew strength from Aaron's solid hold, the simple action far more powerful than I'd ever given credit.

An overwhelming need to *show* him how much he meant to me swept through my spine, and I rose from my cuddled perch in his lap, pressing a desperate kiss to his lips.

There was no softness, no romance, despite what I was trying to convey with that simple touch of skin. I wanted to devour him, to get inside his body; to tattoo myself on his soul, so no matter what happened in the coming weeks, we'd never be apart.

I loved this man so definitively, so purposefully. *mi cabellero oscuro.*

The abrupt shift in mood didn't stop Aaron from returning my kiss just as fiercely, his tongue seeking entrance as if he'd never once tasted my skin. I shifted in his arms, turning toward him to straddle his waist. I locked my thighs with his in a tight grip, needing to be as close to his heat as possible.

His hands rose to my hips, shifting me to slide over his hardening length. He groaned deep in his throat at the contact; the masculine sound shot sparks of heat from the base of my spine to the swelling hood of my clit.

Our lips, our tongues, fused together, unable to stop to breathe in our desperation to become one being. He loosened his grip on my hip and shoved my skirt up to my waist, toying with the damp fabric of my pantyhose as I wriggled above him, encouraging his touch with light bucks of my pelvis.

His cock was now steel, jutting out of the loose sweatpants fabric; the engorged head draped in cotton and teasing me like a too-small dildo.

Aaron broke away from our kiss with a light curse. He looked down at the junction between my thighs with a frown. Then he reached two hands down and ripped the pantyhose in two, right at the crotch.

Impressive, since they were the no-run kind. They probably hadn't been tested by horny killers, though.

Then he lifted me slightly, shoving down his sweats and boxers with one hand. His deliciously swollen and seeping cock was exposed right where I needed it.

His lips were on mine again and he yanked me down on top of him, sheathing himself inside me in one hard pull.

I moaned at the stretch of him inside me. The thickness of his shaft filled me so deeply I'd feel the memory of him tomorrow.

We stayed there for a moment, lost in another depthless kiss of longing and love, our bodies held together like a lock and its proper key.

I became wet to the point of soaking while we held ourselves still in a silent promise; mind, body, and heart. When I attempted to move, to ride him so desperately, he gripped my hips tightly and held me immobile.

"We have a visitor," he whispered against the shell of my ear. I stiffened, my pussy clenching around him as I did so, and he let out another irresistible moan that had my insides quaking.

Before I could turn around to see which of the wayward men had shown up unannounced, Aaron broke the silence.

"Are you joining us, *companero*?"

His question was as smooth and heated as melted butter, seductively influenced by his desire. I turned my head to see Kellan's navy blue eyes fixed on the crease of my ass where our bodies joined, and the outline of his own desire was fighting against his pants.

He licked his pouty lips like he was a lion stalking his next meal, and my pussy clenched again. The idea of being sandwiched between them, with nothing between us but sweat and skin more arousing than anything I'd ever pictured.

"She likes that idea." Aaron chuckled darkly against my neck, and abruptly thrust up, pulling a sharp cry of ecstasy from my lips. "If we are to share her, we can share her, no?"

My gaze flitted between the burning caramel of Aaron's to the stormy blues of Kellan's; their lust-filled stares speaking in a code I didn't need to decipher.

"Kellan?" My voice dripped with want, my arousal soaking Aaron's thighs. I shifted on top of him, rising upward, only to fall back down on his cock once more as a desperate shudder filled me.

With a growl, my fierce Viking protector was suddenly behind me, the heat of his chest against my shoulders. His coarse palms gripped my neck, tilting my head back to claim my mouth in a ravenous kiss, his tongue forcing my mouth open to submit to his exploration.

I lifted my hips and slowly rode Aaron's cock, basking in the waves of pleasure at each filling pass. My clit deliciously rubbed against his pelvic bone as he let me take control of him, while Kellan took control of me.

Too quickly, he broke our kiss and turned on his heel, heading to my bedroom. I watched the retreat curiously while Aaron took control of my body, slamming me back down on him more insistently; an orgasm was building in me so fast it was about to blind me with its ferocity.

"Not yet," Aaron tutted. His hand gripped my chin and turned my attention back solely on him. "Let him see it."

His eyes gleamed with a feral hunger I'd never seen, and I realized he was getting off on this, too. Did he enjoy watching me with the hot blonde Viking, or was it more than a voyeuristic kink?

It really didn't matter. That Aaron was willing for this, willing to love me and share me with another man who held my heart, was more than I could have ever dreamed, and I wasn't going to question his motivations.

He continued to tease me, gyrating my hips over his cock while increasing the pressure of my clit against his skin. I was trapped in a sea of endless tantalizing bliss and the desperate need to let the bliss explode from my core.

"Now, *Mi Reina*," he commanded and, with a sharp thrust upward, he pulled me down hard. I came with a strangled cry, the explosion of pleasure ripping through me and I dissolved into a puddle of goo in his hold.

"Wasn't that beautiful, *companero*?" My Dark Knight's taunt was soft and his eyes shined with Lucky-like mischief. "Shall we give her this gift again?"

A deep grunt came from behind again, and before I came to all my senses, a sharp, wet sword poked against my ass.

"No," I complained on a whimper, rocking against Aaron's still very hard dick, greedy for the two of them. "I want to face you."

Aaron guided my spent body, slowly maneuvering me around with his cock still inside me, until I faced Kellan's pants-less form. His thick, slick cock protruded proudly and ready for me. I reached for it, biting my lip as I considered what I was about to ask.

He quirked a bushy blonde eyebrow at me, no doubt questioning where I was leading the two of them. I guided him to my pussy, where Aaron's cock was still very much buried within me.

"Fuck us both," I challenged, holding the tip of his weeping dick to my entrance. "Make us both submit."

My Viking's eyes flashed with insatiable hunger before reaching down to grip his shaft, placing his hand over mine. He licked his lips again, before flicking his gaze quickly to Aaron.

"Go on, *companero*," was his answering reply. "Yours will not be the first dick I've touched. Make us submit," he echoed.

Whether he knew that was the exact challenge that would turn Kellan into a feral beast, I didn't know, but his words did just that.

With a guttural snarl, Kellan wedged the head of his dick into my pussy. The sharp sting of the stretch melted into a mind-altering fullness that set every nerve ending in my body on fire. Aaron groaned beneath me and bucked his hips, as if seeking more of the tight sensation.

Our blond partner obliged, slowly easing into me. The slickness of his lubed shaft slid against Aaron's cock with incredible friction. Once he bottomed out, he held us both in his grasp. We waited with bated breath for him to take us to the brink of ecstasy and beyond.

"Do you like this, Killer?" He growled and eased back out, then thrust against us with a savage jolt. "Do you like it when I fuck you, while I fuck your boyfriend?"

Holy shit, yes. Yes, I did.

"Fuck, yes." My words were garbled, the tension in my body tight like a bowstring, ready to release any second. He slammed back into the two of us again, and again. His pace would slow, then ratchet back up to one hundred, not giving us a moment to think or to breathe while he tore our bodies apart.

His lips crashed into mine in a savage kiss, all teeth and tongue, before he pulled back to watch the two of us, his eyes alight with dark obsession as his gaze dropped from our faces to where we all joined.

I watched too, in utter fascination, as the three of us partook in the unthinkable; in any of my wildest fantasies, I could never have imagined this scenario, and now that I was literally in the middle of it, it was perfect. Raw, unpolished perfection.

"Look how pretty the two of you are, taking my cock. Tell me how much you like me fucking you," Kellan demanded, his eyes knitted in heavy concentration. Beads of sweat formed at his brow.

He was a god in this state. Wild blonde hair in messy tangles, his blue eyes blazed with the lust of a thousand suns. His thick thigh muscles bunched and bulged with every thrust of his hips. He was a god, and I a mere mortal, desperate for his favor and affection.

Before I could get out the words, Aaron's strangled response came from behind me. "I want to be torn apart by your cock. I want you to fill us with your cum and then use me all over again."

My body spasmed in delicious shock at those dirty words. My orgasm was too close for comfort, my body at the point of pain in anticipation of the release to come.

The beast roaming just under the surface of Kellan's skin raised its beautiful head before sinking its jaws into Aaron's lips.

Their kiss was equally messy, tongues clashing beside my head, a brutal claiming of sexual tension I hadn't even known was there. It was beautiful; two of the sexiest men I'd ever met sharing pleasure in each other's bodies, with me the catalyst between them.

When Kellan bit Aaron's lip in forceful dominance alongside an equally forceful thrust, I shattered, my cry piercing the heated air between us. Every molecule in my body hummed with release. All sound went muffled as I sagged between them, my brain lightheaded and fuzzy from the sheer magnitude of my orgasm.

It was as if I was TNT—Aaron shouted his own release within seconds of mine, his hot cum spilling into me and all over Kellan's cock.

Kellan's growl was animalistic, a rough rumble emanating from his chest as he pumped against us twice more before stilling, sweaty and sated.

For moments or minutes, we sat suspended in time, panting heavily into a dense air of desire. Kellan moved first, pushing away from us to stand. He held out a hand for me to take. I allowed him to pull me up into his arms. Then he offered his other hand to Aaron.

"Let's get the two of you cleaned up." His command was gruff. And he led us down the hallway to my expansive tiled shower.

He turned on the tap and then turned his attention back to me, gently twirling me to remove my blouse over my head while Aaron pulled off my ruined set of pantyhose. I slipped my skirt down over my hips as Aaron unclasped my bra.

The two of them then spun me to enter the shower while they removed their own clothes.

We didn't speak—we didn't seem to need to as we stood under the hot spray to get clean. The euphoria of an incredible fuck and an awakening of sorts had untethered us from our bodies and we floated up in space for a little while longer.

My two men took turns soaping me up, paying careful attention to my very sore and swollen pussy, fluttering light kisses across my shoulders and neck as they did so.

I caught the two of them staring at each other too; apparently the sparks of the heated moment weren't a dying flame—it looked like just the beginning sizzle of what would become a blazing bonfire.

I bit my cheek before the smile could take over my face, oddly satisfied with this little development. If these two men could find love with me, who knew what they could find in each other—even if it was just a fun fling of fucking?

After drying off, Aaron and I put on fresh clothes. Kellan left for the living room to grab his pants from the floor.

"Oy, Conan," I heard from the next room. "Nice arse. You here to fulfill my wet dreams, or Blondie's? How about a two-for-one?"

"Too late for that," came Kellan's cutting reply.

"You gotta be kiddin' me!" came Lucky's response, and I could just picture his childish look of disappointment. "And I *missed* it!?"

I snickered, then resumed a neutral mask to go greet our other roommate. This condo was becoming awfully crowded these days.

I walked out into the kitchen with Aaron in tow. I surveyed the three men I was now completely in bed with. Figuratively, and... literally.

"Good, we're all here."

My tone was bright, my mood considerably content after the best threesome of my life. Marco's world was going to implode tomorrow, and things were looking up for our little group of misfit criminals.

"I'll order takeout. We've got some planning to do."

235

CHAPTER 21

Kellan

"I have another update, and you're not going to like it."

Trish, to her credit, stared down her angular nose at me and didn't even blink. My updates were usually a breakdown of Antonio's latest drug shipments, or information on a new weapon supplier. She had long since been desensitized to the depths of my father's depravity.

She knew about the gang war and Alvarez's determination to take down Antonio's territory, and the retaliation efforts we'd led to wage bloody war against the crews on the ground. My brothers had taken out four more sites in the last several weeks, decimating Alvarez's gang presence in Sequoia. We couldn't do anything about his locations in other states, but Antonio didn't care about those operations, anyway.

If Alvarez was no longer encroaching on his business, the leader of the Carlos Cartel would let him live—until he made my brothers make an example of him when the timing was right. The two rivals had maintained their separate operations for decades. This was the year Alvarez had started pissing in our backyard.

Where my father didn't care, we'd taken up the mantle; Lauchlan and Blackbird had successfully hacked into all of Alvarez's major systems—bank accounts, private chat links with evidence of his underground behavior—the whole gambit. That information would be leaking to the world in the next hour. Alvarez was about to have one hell of a lawsuit on his hands, with his fortune dismantled in minutes.

The worm or spoof or rootkit—fuck, hell if I knew, I wasn't a hacker—would siphon most of his accessible holdings to private accounts worldwide, before being rerouted as anonymous donations to over a thousand women and children's organizations internationally; Killer's directions, and now that I knew the history behind her hurt, I didn't blame her. Blackbird had already parsed through some of the incriminating encrypted text messages and would upload them to national news channels at the same time.

Today, Alvarez was royally fucked. And Trish-the-Fish was going to be royally pissed I'd waited this long to tell her. The last thing I needed right now was to be the next victim on her chopping block.

"And?" she prompted when I failed to speak up.

We were back in the makeshift office again, seated on dented metal chairs around the dinged-up coffee table in the center of the room. Maverick, my number two, was following up on another lead for the international theft ring.

I'd let that ball drop these past few weeks; my attention tuned into the other massive shitstorm on my docket.

Now Alvarez had been taken care of, my sights were quickly shifting to my other family obligation. We were in the last week of January. My debt to my father—the one I'd accumulated by simply being born into this fucked up family—was about to be called in.

"Marco Alvarez is about to be exposed to the world," I said, then laid out the stakes in tidy piles for her to sift through. "You're going to want some agents on standby in the next couple of hours."

Slivered, severe brows rose at that statement. I summarized everything for her; leaving out names and accomplices, and spun the story to look like the Carlos Cartel had arranged the cyber hit. It wasn't a stretch of the imagination, and I was determined to leave Hillary's involvement entirely out of it. Blackbird would remain anonymous too—she was a useful card to play, and I planned to keep her in my back pocket.

"And you didn't think I deserved a head's up on any of this?" Trish barked when I finished. Her face had collapsed into a disapproving frown. She didn't wait for me to answer, choosing instead to grab her phone and deliver orders for several of my colleagues to return to base.

"I made a judgment call." I shrugged unapologetically as I faced her ire head on. "I need to be several steps removed from this, and the media shit storm is going to be a frenzy. It won't matter how the information came out—he's guilty, and the evidence shows that."

"You know damn well it matters!" she hissed, her eyes flashing with a healthy dose of anger, tempered with a slip of fear. "They committed a hundred felonies to get that information!"

"So, what!?" My voice rose, hovering on shouting; I took a calming breath and tried again. "Antonio doesn't give a fuck if he committed a thousand felonies. You're telling me that our justice system is going to care more about the method than the madness? Human trafficking is one of the worst crimes on earth. *That's* what we should talk about!"

Years of polished frown lines forced her face into a heavy scowl.

"What sort of justice system gives a sixteen-year-old child soldier an ultimatum to work for them, Kellan? Are we talking about *that* justice system right now?"

I scrubbed my palms down my cheeks and through the scruff of my beard, not liking where this conversation was going. Sagging into the creaking chair, I released a long sigh and met her eyes. All colour leached from them the longer we stared at each other.

"I don't know, Trish. That ultimatum gave a young man the possibility of a conscience and an entire world outside of gang doctrine. Sometimes, evil deeds have good consequences."

She remained silent and stared through me, as if searching for the answers to life's secrets under the surface of my skin.

"Do you remember what I said to you the day I found you, Kellan?"

The day she found me. The day my father had sent me to kill her as my initiation into the position of my birthright. She'd been a junior agent back then; a fierce fighter who'd thwarted my advantage by punching me in the temple and whipping out the second gun at her ankle— the illegal weapon agents weren't supposed to carry.

We'd been caught in a stand-off—my handgun to her head, her tiny pocket pistol trained on my crotch. Perhaps the most terrifying threat to a teenage kid who'd recently discovered his cock was to permanently mangle his dick.

Maybe she saw the war within me; I wasn't thirsty to take her life like some of the younger gangbangers in Antonio's training ranks. I hadn't wanted this life at all.

She took a chance that day, lowering her gun while quoting a phrase, her eyes never leaving mine as she dropped it to the ground. It was the day she'd saved me from a completely scorched heart, but she hadn't been quick enough to remove its discolored tarnish.

Some days, I didn't know whether to be grateful or to curse her interference to the high heavens—those days I ached to carry out my father's bidding without the burden of a heart to feel.

"*The greatest good is often born of the greatest evil,*" I quoted, rolling my eyes up to the drop-tile ceiling. "You quoted King Lear to a teenage Cartel hit man."

"I did," she agreed, and the tiniest shadow of a smile traced her lips. "And that teenage hit man knew the quote. So what does that tell you?"

"My father valued an English education?" I snarked.

"We only remember quotes that *resonate,*" she emphasized, her stern gaze that of an annoyed parent. "Why would a shit-for-brains gun-slinging teenager know and *remember* that quote? I had a choice to offer you something outside of a bullet to the brain, and I fought for you. You had to choose to fight for yourself."

That assertion sat like a stone in my gut. I didn't feel like I'd fought for myself. My entire existence was purgatory; torn between two worlds where 'good guys' and 'bad guys' often got confused, where one step forward was always two steps back.

I fought to be redeemed when I was irredeemable.

"And what are we fighting for now, Trish?" I challenged, the pain of those memories creeping up my spine like the icy fingertips of death. "Who are we fighting for? I play so many sides of the fence; I don't even know anymore."

Her weighted stare held a thousand words she wanted to say, but wouldn't. Trish wasn't big on platitudes or reassurances. She practiced tough love and trial by fire. Even though I knew she would have my back in every circumstance, she wouldn't be doling out warm praise or pats on the back.

"Trust me when I tell you that your presence here has saved a hell of a lot more lives than you would have killed as Antonio's puppet."

She stood and walked to the dingy window to look down.

I followed her over, taking in the gray carpet of cars and the dots of people, none of them even aware their world and everyone in it could collapse at any moment.

"He's ready to hand over the flesh trade," I admitted, finally coming to terms with the inevitable ask; I wouldn't be able to follow through with it, I realized I didn't have enough protection on either side of my fence to walk away from Antonio's desires.

I didn't want to disappear from the world like Rodriguez, or have Hillary try to jump in to save me from a world I couldn't be saved from. But I wasn't seeing another option—that didn't end with my head on a spike—so I'd serve as the proper example to anyone else that dared to defy Antonio Carlos.

Her reply was quiet, but a challenging question, as if I somehow had the answer and just hadn't said it out loud yet.

"And what do you suggest we do about that?"

Before I could respond, Maverick strode through the glass doors, a cocky grin on his face.

"I think I found our perp!" he exclaimed, waving a paper printout in the air. "Well, one of them, anyway. This organization is *huge*. Their primary base is out of Europe, but they have separate operations across four continents."

I guessed he was reviewing all of this for Trish's benefit, since yes, I knew full well how big The Six was, given it was *my* file. Still, I hadn't figured out who the perp was, so I should be more grateful my chief agent had found a lead we could actually use.

"We identified a liaison out of London," he continued excitedly, holding the piece of paper up as if it was the holy grail. "A Bellamy Graves. Hacked his phone calls and traced the phone numbers back to several sites across Greater Europe and North America, but this one was local. Got a picture of the perp off a sat using his GPS location."

He handed me the grainy gray-scale picture and my heart crystallized to ice in my chest.

The man was dressed in a tight, tailored jacket, holding a cell phone up to his ear while he checked his watch outside of a popular coffee shop in the downtown core.

Fucking *Lauchlan O'Donnell* was the perp? He was the one playing my Killer as the patsy all this time?

The sneaky, lying, *dead* mother fucker.

I forced the anger out of my voice and swallowed down the heat in my blood. "I've never seen him before. But this is great work, Mav. See what else you can find out about it."

Trish cocked her head in question. She would know me well enough she could probably see I was hiding something. But now wasn't the time to admit the man I'd been forced to spend time with—a man I'd *fucked* more than once—was the very reason I'd been called to Carlisle in the first place.

"I need to get moving." I shot Trish a meaningful look. "The feeds go live at three—you'll want to be ready."

"Yeah, thanks for the"—she glanced at her watch–"one hour's notice." Her tone was sharp, as if remembering she was pissed at me for withholding the information. "Maverick, I need you on another assignment for the rest of the day. You"—she pointed at me with a blunt nail—"go take care of your shit, and we'll talk later."

Nodding respectfully, I brusquely stalked out of the office and down to my car, ready to set things right. I knew where the fucker was holed up today—the three of them were working from Hillary's condo, waiting for the metaphorical shoe to drop on Alvarez's ass.

Cora Flynn

I seethed the entire way there. The anger in my veins bubbled to a fiery rage as I considered every fucking moment since I'd met the man masquerading as a Skittle-loving jokester when he was actually casing Hillary for all she was worth. He knew her deepest secrets. He'd watched her *kill* someone.

He'd wormed his way under all our skins with his irritating positivity and charming fucking smiles, and now he had exactly the leverage to threaten Hillary.

I slammed my palm against the steering wheel, the rage spilling out in ravenous waves. Mother*fucker.*

I stormed into the building, vibrating with vengeance, jiggling my leg as I waited impatiently for the elevator up to her penthouse. I had started to consider taking the stairs up the thirty flights to work out a fraction of my wrath when the doors opened up with a ding.

Suddenly, every little quirk and ability of Lauchlan made sense. How he could resist my torture session, the way he noticed the tiniest of details, his connections all over a state he'd never been to before... micro details I missed because I hadn't connected them together.

Either he was very good at his job, or I was seriously fucking stupid. I had a feeling it was a combination of the two.

"Hey, Viking," Hillary greeted with an anxious smile as I stalked into the living room. Her smile faltered at the no doubt thunderous look on my face. "What's wro—"

I yanked the sniveling fuck of an Irishman from his lazy perch on the couch and punched him in the face. My fist crunched against bone as his nose broke into smaller, less-smug pieces.

"Whart du farck!"

Blood poured down his face and into his shirt. I glared at him through slitted eyes, nowhere near done with defending my Killer's honor.

"Kellan!" Hillary shrieked, her tiny hands tearing at my biceps to pull me away from punching him again. Aaron was at my other side, hovering, waiting to see if he needed to assist Hillary, or assist me.

"He's playing you," I growled, not bothering to turn to her with the explanation. "He's fucking playing you, and playing us. Do you know what happens to liars, O'Donnell?"

I stepped back into his personal space, overpowering him with my bulk easily. He stepped back to get away and fell into the couch cushion behind him, completely trapped and perfectly positioned to take another punch to the face.

"Me!" Lucky exclaimed, his hands cradling his mangled nose. "Yurf a fraghen FBI!"

I stilled, my clenched fist halfway in the air at that accusation.

"And how did you fucking know *that?*" I spat, ready to pummel his pretty pout into a mess of bloodied mashed potatoes.

"Kellan!" Hillary repeated forcefully, catching my arm with a tight hold of her own. "I know. I've always known. Lucky and I have been playing a little game."

My furious stare turned to her, disbelief briefly softening the rage coursing through my muscles. "Someone explain before I kill him."

"I've known Lucky's been trying to con me from the beginning." She shrugged, as if playing footsies with criminals was a part of her daily routine. "But he didn't know that I knew, and when I found out what he was after, I gave him the chance to walk away, or stay on board. He stayed."

"And why wasn't I aware of this?" I demanded through gritted teeth, the need to punch *something* still rioting through me.

"Hasn't been a whole lot of time for a debrief, Viking," she explained cautiously, another hand coming up to my back in an attempt at a soothing stroke. "He was the lesser demon of all our demons right now. And he's the cutest of the bunch, though his face might not be as pretty anymore."

She swung her head around to examine my victim's face, scrunching her nose up at the swelling already filling out his shattered nose and cheeks.

"Yeah, you're no longer the prettiest, Lucky." She tsked, as if this revelation was a joke to her. "Guess you should have fessed up to Kellan before now."

"Me?" Lauchlan exclaimed, his voice a little less muffled as he pinched his nose to stop the bleeding. "Yourf a fecking double agent. Did youf tell this lot that?" He swung a hand up toward Aaron and Hillary.

"We knew this, Irishman," Aaron stoically announced. "You are the last to know."

"Well, I guess we're *all* in the know now." His slitted green eyes fell on Hillary. "Am I actually a part of the club now, or is Conan going to punch me again?"

"I'm going to punch you again," I answered with a sucker punch to the diaphragm, knocking the breath from his lungs. He wheezed and clutched his stomach, causing more blood to rush down his face and soak into his shirt.

I uncurled my fists and crossed my arms against my chest in satisfaction. I wasn't done with the fucker, not nearly. But knowing he hadn't actually hurt my Killer and she'd been aware of his motives this entire time made me hate him a little less.

Rodriguez left the room and returned with a warm cloth, handing it to the bleeding sap, who accepted it with a grateful grimace. I got comfortable on the opposite couch and turned the television on; we all settled in for the news.

Hillary sat next to me, with Aaron on her opposite side. Lauchlan stayed as far away from me as possible on the far side of the room, nursing his wounds as if he was near death.

Good fucking riddance.

Rodriguez caught my eye over Hillary's nestled head as we waited in stilted silence for the broadcast, his expression one of quiet solidarity.

The threesome we'd shared the other evening had caught me by surprise; Rodriguez wasn't a man I'd ever pictured myself with, let alone with Killer writhing between us, and yet, the chemistry had been fucking explosive. With everything else on our plate, I hadn't stopped to consider what it actually meant, but the heated, appraising stare he was shooting at me told me it was a moment that might bear repeating.

"Breaking news," the Channel 9 announcer declared, forcing me to face the screen. "Marco Alvarez, President and CEO of Alvarez International, a subsidiary of Predrolas Oil & Gas, is being taken into custody for a series of leaked photos and incriminating messages that appear to show Alvarez involved in some kind of sexual exploitation ring. Investigations are ongoing, and we'll continue to report on this as they come in."

Video footage of a frazzled Alvarez with flyaway hair and a rumpled shirt being carted away outside his office building by a few of my colleagues was satisfying to watch; I'd have preferred a takedown by bloody force, but this was the best we'd get given the circumstances.

Squeezing Hillary's shoulder, I turned to look at my cohorts in the room—even the fucker with the Rudolf nose. "This isn't even close to being over. We need to be prepared for any retaliation."

"We'll be ready," my Killer assured me, a grim smile and steely resolve creeping across her features. "Alvarez is tumbling down."

Her blue eyes shone at me, a cocktail of determination and malice.

"Next stop, Antonio."

CHAPTER 22

Aaron

Content warning: This chapter includes descriptions of sexual violence.

I was restless.

The caged tiger within me had prowled its cell long enough; my skin crawled from the monotony of security. I wasn't used to such a mundane life.

Mi Reina's basement apartment suited me well when it had only been a few weeks. Her condo was a vast improvement, with natural light and breathable mountain air, but a glass cage was still a cage.

Cora Flynn

Possibly, I had been a fool to believe in this arrangement. I trusted my beautiful cage master with my life; Kellan as well, but the execution of this plan was taking much longer than I'd given credit. Yet, I was a patient man.

I'd been born into a life of luxury and excess; despite not choosing my path in this world, I'd wanted for nothing. I'd endured the pain of torture, the guilt of disappointment, and the tormented fear of failure; Vicente had scarred my flesh while Veronica had scarred my mind—yet this feeling of helpless entrapment was its own form of mediocre agony.

The twitchy *Rojo* Irishman and I weren't so different after all.

Or perhaps, it was the encrypted message I'd received on my private dark web server. I was not an expert in such things; I only knew how to use the underground internet to reach out to our many associates in underground industries.

Someone had found me.

Veronica is hiring underage girls. Vicente is raping girls. If you're out there, please save us.

I had received the message four days ago, but the last four days could have been four years.

I hadn't had time to review with *Mi Reina*, nor was it the most appropriate use of time. Alvarez's tear down would inevitably bring down my parents with him, and I would bask in their demise long before I put them into coffins.

Veronica and Vicente would oversee the damage from their iron thrones, desperate to claim their power back. They had hitched their wagon to Alejandro, not Marco, but the media had not been kind to their associations. My parents did not entertain such human emotions as regret; they'd retreat into their anger before unleashing it into the most convenient outlet.

How fortunate for me that I was dead.

I signed onto the dark web to see if there was an update. A new file awaited me with several encrypted videos from the same source. I opened one, unprepared for its contents.

Three women, one looking barely older than a child, were cuffed in metal bondage straps in a dark room. The footage was dark and grainy, but the space resembled our questioning rooms in the basement of Club 7.

Two men stood behind them, brutally sodomizing their bodies as the women screamed out in anguish. The child-like woman sobbed as she watched, tears falling down her face in buckets.

This was not fulfilling a fantasy. It was brutal ownership in the most violent of ways, meant to tear down a human being to assert one's own puny idea of power.

Visceral rage raced through my veins and into my heart, its beat erratic and ferocious in my chest. Rape and assault were not the foundations of Club 7, or any of the other clubs. This abomination must be stopped.

Mi Reina was leading the Board of Directors in an emergency meeting since her company had signed agreements with Alvarez International. *Rojo* was cleaning out his desk at the office, and Kellan was meeting with his brothers to disband the rest of the men loyal to Alvarez's operations.

I was alone.

My gaze flitted back to the message on my screen, sent yesterday. Whoever had sent it left no trace of their identity. Perhaps I could use our resident hacker to identify the source.

That would take time, though, a luxury I could not afford. I'd made a commitment on my honor to the employees of Club 7; no harm would come to them at the hands of someone within its walls; that included the wandering eyes and hands of management.

Leaving now was a weighty risk; weekdays were quieter at the club, and I could enter via the back entrance to hide my arrival. Provided the electronic key pad remained the same, I could slip in, verify the truth, and come up with a plan to save the women before burning the building to the ground.

I had to consider *Mi Reina*'s fury for putting myself in harm's way. But did my life have more value than the people in my care?

I had to ascribe to her beliefs—we were more fortunate than most, with our wealth and influence, but our fortune at birth did not dictate our value above others.

She would understand after her rage subsided and she'd made me pay my penance in blood. It was a risk I was willing to take to ease the weight of my conscience.

I could not leave the condo myself. I had no vehicle here, or access to any of Hillary's which lay dormant in the garage.

I would have to phone a friend for my errand. 'Friend' was surely a loose term, but the only person I could think of who would entertain such an idea without deterring me from my mission. A skilled arsonist accompaniment would also be an asset.

Reluctantly, I texted *Rojo*.

Aaron Rodriguez: I am in need of your assistance, Caperocita Roja.

Lauchlan O'Donnell: King Strippy! What can I do for ya?

Aaron Rodriguez: Please come pick me up.

Lauchlan O'Donnell: Am I going to get a reason, or did the Robot just run out of juice?

Aaron Rodriguez: I will call Kellan.

Lauchlan O'Donnell: Just putting ya on, King Roboto. I'll see ya soon.

Lauchlan O'Donnell: She's gonna kill you.

I looked at my clothing and my brow wrinkled in distaste. After years of wearing fine tailored suits and Italian shoes, I was now a casual clothes man. I had never shown up to any of our clubs in anything but my best clothing; I would stand out like the sorest of thumbs.

Lauchlan had a collection of suits still hanging in the closet in the bedroom he'd vacated since I'd moved in; perhaps he had something I could wear.

I rifled through the racks of suit jackets and pants, finding a charcoal gray suit similar enough to my previous collection to pass for the day. I was taller and slightly broader, but not by enough that anyone should notice. I borrowed a freshly starched dress shirt and put on the ensemble as I impatiently waited for him to arrive.

The longer time passed, the more unsettled about this decision I became, but I had a duty to fulfill. If the demons that spawned me were indeed abusing their power in the most egregious ways, it was up to me to right their wrongs in whatever way I could.

Lauchlan texted me when he arrived, directing me to the private parking garage level that only housed Hillary's many cars. He met me with an infuriating smirk, but the guarded stare in his eyes showed he was troubled.

"Are you sure about this?" he questioned as I lowered myself into his ridiculously low muscle car. "Blondie's likely to kill us both, yeh know."

"She will understand," I replied smoothly. Uncertainty lanced my gut, but I pressed onward. "My employees are in danger."

Lauchlan's gaze blazed with determined fire. "Then let's go save some worker bees, yeh?" He gunned the engine and roared out of the parking garage in a spurt of obnoxious smoke, but I appreciated the sentiment of the childish Irishman.

"Wait a minute—is that my suit?" His attention left the road and his accusing stare swept over me as if I'd attended the murder of his puppy.

"It is now *my* suit." I smoothed my hands over the mid-level fabric and shifted uncomfortably in its tight confines. I did not want this mediocre suit in my wardrobe repertoire, but as it was now all I had, I would suffer the consequences. "I will not need it after today."

"Might need it for your funeral," he muttered under his breath, but he said nothing more about it. "Where to?" he asked instead when we came to the roundabout leading through town.

"Club 7," I directed, and he weaved through the Carlisle streets as if we were in a cliched Los Angeles Street race. "I will tell you when to turn."

Admittedly, the man got us there more quickly than Jacques would have. He likely had sensed the urgency in my tone and body language because he continued to glance at me from the corner of his eye. I was concerned about the lack of eyes on the road, but I felt safe in his care. Lauchlan was reckless and woefully ignorant, but his skills were vast and often underestimated.

I was learning not to underestimate him.

Instead of pressing me for more information about the brothel's activities, he broke the silence with a different question.

"Why are you trusting me with this? I'd have thought you'd want my head on a spike."

Ahh, yes. His game with *Mi Reina*. I was surprised to learn of such a game, but I was also learning my love thrived on unpredictable challenges; *Rojo* embodied that like pliable silicon.

"You did not betray her, no? She was aware of your intentions and played with you, anyway. What is to come of you and her is between the two of you." I caught his wandering eyes, forcing his gaze from the road once again with the hardened malice in my stare.

"You choose to play me, little Irishman, and I will chop off your limbs and feed them to mountain lions while you watch, slowly bleeding to death."

He nodded as if this were an appropriate punishment for such a crime.

"Noted," he responded with ease; threats on his life were normal for him, it seemed. "Kellan will beat you to it, though. I might be bled out by the morning."

I watched the traffic with blind eyes, the unfamiliar feeling of anxious energy worming its way beneath the folds of my skin.

"Kellan is a protector, as am I. I choose to trust that *Mi Reina* can take care of herself, and will request me when she needs me. Kellan is an impatient man and does not wait for her to ask. He will learn to trust her in time, or he will not. What is to come of them is between them."

"How are you so calm about all of this?" *Rojo's* voice took on an incredulous tinge. "You're really are Mr. Roboto."

I did not love this nickname, but I had been called far worse insults in my lifetime. This man would not gain the satisfaction of riling me in the way he excelled at riling Kellan.

"There are two things I am most certain of in this life. Hillary Lane and my love for her. The rest is immaterial. You will be here next week or you will not, and that is at her discretion."

I turned my whole body to face him, which was difficult in the confines of his sporty clown vehicle.

"You were going to thieve from her and she chose not to harm you. Perhaps you should express more gratitude to the woman who spared your life, when she can take the air you breathe and force you to choke on it."

I didn't give him time to respond. Club 7 was in my sights, and I needed to focus on my mission ahead. No other woman in my care would be touched without her permission.

"Wait here," I commanded once he had pulled up to the darkened private employee entrance at the rear of the building. He gave me a two-fingered salute, and I hurried toward the building I'd swore I'd never see again.

To my relief, the code still worked on the keypad. As a precaution, I did not use my own—I chose a generic one we kept for emergency use when an employee got locked out of the building. I slipped into the familiar hallway; its dark, glittering walls now foreign to me as I crept down them towards the staircase to my old office.

I wasn't used to creeping about like a thief in the night; I commanded this space and everyone within it. It may have been more suitable for Lauchlan to complete this mission on my behalf, given his proclivities.

But no—this burden was mine alone to bear. My birthright made me my parent's insufferable keeper until such time I made them suffer themselves.

I saw no sign of Rosa near her usual perch by the stairwell; I didn't have the time or opportunity to search the building and remain unseen. If I were to find an employee and pay them to remain quiet about my appearance, I could verify if the message was true. My arrival was too big of a risk to not leave with answers.

The hallway opened up to a series of doors; all private rooms for our—their—most profile clients. I jiggled the door handle on the first one and found it open. These rooms had automatic locks if the room was in use, so I moved to the next one in sequence. I had no use for empty rooms.

"Mr. Rodriguez!"

A high-pitched voice squeaked behind me, and I turned quickly to press a finger to my lips. A woman's wide blue eyes peered back at me in wild surprise. For the first time, I cursed not knowing the employee's names; it would have been useful to call her by name to coax her into spilling her secrets.

She looked vaguely familiar, but the outfit she wore— the black skirt and sequined bustier with red sequined stilettos, told me she was one of our attendees, hired and designed to service the fantasies of other men and women on the floor.

I beckoned her into the vacant room. She hesitantly followed me into the sexual fantasy space, where a bondage bed lay amidst black and red painted walls.

"I have not been here. No one can know the truth. Can I trust you with this?"

Fearful eyes, clouded with confusion and apprehension, stared up at me through the dim light. I stepped back from her to give her space. I had unintentionally crowded her with the magnitude of my anxiety.

When she confirmed with a nod of trepidation, I continued. "I have heard rumors that my staff are being abused. Is this true?"

I had no time to ply her with compliments or enter small talk designed to set her at ease. An uncomfortable itch under my skin grew hotter with each passing moment; I was aware of the limited time on my clock.

"I—er—well..." Her gaze flicked nervously to the door behind us. "Nothing has happened to me," she squeaked out in a rush, and her cheeks flushed crimson under the amber pot lights. "But I know of a few girls—er—women, who've been touched... inappropriately."

The itch mutated into a searing burn beneath my flesh. In the several years I'd overseen and built this thriving business, I'd been forced to rid the brothels of opportunistic men who'd felt entitled to unwilling bodies; who abused the fantasy of rape by bypassing the several safeties put in place for the workers willing to entertain such fantasies, instead taking their power and choice away altogether.

I'd stripped the flesh off of a client who'd taken my employee's rights into his own hands. Another, I'd broken every bone in the hand he'd used to strike an unwilling attendee. I had no such patience for men who broke the rules. *My* rules.

"Explain," I growled, the word dipped in acid as I barely held my anger in check.

"Vicente has brought in some... friends," she stuttered, desperate fear burning in her gaze as she peered back at me on trembling feet. "They haven't been following the... rules," she finished lamely, and my impatience grew to irritation.

"Elaborate," I insisted, using all my self-control not to step into her personal space to threaten her with my size. I was not willing to burn down the house without direct confirmation of misdeeds, and "not following the rules" was not enough to give me what I needed.

She shrunk in on herself despite me staying well out of her comfort zone; the rage emanated from every pore of my skin, the vibrations of it pulsing into the surrounding air.

"My friend Chauntelle was raped." Her head hung, gaze glued to the floor, as she spoke the next words. "And they've brought in younger employees. Last shift, they forced me to work with a fifteen-year-old."

Vicente was going to die. *Today.*

"Thank you," I gritted out between clenched teeth. "I will pay you to keep my appearance here quiet."

She met my stare and the fear faded for a brief moment, replaced with proud defiance. "Mr. Rodriguez, save those girls. Save me. I don't need any money from you."

"It is done," I replied, tone resolute. The determination to rid the earth of the scourge of my father and his desperation to prove his tiny cock was something to be admired filled my every blood cell. I held open the door for her and gestured for her to leave.

"Speak of this to no one," I reminded her as she scurried through the opening, fear lacing her posture once more. "I will put Vicente in his place."

Once she had vacated the corridor, I quickly fled down the opposite way, urgency biting on my heels. Lauchlan was still waiting for me, and I would need an hour off the premises to formulate a plan. My favorite dagger was not enough to exact the justice needed here.

My footfalls echoed down the polished concrete floor of the rear hallway. I had rounded the corner to the door when an icy prickle swept down my spine. Someone was watching me. I felt their presence in the shadows like a dark cloud covering the sun.

Before I could turn to confirm my suspicions, a warm hand and sharp prick bit at my neck. I crumpled to my knees and my world faded into inky blackness, all sounds muffling save for the final few words:

"Welcome back, Mr. Rodriguez."

I was not a man who indulged in drugs. Vicente had subjected me to many illicit substances over the years to understand their effects and to coach my brain into working through their cloying strength.

I'd been injected with a depressant of some kind. Designed to incapacitate me and make me pliant in the users' hold. I'd been trained to fight the drug's effects, and the dosage was too low for a man of my size. I was groggy, but aware; aware enough to know I was still in Club 7, in one of the basement rooms designed for torturing the abusive clients. My limbs were trapped in the grip of bound ropes, my arms and legs tied to the arms and legs of the chair.

How ironic it was I who was now in the chair when I had come to save them.

"You are a tricky man to find, Aaron," a sultry voice purred in my ear, and I jolted at the warm breath against my skin. Perhaps I was more out of it than I'd expected.

I fought against the nausea, breathing large gulps of stale air through my nose to settle the roiling acid of my stomach.

I said nothing, choosing to wait out the woman who spoke so candidly to me, waiting for her to show her face. She did not disappoint; tanned, creamy skin, long dark hair and even darker eyes came into view as my attendant, the one whom I'd rescued from my father's deplorable treatment, stared back at me, her expression a mix of satisfaction and curiosity.

Though surprising, I was relieved to see it was her and not Vicente or one of his loyal men. Vicente would murder me within moments to set the example and remove me from his list of challenges. This woman might not have such vehement motivations.

"I wasn't sure if that ploy would work," she mused. She toyed with the sharpened blade in her grip, holding it casually as if she knew how to use it. "We weren't convinced you were still alive, but I knew when you tried to rescue me from Vicente that you had a weak point. I've been working double shifts, just in case."

Perhaps her motivations were not so pliable, after all. I had considered the message was a trap to draw me out of hiding, but her involvement was certainly a surprise. How she'd known to manipulate me was another thing altogether.

A brittle laugh escaped her full lips as she assessed my dubious expression. "I know I'm not your weak point, Aaron. You didn't even bother to learn my name." Her tone bordered on playful, its upturned lilt suggesting this was all a game. "It wouldn't have mattered. It wouldn't have been my real one."

The fuzz in my brain waged war as I pulled the strand of a murky memory. She had shown up to our ribbon-cutting day. I had only glimpsed her, but I'd known she was there.

"Who are you?"

I folded the words over my tongue as I stared back at the beautiful woman who'd once satisfied my every sexual need for a healthy paycheck. We held no loyalty to each other, no pretense of connection, despite the connection of our bodies once upon a time. Simply a transactional relationship.

How could I use that transaction to my benefit? I worked through the puzzle pieces of my thoughts as my brain fought to put them back together.

"My name—my real name," she corrected, "is Carmen Delgado. You have been my prize for a long time, Aaron Rodriguez."

The name was not one I knew.

"I'm afraid your name means nothing to me." I shrugged one shoulder in both an admission and to loosen the fibers against my skin. I'd trained to release myself from such devices, though I hadn't been tied up for anything but bondage play in two decades. My lack of practice would be my downfall.

Her smile widened, her straight teeth resembling fangs in the ominous air. "Of course it doesn't, you uncultured bear," she cooed, condescending to me as if I were a child. "Why would you suspect the woman you paid to wet your cock would be the very assassin hired to kill you?"

A lesser man might cower in fear; I was not trembling in my boots—my interest was piqued. Who would hire someone to assassinate me when Kellan had already been tasked with the job? We'd kept our list of enemies small over the years, and we held most of the power. I was at a loss.

Unless...

"Who do you work for?"

Her grin mimicked a shark's maw, with far more menace. "For a man who needed such assurances that you would *actually* end up dead. There is some mistrust in the family right now, I'm afraid."

She waved her hand airily, and the dagger glinted in the soft golden light with each movement.

So, Antonio then. Kellan had admitted the relationship with his father was eroding; we had commiserated over our parentage together one evening. Our fathers would certainly put failsafes in places to ensure our follow-through. Had I been tasked with the same directive, no doubt Vicente would do the same. Familial trust was a myth in this business. Our blood was not thicker than water or wine; it thinned with every breach of disappointment until the bond was broken altogether.

I continued the micro-shifting of my muscles against the nylon cords, grateful for the cheaper suit wool that would work against the rope on my behalf. A more expensive fabric would tear. *Rojo*'s suit may become the luckiest garment in my possession.

"And what is it you plan to do with me?" My voice remained calm—disassociated from the panic of the situation and the ravenous gleam in her eye that hungered for my death. "And what can I do to change your mind?"

"Oh, you won't be changing my mind, *cerdito*," she taunted and held the shimmering blade to my throat. "But I get paid more for prolonging your suffering, so we will be here a while."

Without pause, she plunged the dagger deep into my abdomen. White hot pain consumed my insides and I fought to maintain consciousness. My hands almost free from the cords, I pasted my lips shut, determined not to give her the pained cry she was craving, but the action took every ounce of self-control I bore.

She stepped back, cocking her head to admire the blood staining through the crisp shirt.

"Beautiful," she breathed, the sadistic gleam of a killer finally entering her gaze. "You're about to become your own work of art, Mr. Rodriguez. I hope you enjoy painting with blood."

The knife drove into the muscle of my thigh, ripping the flesh into jagged tissue before I fell back into the bliss of unconsciousness.

CHAPTER 23

Lauchlan

*T*ap, tap, tappity, tap.

Tap, tap, tippy-tap, tappity-tippy, tap, tap.

Tap, tap, tap—Christ, this was boring.

How Mr. Roboto had convinced me to be the driver of this rescue mission that was sure to get us both killed—by Blondie, *not* any baddies—was still a mystery to me. I'd been wrapping up a goodbye lunch with Gertie, using the very bogus excuse that my work visa was no longer valid if my employer was incarcerated, when I'd received his text.

That the Robot had no one else to call on for this madness was not lost on me, but you could bet I'd take advantage of some bonding time with the broody no-longer-a-businessman. And we had a nice heart-to-heart alongside the mission. I was gonna be calling him Daddy in no time.

He'd been fucking forever, though. Nearly an hour, and unless he'd risked castration and get a rub-n-tug while he was in there—something that would *really* get him killed by Blondie—my spidey senses were telling me something was off.

I'd parked out of the way from the parking lot cameras peeping eyes at the rear of the building with a full view of the back door. For the first time in my life, I wished my car was a wee bit more discreet than M&M blue, but I hadn't considered my work would evolve into hacking with assassins.

I still didn't have a plan for my painting situation. I'd placed all my eggs in Hillary's basket like a happy little Easter bunny, but now I had to come up with something to get out of my contract with The Six. I was conniving on the best of days, but I was still sitting on a fat zero for a solution. And I wasn't going to find it in a brothel parking lot.

I'd turned on the radio to bide my time; Americans loved their talk radio. News, news, and more news, except none of it was *actually* news—just the same rubbish shyte on repeat.

A shadow filled my driver's side window and nearly tore me out of my skin. The door was yanked open and two large hands gripped my jacket and lifted me off my seat.

"What. In. The. Fuck. Are. you doing here?" Kellan snarled through gritted teeth, his voice hovering between murderous and double murderous. I should be terrified of him—this Cartel killer who broke my beautiful nose and was double my size with triple the Big Dick Energy—but I wasn't. The man was becoming a growly teddy bear toward me.

I was in for a world of pain, though.

"Before you kill me..." I held up one finger to stop him, as pointless as it was. "Yeh should know this was not my idea," I pointed the finger toward the building behind him, "and Roboto hasn't come out in a while."

"Fuck." The Viking released me and dropped me to the ground, turning toward the building instead. "Fucking Rodriguez," he cursed again. "Grab your fucking gun. We're going in."

Three musketeers for the win today. Never would have predicted this outcome, but I was down to clown.

"Okay, so there'll be three funerals on the docket today." I reached for the gun under my seat and slid out from between the car and Kellan's massive bulk, ready for the showdown of a lifetime. "Fucked if I do, fucked if I don't. Might as well go out with a bang."

The blond baddie was ignoring me, glaring at the building like it owed him money.

"I know the layout of this club," he said in a low growl. "It was originally built with Antonio's blessing. We'll start with the private suites on the lower levels—it's where they beat the shit out of the Johns who get too carried away."

"What makes you think he'll be there?" I followed his lead as we walked casually to the rear door as if we belonged there. I attempted to hide my face from the cameras by burying my nose in my coat collar.

"It's where I'd take him."

Fair enough.

He attached a slick device onto the electronic keypad, and numbers lined up in sequence like we were in the mafia version of the Matrix.

"Fecking sweet!" I exclaimed, impressed. "I need to get my hands on one of those."

"Come on," Kellan beckoned me inside, then closed the heavy steel door behind us. We were at the end of a long, dark corridor, with not a single soul to be seen.

Thank you, universe.

Cora Flynn

I enjoyed a good adventure like the best of con men, but I was unprepared to die today. I'd suddenly found a few things to live for, and I hoped to enjoy a few more tastes of Hillary's heaven before I was put into the dirt. Or a pond or… whatever method of death Aaron's family liked to deal in.

I really wasn't keen to find out either way.

"Wait," I hissed, realization dawning on me. "How did you find us? Weren't you with Tweedle-Dee and Tweedle-Dum-Dum today?"

"I had them come to me," he grunted, creeping down the hallway on stealthy feet for such a big fuck. "I don't like being too far away from Killer right now."

"And you tracked me?" I guessed as I pointed to my arm, knowing full well the broody, controlling motherfucker would have been watching my every move now he knew my true identity. "Can't keep your eyes off me, eh, Conan?"

I received a serious case of pissed-off mafia man side-eye, and it only made the man hotter than Hell in a heat wave. But he ignored me, because the man had the self-control of a vegan on a bacon farm.

We rounded a corner, still seeing no one—did anyone actually *work* here?—and he led us down another short hallway to a gloomy concrete set of stairs. "Good thing I am. Thanks to you, this stupid fucker is going to get himself killed."

We descended the super creepy steps into the sex dungeon below. The Barbarian was riveting to watch in action. All muscles bunching and radiating "don't fuck with me" energy while he prowled through the building like we were on an episode of *Blue Lights.* Had there ever been a mafia-man/FBI combo before? Stuff of a Hollywood movie, that. And fuck me, I wanted to know the story.

At the bottom of the stairs was another windowless corridor that looked like it had been intentionally left to look creepy, down to the swinging bare bulbs from the ceiling and the crumbling plaster walls. I held my gun tighter, keeping my guard up as I heard the soundtrack in my head to some horror film where the daft brunette gets gutted by the killer.

I covered his back while he peered into the tiny windows at the top of each metal door on either side of us.

"Mr. Roboto doesn't feel much for anything," I whispered conversationally, despite the creepy murder vibes. "Gotta wonder why he'd risk it all for this—"

"Hold it," Kellan hissed as he peered through a metal door's teeny window. "We're here."

Adrenaline burst through my brain like tiny little fireworks. *We're here?* Did that mean Aaron was just sitting back, having a yarn with another baddie sexpot and forgot the time or—

Kellan let out a string of colorful Spanish curses as he kept to the side of the door, motioning for me to do the same.

The glass shattered outward and smothered the two of us in teeny shards. I rolled to the left while Kellan leaped to the opposite side as a tiny bullet lodged itself into the opposite wall.

Without pausing, the Viking crept low and shot the door handle clean off. He only made eye contact with me for a split second before he kicked in the door and rolling through it like Mark Wahlberg in—anything Mark Wahlberg's ever done.

Another stifled pop of a silenced pistol echoed through the chamber, and I cursed colorfully in English before crouching low and following in after him to cover his arse; I didn't even think these two liked each other, and now my blond buddy was just going in, guns-a-blazing, to rescue a bloke who'd brought a knife to a gunfight.

Bet ya he wouldn't be risking his neck to save *me.* Good thing I was the hero type and would throw myself into chaos to save him instead.

I mean, don't threaten a mate with a good time.

The dark room reminded me of the basement Kellan had attempted his sexy torture session in—dim, dank, and dirty. A lone figure slumped in the center, head hung like he was already a corpse.

Fuck.

Kellan fired another shot, and in a blinding blur of motion, a tiny figure slipped behind me and wrapped dainty little arms around my neck. Before I could fight them off, cool metal kissed my temple.

"Drop it, Kellan," a calm, feminine voice commanded as she wrapped her arm tighter into my windpipe, choking me out and bringing me to my knees within seconds.

Not even in the action for two seconds, and I was already the sitting duck. I needed to up my assassin training skills when I got us out of this one.

I was a wee bit worried about me, but more worried about the man who hadn't even moved since we'd come into the room. The air smelled of gunpowder and metal, and whatever sweet perfume the lass behind me was wearing. Not like death yet, but that was coming.

"Carmen," he replied, his gruff, growly voice his version of calm. "Care to explain what you're doing with Aaron Rodriguez?"

What the—he *knew* this woman? If air wasn't being cut off from my brain, I might have put two-and-two together but—

"Care to explain why you are after a dead man that you were already to have killed?" she countered, her lips purring the words into the shell of my ear as her grip tightened even further.

Ahh. So, she was a baddie for the Cartel. Didn't need the old oxygen to make that connection. That wasn't good. If they knew Kellan hadn't killed Aaron like he said he did then...

Time for Plan B.

Kellan, if you can read my mind right now, you stall her while I play dead.

I willed my muscles to go limp in her hold and dropped to the concrete floor like a stone, pretending to pass out sooner than she expected. Her grip loosened in surprise, giving me just enough wiggle room to buck her off my back. The move propelled her forward into the empty space between me and the big oaf.

She was quick for a tiny thing. Before I could re-grip my weapon and point it at her, she sprang to the side and whipped around, her gun pointed at me, and another smaller pistol pointed at Kellan.

It'd be fucking impressive if it wasn't my life on the line. We were in a triangle stand-off, and currently, one of us was going to end up dead.

I finally got a good look at her. Pretty, with long dark hair and dark eyes, and a snarl that rivaled my Blondie's when she was pissed off. I'd hedge my bets with the woman of my dreams, but somehow, I didn't think that sort of charm would work on this one. She seemed more of the psycho-twin type.

Everyone, remain calm.

To be fair, I appeared to be the only one freaking out.

"Carmen," Kellan commanded again and his voice rang with authority like a true cartel king. "Stand down on this one. You don't want to make an enemy of me."

"You are wrong, *Careverga*." Her gaze trailed over to Aaron's lifeless body; while she was distracted, I snuck a peek, too. His head hung limp to his chest, with bloody gashes showing through his clothes all over his body; my favorite suit ruined.

Not the point, Locke.

The brunette turned her attention back on us with a hard, no-fucks-to-give stare. "I do not want to make an enemy of Antonio. And since he has already signed this check, I intend to follow through."

Before I even blinked, she dropped to the ground, swapping out the tiny pistol for a knife in her boot. She threw it in Aaron's direction at the same second Kellan shot her in the shoulder.

She let out a howl of pain, but before she could retaliate, I shot her in the thigh. The small-caliber round pierced through her flesh, crippling her and sending her to the ground. Kellan's gun had a silencer; mine did not. The sound ricocheted in the small room and blasted my eardrum, definitely letting everyone know in the building we were here for a not-good time.

We needed to get the fuck out of here *now*. I didn't think brothels would call the police, but they probably had their own reinforcement, and I wasn't keen to meet them.

I turned to my most unlikely partner in crime. "You deal with her, I'll get the Robot."

I spun on my heel to run to Mr. Roboto's aid, only to see his body curled into a ball on the floor, his arms and legs unbound. In the chaos, I hadn't heard him crash out of the chair.

Had the fucker been *pretending* to pass out? Or came to while we were there? It was the only way to explain how he'd avoided a knife to his chest. He'd fooled me—but that older stab gash in his stomach was definitely not a sham. It was too close to his liver to be a flesh wound.

His skin was as pale as mine, which on the well-tanned Colombian, meant he was in a *very* bad way. Panic, real and raw, crept into my belly.

"He needs a doc, Kellan, *now.*"

The man was at my side in an instant, moving me out of the way before gently hauling Aaron upward to carrying him bridal-style. I ripped off the sleeve of my jacket and held the fabric to Aaron's stomach, but the blood loss was already so great I didn't know if pressure would make a difference.

I didn't want Aaron to die. I didn't want Hillary to kill me, and I didn't want him to die.

Carmen—whatever the hell her name was—laid out on the floor, weapons removed, with hateful eyes watching us. Her wounds would heal, and apparently the Barbarian was more concerned about saving Aaron than killing her. I was on board with that plan.

"This isn't over, Kellan," she spat, her threat so jagged it could slice through steel.

Instead of replying, he took off on a light jog down the hall. Should I kill her, or...?

"Kill her!" Kellan bellowed, his voice carrying down the hall as I stared dumbly at the beautiful assassin.

Answered that question, then. Fuck. I'd never killed a woman before. Never actually murdered *anyone*—injured, sure. Maimed—once or twice. The most brutal I'd ever been was stabbing that fucker in the dick who'd hurt Blondie, but he'd already been dead.

I'd never taken a life. That wasn't my bag—I ruined rich lives by taking their precious little billionaire possessions, but murder...

I stared into her violent eyes; loathsome hate stared back at me, like I'd already killed her entire family and stolen her puppy, too.

A kill shot would be a kindness. I wanted her to hurt for what she'd done to our third musketeer, but I couldn't watch the life leave her eyes while I did it.

I aimed at her heart, fired, and spun on my heel, unwilling to see the aftermath of what I'd done. Watching Aaron strip another human differed from putting the bullet into the heart myself.

Apparently, my stomach wasn't as iron as I thought.

I chased Kellan back up the stairs, keeping my gun at the ready in case we encountered anyone.

We didn't see a soul until we got to the second corridor. Three women in skimpy suits screamed in fright when we raced through the hallway to the rear door, but they did nothing to stop us. I ran in front of Kellan to hold open the door for the two of them, and we rushed out into the parking lot.

Aaron had passed out again, his limp head bobbing up and down in Kellan's arms.

Fuck, fuck, fuck!

Kellan raced to his own vehicle, and I followed him, climbing into the driver's seat of the Jeep while he laid Aaron down on the backseat. He jumped into the passenger seat without complaint.

"Where am I going?" I was desperate to get out of here, but had no idea where to go. We couldn't risk being followed back to Hillary's condo, and Kellan's house was too much of an obvious target.

Kellan reached back to press his hand on Aaron's wound, applying pressure as our passenger let out a groan of agony in his barely conscious state. "Hillary owns his old warehouse now—the one you followed us to. She finished the construction contract, so we'll lie low there for now."

"He'd gonna die without a doctor, Conan." I couldn't keep the worry out of my voice, my heart actually tugging for our android side-kick.

"I have someone I can trust," Kellan grunted, pulling out his phone with his other hand. "I'll have them meet us there."

"Tell them to bring blood—loads of it. He's gonna need a transfusion."

I received a somber nod as I peeled out of the parking lot toward the warehouse; that one night changing my life all those months ago. I'd chosen my fate when I joined Fight Club then—and now that we'd been bonded in blood, I wasn't willing to let him go just yet.

We'd get Aaron the medical attention he needed, and then when his life wasn't on the line, we'd come up with a plan.

Fuck... who was going to tell Blondie?

Cora Flynn

CHAPTER 24

Hillary

Directing men in every corner of my life was exhausting.

Admittedly, the Board of Directors for Lane Enterprises was almost a fair 50-50 split of genders, with a non-binary member as well, but there was something about veteran businessmen who thought they knew it all that grated on my nerves like a lemon zester to the nipples.

The one-hour defensive planning meeting had turned into three. Because I'd known what was coming, I'd already put together a PR plan, but it had taken hours to convince certain curmudgeons it was the best option. They were useful curmudgeons—poking holes in my theories to come up with the best decision was far better than a team of sniveling 'yes men'—but their pointed questions and need for answers I couldn't admit I knew had been an irritating game of shells, when I had far more important things to do.

Important things, like protecting my own ass from Alvarez.

I wasn't naïve: this wasn't anywhere close to being over. Alvarez had been released on bail and placed on monitored house arrest. He'd spend the next few months fighting every tiny legal loophole of this case, and unless they froze his assets—which Kellan was fighting for on his side of the fence—he'd have a bottomless pit of money to throw into his appeal.

He had millions at his disposal. I had billions, though, so no amount of bribery was going to get him a winning verdict. When he'd exhausted all his resources and he was finally thrown in prison, Kellan would arrange for a very painful death through one of the incarcerated Carlos Cartel gang members. Aaron had voted for disembowelment, but I was still vying for castration with a slow bleed-out from the femoral artery. Time would tell.

We'd taken all precautions to be untraceable, but very few things remained *actually* untraceable in this era of technology. It was a fool's errand to think we were invincible. I was just waiting for some form of retaliation from the Alvarez family and planned to lie low over the next few days to watch his next moves on the board.

Joey glanced at me every few minutes in the rearview mirror as we drove back to my condo, her brows knitted in a frown. I'd informed my teams the Palace had burned down because of an unforeseen electrical issue, and she'd digested that information without question. The people I hired were intelligent, and she knew a storm was brewing in the electrically charged air around us, but I was having a hard time telling her which front to expect it from.

Alvarez? Antonio? The Six? Due to my merry band of murderous men, we now had an entire fleet of enemies at our back.

My men. A few months ago, I wouldn't have called any man in this world "mine," but now, I had three who'd showed they'd move the world for me—or at least murder my enemies with just cause, and truthfully, that meant a hell of a lot more.

Kellan's overbearing protectiveness drove me up the wall; it also made me feel a sense of safety and security knowing his watchful eyes would never stray too far, and he'd leap to be my sword or shield at any cost.

Aaron's devotion made me feel precious and cherished; his unwavering commitment strengthened my resolve. I knew I could break into a million pieces and he would glue every single one of them back with perfect care.

Lucky's casual approach to life disarmed me; he coaxed me out of my protective casing and knew how to show me the lighter side of the darkness we tread. He balanced my sharp edges with his smooth lines and soft smiles, and I craved his whimsy, even when I wanted to punch it out of him.

Four dark souls exorcising their demons through an unlikely combination of revenge and sexual tension—it was the plot of an excellent book.

I'd cautioned all my men to be vigilant. I was grateful they had the skills to take care of themselves, but the roiling sensation of sparklers going off in my gut all day had been enough to put this seasoned vigilante on edge.

Thankfully, the world believed Aaron Rodriguez was dead. Veronica and Vicente were currently being raked naked through burning coals at their recent shift in allegiances. Had he been alive to see it, Aaron would have been coerced to take the fall—or planted as the scapegoat without his knowledge. We would watch their palace burn together from the comfort of our own. Then, once it was nothing but a pile of powdered ashes, we'd take out their brothel network, too.

I'd tasked Lauchlan with his own plan for dealing with The Six. We couldn't afford an additional war front with another criminal organization; he'd find a way to charm them the way he charmed everyone else when he couldn't come up with the painting. Then we'd run some of our own reconnaissance in the background. I wanted to know who'd hired him.

You didn't get to be rich and powerful without a lineup of enemies waiting to take their swing at you with maces and pitchforks; the list of culprits was as long as the Nile. When we found them, they'd learn the true consequences of fucking with Hillary Lane.

My long-term plan for Antonio was still very much in play, and ruining Alvarez's company would only make for an easier transition to attack mode when the timing was right. Right now was most definitely not the time to piss off both mobsters in my backyard—but it was coming.

Traffic was significantly backed up in the downtown core, so I browsed through my messages, surprised I had seen nothing come through from Aaron or Lucky. Kellan and his brothers were disbanding the last few outposts for Alvarez's gangs in Sequoia, but Lucky should have been home by now after clearing out his desk.

I really didn't like this Mother Hen hat I was wearing. It was as unfamiliar to me as an Amish bonnet, and it did nothing to complement my killer outfit.

Still...

I sent them all a message on the new group chat I'd created, asking for a check in. Then I shoved my phone in my purse, desperate to unplug for a few minutes. I'd convince Kellan to spar with me this evening to rid my body of some of this tension. Then I'd convince him to use me for his pleasure and we could escape into each other for a little while.

Or maybe we could re-live the threesome of the other night. In my darkest sexual fantasies, I'd never considered these two Alpha males sharing me between them, or ever sharing themselves with each other, but the moment had been the perfect melding of sweat-slicked bodies and desperate desire. I replayed every delicious second in my mind as Joey weaved through the stalled cars along the freeway, closing my eyes to relive their taste on my tongue and their cocks stuffed into my—

"Ms. Lane, are you hearing this?" Joey interrupted the best part, but when my eyes flew opened to see deep concern saturating her stare, I straightened in my seat.

"Sorry, what was that?"

She wordlessly turned up the sound on the radio she had been listening to quietly up front, and a male news announcer's voice flooded the cab of the G-Wagon.

"They're calling her the 'Mutilation Mistress.' Anonymous sources report that this woman has been targeting high-profile men in Sequoia county for over a year, forcefully castrating them with a team of mercenary killers, and then blackmailing them once released. Three victims have come forward, and local police are investigating what they are calling the most gruesome serial mutilator since Jeffrey Dahmer, although at this time, there is no confirmation that she's actually killed any of her victims."

A ravenous fear gripped my belly, its familiar claws holding me hostage as I listened to the radio with rapt attention.

"David Owens, recognized military hero and husband of Sandra Owens, reported his wife missing just two weeks ago. In an updated recount, he asserts that she'd called him from a truck stop north of Carlisle, claiming she'd been drugged and captured by a team of masked men, then held captive and tortured in a padded cell by a woman. Sandra had escaped her captivity and was waiting for her husband

to come meet her, but she never arrived at her destination. It is unclear if these two cases are related, but we've learned that this is also an active investigation. An anonymous tip from Carlisle Police indicated that the Sequoia office of the FBI will be brought in to take over from here."

How in the ever-loving fuck was I not informed of this? I had eyes and ears everywhere; Kellan had eyes and ears everywhere. How had he missed this?

I sought Joey's eyes in the rearview mirror once again, catching the fierce stare of solidarity. Whatever this was, we were in this together. "Get home as fast as you can."

She gunned the engine and squeezed through impossible spaces while I frantically dialed Sammy.

"Shut everything down," I ordered brusquely when he picked up on the second ring. "Disband the team, offload the equipment. We're going underground for a little while."

"On it, *Ojitos.*"

I hung up and called Kellan. I was sent directly to his voicemail. I dialed Aaron; after six rings, I heard his smooth tenor come through the line, his answering machine tricking me for the briefest of seconds into thinking he was on the other end. Lucky didn't answer his phone either.

Panic seared through my guts in burning waves. Something was very wrong.

When we arrived at the condo, I raced through my private lower-level parking garage, Joey on my heels, before the agonizing elevator trip up to my floor stalled us.

A jumbled mass of thoughts tumbled through my mind at light speed. Where were they? How had the media found out about us? Had I covered my tracks enough so all leads couldn't be traced back to me? Where were they?

I'd check their trackers as soon as I got inside my condo. I wouldn't feel any semblance of safety until I was within the walls of my home.

Withdrawing my gun from my purse, I readied myself for whatever lay on the other side of the elevator door. Joey and I exchanged a solemn nod, her controlled calm a much-needed balm to my raging insides.

"Aaron?" I screeched as the door opened and I raced through my condo. Joey and I moved from room to room with our weapons raised, finding no one waiting for us in the silence of the rooms. "Lucky!?"

I stood in his empty bedroom, the faint crease of Aaron's body on top of the duvet still an imprint in the bed clothing. I fought my body to get my breathing under control. In the last two weeks, panic had become a clinging force holding me in its clutches and tethering to my soul. I didn't panic. I was *Hillary Lane*, for fuck's sake.

"Ms. Lane, you're going to want to see this," Joey called, her usually stoic voice grim.

I retreated from the room and found her standing at the entry to the living room with her arms folded across her chest, as if shielding me from what lay behind her. My gaze moved past her to the room beyond.

A blueish lump nestled in pink was set on the coffee table. As I moved closer, I realized the blue was strands of cobalt hair, the lump a severed head, the pink congealed blood that had hardened to the glass.

Blackbird's lifeless eyes stared back at me, the blank eye sockets pulling me into their terrible, barren void.

I screamed.

CHAPTER 25

Kellan

I paced the floor of the long ballroom, the original space just plaster and plywood the last time I had been here.

The doc was working on Aaron now. For all Lauchlan's faults, the man had skills, and when he started speaking to the doctor in medical terms and offered himself as the helper, Doc gladly took him into the makeshift infirmary of a co-opted office space and a stretcher.

Hillary had taken over the construction contract when Aaron disappeared, and turned this place into a massive entertainment space that would have been warm and inviting—if I wasn't terrified the man I'd been sent to kill all those months ago was actually going to die.

I'd missed three of her calls, and knew I had to call her back. She was going to kill me for waiting this long, but I couldn't answer until I knew Aaron was going to be okay. I couldn't be the one to tell her the man she'd admitted to loving was dead.

Carmen Delgado had targeted Aaron Rodriguez, which told me two things: she'd been hired to do it, even when Antonio directed me to make the kill, and that she or my father hadn't believed Aaron was actually dead. She'd lured him out of his hiding spot today, and she could only do that if she'd suspected him to be alive. Which meant my father knew I hadn't killed him after all.

We'd prepared for the possibility of needing to bring Aaron back from the dead—but not with Antonio in mind. The car crash was flawless, the cover story air-tight. If my father had trusted me, he never would have put her up to this.

Which meant I'd fallen out of my father's favor, once and for all.

If I'd fallen out of my father's favor, everyone around me was now in danger.

Thankfully, Lauchlan had killed Carmen. I would have preferred to put the bullet into her brain myself, but seeing Aaron bleeding out had made me panic. It was bad enough when I had to keep sharp eyes on Hillary's every movement to keep her safe—now I had two people to worry over. When I wasn't being a prick about it, I didn't want Lauchlan dead either, though the man was a complete menace to everyone around him.

I wanted to blame him for Aaron's injuries, but I'd seen how fierce Aaron was when he wanted something. The Rodriguez family had been allies with the Carlos Cartel for decades, and I'd watched from a distance as Aaron grew into a feared man as he took over his family's brothel businesses. Lauchlan was his patsy—he would have found a way there, with or without him.

Which meant we'd just gotten on top of one enemy, and had sped up the wrath of the other, *bigger* enemy. And as long as I stayed close to Hillary, they'd be in the direct line of fire when Antonio decided I was no longer useful.

I'd protected her from too much to get her killed now.

Hillary Lane was the woman I would die for; the woman I'd risk everything to save. I'd been running from my feelings for years. Why was it only when the world was falling around me, I could finally get my head out of my ass and admit I loved her?

But loving something meant letting it go. There was no way I could fight by her side in battle and be the sword and shield she'd claimed me to be. I would need to bring the war front to Antonio and leave her entirely out of it. She couldn't wage war on an enemy already dead.

First though, I needed to know Aaron was okay. Hillary would kill me herself if I left her alone with the corpse of her lover and the cocky leprechaun for company. But then...

My phone rang again, its shrill sound breaking through my racing thoughts. I glanced at it, preparing myself for Killer's number and how I was going to respond. But it was Antonio's name flashing across the screen.

Fuck. Either I answered this and faced him like a man, or I cowered in the darkness until he found me like Carmen had found Aaron. My fate was now sealed in blood either way.

I answered the phone with a barking command. "Yes, sir?"

The familiar velvety tone came through the line.

"You have chosen your side, *traidor.*" My father's voice held grim menace, a solemn vow of retribution. "I hope you are prepared to die for it. Your brothers are coming for you."

Cora Flynn

Our Knight is on his last legs, but if they manage their
moves, the King and Rook might save him.

How will Lucky get out of his contract with The Six?
Is Alvarez unreachable, or will the Queen bring him to his
knees?

Will Kellan, Aaron, Hillary, and Lucky get their ultimate
revenge against their parents?

Order your copy of To Claim A King, the final book in the
All The Queen's Men series today!

Other books by Cora Flynn

<u>Cascade of Lies (series)</u>
Days of Winter
Nights of Winter
Winter's End